Dog
in the
Road

A Novel

DAVE BAEHREN

STATION
SQUARE
MEDIA
NEW YORK, NEW YORK

For Sonja

Advance Praise

Fast-paced and riveting, Dog in the Road resonates with an authenticity that is grounded in author Dave Baehren's stellar career in emergency medicine. As his characters' lives play out in these pages, it's clear that this is more than a story about the world of medicine. It's a story about life.

— *CHRISTINE BRENNAN, USA TODAY COLUMNIST*

I count myself lucky to have read *Dog In The Road*. This book is fundamentally perfect about life and self-discovery that words alone are not enough. It is something you need to experience and feel. The book goes beyond storytelling. It's a light in the dark, the up when you're down, a balm to soothe pain. It's a thread of providence that invisibly binds life's challenges and how others positively impact our journey.

— *COLONEL DAVID W. SUTHERLAND, US ARMY (RETIRED), AUTHOR,* BEDU: BEDOUIN BOY, POET KING

Dog in the Road provides the reader a chance to go on a journey with Dr. Sam Buchanan, an Emergency Room Physician, whose life in the trenches takes him from corporate Emergency Medicine, to alcoholism. You follow Sam through the collapse of his marriage, his road to recovery both physically and spiritually and ultimately his redemption through reconnecting to care giving, his wife and the people around him. It is a compilation of all the experiences most every ER doctor in America encounters during their career.

Whether it's the rich executive, overly enthusiastic about befriending the physician they credit with saving their life, the carpenter or painter you hire from a patient encounter, the felon with no vision of his future, or the weathered whims of simple stray cat, you will get a chance to experience the real soul of Emergency Medicine through Sam's life story.

Dave Baehren writes with refreshing imagery, without resorting to cliché medical metaphors that often flood the works of physician writers. He makes me want to get up in the morning, put on my scrubs and go back to work, to see what beauty a day in the ER has in store for me.

— *Louis M. Profeta MD, Author,* The Patient in Room Nine Says He's God

Dog in the Road is a timely story given the increasing issues of burnout, substance abuse and suicide among medical practitioners. But it is not just a story for physicians. It is a reminder that humans have the capacity to overcome troubles and move forward, but that it will always require self-examination, forgiveness, hard work and most of all, the love of others. And that things may turn out well, but not always as we expect.

It is a reminder that the past is not a sentence, and the future is not always what we expect. And that it can be worse, and ultimately far better, than our failures and tears would lead us to expect.

— *Edwin Leap, MD, Author,* Cats Don't Hike

1

THE THICK WOODEN gate clicked closed behind me as I stepped into Elysium. Alone, I admired the expanse of lanky grass and blooming trees. New sun filtered through dense pines. Dew-soaked blades littered my toes, yet my feet felt warm, as if stepping from an evening bath onto terry cloth. A light breeze floated the aroma of gardenias. I breathed the peace. Slowly. Deeply. Quiet, as if underwater, until an unfamiliar urgent yet distant voice caught my ear. No one appeared. I closed my eyes, willing it away. Willing this increasingly annoying voice to leave me to my solitary journey.

"We need a doctor in first class immediately."

I opened my eyes and gazed at the shrimpy speaker next to the call button, trying to orient myself. The message repeated. My loafers lay askew under the seat ahead of me, so in my stocking feet, I bounded from the last row of coach, sensing the heat from every expectant and curious eye. Like a bride running the wrong way between the pews. A flight attendant pounded the back of the man in an aisle seat, center row. There was no need to explain. This guy, who looked to be about sixty-five, seventeen years my senior, held his hands up to his neck, TAG Heuer timepiece on his wrist. The blank expression on his flushed face revealed all I needed.

"I'm Susan, I think he's choking."

I ignored the flight attendant not out of rudeness, but for the expediency of dislodging the offending material from this man's hypopharynx. Lost in his distress, he gazed ahead, neck craned forward.

"Hey," I said, loud enough to startle the onlookers. I shook his shoulder and met his dull eyes. "Stand up now or you will die."

His wife, upscale makeup and nails, shrieked and pulled up on his arm, yelling his name, "Stan!" I lifted the other as we hoisted his long frame from the ample leather seat. The second officer, with the silver hair and cowboy mustache, pushed from the cockpit as I turned Stan away from me. He supported one side and Susan the other. I reached around Stan's girth, made a large fist with hands clasped and snapped upward under his ribcage. Once, twice, and at the third try he and I collapsed to the deck. Shit. I extricated myself from beneath Stan's weight and rolled him on his back. His wife sobbed, and her fear was palpable. I pushed that away to concentrate on Stan.

There was no thinking. Twenty years of practice, like gravity, produced automatic action. I placed my thumb under his tongue, a risky move in someone approaching an anoxic seizure, and my index under his chin. I lifted, and his lower oral bridge ejected from his mouth as a dental Frisbee traversing the aisle and resting on the foot of a lady two rows back. Again. A golf ball-sized piece of partially chewed chicken lay deep behind his tongue. Had I possessed Magill forceps, the removal would have proven facile, but like the police or the correctly sized screwdriver, they are never beside you when you need them. Taking the risk of pushing the slippery stoppage back to his larynx, I pinched as if picking up a sliver of glass from behind the couch. On the fifth try I caught a strand of connective tissue and drew the slimy mass forth, flicking it under the adjacent seat.

Stan lay motionless and ashen, a pre-autopsy state, and I pondered if this would be one of these deals where the operation was a success, but the patient died. I knew the next step but desired this no more than slamming my hand in a door. A smart person invented a product to use for mouth-to-mouth resuscitation, so you didn't get their slobber on your mouth. Police and screwdrivers. I pinched his nose and expired five breaths into Stan. Time and sound, save for the drone of the engines, stopped. I placed my index and long finger against his carotid artery. Dangerously slow pulse. Guttural breathing resumed, face regained a ruddy complexion, and for the true prize he opened his eyes.

I looked at his wife, pixie body, button nose, brunette hair cropped at her shoulders, perceptive eyes. "He's good now." I used my sleeve to wipe my beard. "I'm Sam."

"JoJo. Thank you so much, Sam."

I dribbled the ball, stopped at the top of the key, five

seconds remaining, and launched the ball. Nothing but net. Cheers of relief filled the first-class cabin and spread to coach.

"Stan. I'm Sam Buchanan. You're flying to Honolulu. You choked on food."

He nodded and closed his eyes. Tears streamed across his temples. I remained kneeling, stroking his forest of dense white hair, watching his barrel chest rise and fall. Like a computer losing power, his brain needed time to reboot. While I savored saving his life, it's different when a lay person saves someone. What I do for a living comes with an expectation for success. When an eighty-year-old George Bush throws out the first pitch, nobody cares if it goes in the dirt; if he nails the glove, the crowd goes wild. When Greg Maddux gets the nod, he better burn a strike or expect cat calls. The fulfillment came in not failing.

"JoJo and I honeymooned at Waikiki." He coughed a few times. "We're celebrating our twentieth. We were reminiscing, and I laughed about something at our wedding, and that was it."

"No worries. You'll be fine."

"Can I get up now?"

I helped him to his feet and steadied him as we walked to the galley. Another round of applause as if for an injured cornerback raising from the turf. Stan and JoJo held a long embrace. I noticed the wet mark on his shorts. I should have been the one pissing my pants.

JoJo stepped close enough to kiss, pressed herself against me, on her toes, and sighed. Her mouth nestled near my ear and softly, "I need to ask you." Two stuttering breaths. "Why are you on this flight?"

This is a long and, complicated story. I did not want to reveal personal details but also did not want to dismiss this heartfelt question. She released me but remained near.

"I'm going through a transition in my life. Leaving some things behind. New job. New city. I'm taking a few months between jobs."

She rested her hand on my cheek as you would a child's. "Thank you, Sam Buchanan. Your presence here is a gift from God. You'll think I'm a nut, but He is with us. Right here."

I raised my hands to hold hers and nodded. My chest tightened. I'm the last person God should send.

2

THE SECOND OFFICER approached and patted me on the back. "I'm Spetka. Thanks for coming to the rescue, doc. We okay to continue?"

"I'm happy to help. Yeah, he'll be fine."

"Okay. Call if you need anything."

I leaned toward JoJo. "This seems pedestrian considering what just happened, but Stan wet himself. Did he pack another pair of shorts in his carry-on?"

JoJo left to inspect luggage and Stan stuck his paw at me. We shook and then the bear hug. "Can you give me your address? I want to do something for you."

"No. I mean, yes, I'll give you my information in New Orleans, but I don't want you to do anything for me. Give a thousand dollars in my name to your favorite charity." I figured someone flying in the front row spends a thousand like most people spend a hundred.

"What's your favorite?" He rested his hand on my shoulder.

"Boy Scouts." I joined the scouts for a few years. If I persevered, I might be a better person. The whole trustworthy, loyal, helpful thing penetrated only so far with me.

"First chance I'll send a check."

"Sounds good."

Susan touched my elbow. "The captain requests a word."

A word. Usually this means trouble. When your wife or your boss wants *a word* there is often some explaining to do. You didn't do that thing you promised, or somebody complained. I figured nobody complained about me saving Stan's life. Well, maybe the false teeth on the shoe lady. We left the galley to give Stan privacy to change into swim trunks. Spetka sat at the controls and Captain Walt Glosser stood at the cockpit door. He set a pitched smile on his balding head. He appeared to be an unflappable sort that could land a jumbo jet in a corn field. We shook, and he expressed his gratitude.

"We'd put you in first class, but the cabin is full."

"Yes, I saw that when I booked."

"You know," he said in a Texas twang, "several things can make for a crappy day in this business. Engine failure, two feet of snow, near collisions, et cetera. Dead passenger, especially this one, is high on the list. Does the name Stan Hayes mean anything to you?"

"No. I'm assuming he's a VIP of some sort."

"Tenth richest man in Georgia. Timber. Good person to have on your side."

"I'll keep that in mind." I held his gaze and considered the VIPs that came through my ER. Worse than the urge to crap twenty miles from the rest stop, I hate it when rich people try to jump the line.

A drunk can call me a flaming SOB and it bounces off the Teflon. Some blue-haired socialite with nausea threatens to call the CEO and I want to spit. "You know, I would give the guy that cleans the airplane the same treatment."

"Right. No question." He turned then looked back. "Listen, we are at the Hilton Waikiki tonight. Dinner and drinks are on Sparky and me." He thumbed toward Spetka.

"That's generous, thanks, but unnecessary. I'm way over in Kailua, anyway."

In the galley I found Susan, a sharp-looking Asian gal with black hair to the mid back, athletic body, and an air of sophistication.

"Dr. Buchanan."

"Sam. Please."

"Sam. Everybody on this plane wants to buy you a drink. Plus, two women, and one man, want your number." She winked and smiled. "They're happy the guy lived but even happier the captain didn't divert us to LAX."

Gallows humor. This chick could work in the ER.

"Ah, yeah. I'll pass on giving my number, but I will take a scotch and water. I just want to return to my seat and the weird dream I was having. But first, I'm hoping for mouthwash."

"Right." She made that face you make when bird shit lands on someone's shirt. She pulled a travel-sized bottle from a drawer. "See the gate agent when you deplane. Give them your return information. Walt said they will comp that segment and upgrade you to first class."

I stopped fending off the attempts to thank me. I started to the sink but turned back. "Do I look gay to you?"

She laughed with no sign of embarrassment. "No. It's a Babe Ruth."

"I don't follow."

"Babe Ruth hit a zillion home runs, right?"

"Sure."

"Also struck out a ton. If you want to hit a home run, you swing for the fence. And not cry if you strike out. I think they like your accent. Georgia?"

"South Carolina."

After swishing Stan's spit out of my mouth, I crouched next to him on my way back to the cheap seats. "How are you?"

"Like it never even happened."

"Great. I'll check on you one more time at baggage claim."

"JoJo and I talked. You gotta come to dinner. Where are you staying?"

"Kalaka Place in Kailua. Tree Tops."

They looked at each other and smiled. JoJo said, "Walk north on the beach until it ends, and you'll find us."

I handed Stan my card. "I'm here through Christmas. Call me with the day."

I limped back to coach. More applause and high fives. Enough already. I know Kailua well from an earlier visit. As I walked, I remembered that house and the Secret Service tent. That's the house where Obama stayed when he was president.

3

I ROLLED MY SUITCASE toward ground transportation. Ahead of me stood a handsome native who
sported a generous smile, floral shirt, yellow plumeria
lei, and a white placard.

DR. SAMUEL BUCHANAN

Stan is a man that can make things happen. I reclined
in the rear seat of the limousine, sipped Perrier, and
browsed the Star-Advertiser on the thirty-five-minute
trip to Kalaka Place. We took the H-1 to the H-3, and
I inhaled the mountains. The odd and rare realization
came that I had no plans for the next three months. I
wondered if I would tire of being with myself.

My life was a well-orchestrated affair. My mother
was a planner. Dad and I, not so much. We went
along for the ride. High school, college at USC,
medical school in Charleston. I hardly took a breath.
That's the original USC in Columbia; the one founded
before California slipped into the union. Then I married my soon-to-be ex-wife. She is a planner too.

Three months of my life unscheduled evoked feelings of unease but joy of newfound freedom prevailed.

The tires popped stray gravel on the narrow lane as we passed cottages and bungalows dressed in bright colors. We stopped three back from the shore. The driver declined my offer of a tip.

Though I could well-afford a place with a view, the one-room apartment with kitchenette provided the minimalist environment I desired. It perched atop a canary-colored three-bedroom bungalow shaded by almond and banana trees with one koa tree in the back corner of the lot casting a broad canopy. A cozy lawn spread below a sweeping deck surrounding two sides of the dwelling. A wrought-iron spiral staircase at the rear of the deck provided solitary access to Tree Tops.

The electronic lock opened with the code provided by the owner. Rattan furniture with flowered upholstered cushions circled a teak table upon which sat a bottle of 2014 Dos Lagos Cabernet and a card. I figured the owner had done it. This was not Two-Buck Chuck.

ENJOY
SEE YOU TUESDAY 6PM
STAN & JOJO

Though Stan was a step ahead of me, there was no way he could have anticipated the seduction of that bottle. I put a few away on a regular basis. More than what was good for me. Whiskey, but I wouldn't refuse a full-bodied Cab along with a hunk of prime rib. Recent events caused me to consider the wisdom of my heavy booze intake. Drinking pushed the bad feelings away, along with my wife. I delayed the decision to quit. After all, I saved a guy's life. I would offend Stan to reject his gift.

I opened the bottle and filled a glass. Island pour. I swirled it a few revolutions and sniffed. Nice aroma. As I downed the first glass, I inspected the various grocery items and liquor bottles populating the stretched counter in the kitchenette. I found the fridge packed with a variety of fresh fruit, juices, cheese, yogurt, and deli meats. I wondered what I would find if I angered Stan. Possibly a horse head. It was a superb gesture, but it freaked me out. In less than an hour, he found my landlord, called a grocery store, and arranged this delivery.

My soon-to-be ex-wife and I are the wealthiest in our sphere of friends. I'm a card-carrying member of the one percent and am accustomed to having premium belongings and service. I casually know a few ultra-wealthy folks but never enjoyed a social relationship until this brush with the point-zero-one percent. Unless you are Jeff Bezos, someone has more money than you.

I removed my shoes and socks, refilled my glass near the brim, and followed the narrow sand path past thick foliage, which shielded the estates on either side. By Hawai'i standards, the day was chilly so I shared the late afternoon, on one of the most beautiful beaches in the world, with a few dog walkers and a guy surf casting. October is not a popular month for tourists because of the cooler and rainier weather, plus the whales come in the winter. Fine with me.

The crescent sliver of gritty white sand runs almost to the Marine Corps Air Station on the left, which tips the peninsula making Kaneohe Bay on the opposite side. The sand runs to Lanikai on the right. I'll never tire of seeing the Mokes. The Mokulua Islands. About three-quarters of a mile off Lanikai, Moku Nui and Moku Iki rise from the azure sea like two breasts. That unoriginal observation was likely made by the first two Polynesian teenage boys to walk on Lanikai Beach. I can picture one elbowing the other and cupping his hands.

I sat on a weathered log and dug my toes. Stan's choking episode replayed, and I considered the heartache and disruption had I failed. I would have dragged that defeat around for decades. There was enough to drag around anyway, so I didn't need to add to the load. I saved plenty of people but most of those memories hide in dark corners. It's the bad ones that come to you at two in the morning.

> Quick pulse, sweaty and cold, sleep abandoned to the memory. A twenty-year-old college student. He drove his car into a tree. Blood gushed from his face. Chest was caved in. I struggled to place an airway, but I got it. I placed chest tubes. More blood. Then we lost his pulse. He would have died regardless, but I wonder what I might have done to improve his chances. I remember

standing in the doorway watching the nurses clean the blood from his face to make him presentable to family.

These patients rest askew on a mental shelf and fall into dreams like a random gust from the north. My shelf sagged from the weight.

I saved a man who would have died and found no real pleasure in it. The only person on that flight capable of saving Stan was me and I viewed it as a perfunctory performance. What the hell. I knew my brain was scrambled and I needed to do something about it. Twenty years of seeing shit you're not supposed to see piled up in my head and it was about to shoot out my ears.

Most of my work is done in clandestine cubes, actions known to few. Taking the stage on the plane caused a rare unsettling look at the reflection of my work.

I walked southeast, toward the Mokes, to the public beach. Thoughts of happy times with my wife rushed like a chance wave threatening towel and book. I treasure a photo of us standing in the shallows with our kayaks, Mokes in the background. The collision of colors along with our bright faces composed a stunning shot and captured one of our happiest times. I saw the magnificence with fresh eyes. I found beauty in the landscape and in my wife's face. The Christmas Eve feeling of a six-year-old lived in me. I mourned the loss.

I knew I couldn't relive those days, nor could I share steps on that sand with my wife. My emotional bank account with her dwindled over many years. Then she emptied hers in a morning. We squandered the capital of twenty years of marriage and I hadn't waded to the depth of it. My bitterness kept me from taking it in. Truly feeling it. Seeing the islands made our division tangible and I shivered.

> I shivered again and saw myself sitting in my car watching a torrent beat the windshield. No umbrella. I sprinted to the red door of the funeral home and shook off the rain. My mom told me he died, but it wasn't real until I touched him. Cold, lifeless, gray. The full emotional release came only after I smoothed my father's hair back with my hand. And I shivered.

The disappointment and anger regarding my wife were still along for the walk but I let them rest long enough to touch the loss and smooth its hair back. If I looked past the anger, I missed her. And there was no way to fix that. Coulda, shoulda, and woulda needed to be tossed to the surf, but I was still pissed at my wife and there was no tossing that to the surf.

The sun fell past the mountains behind Kailua setting them afire and dropping the temperature at the coastline by five degrees. I walked the water's edge to the pathway home and the fatigue from travel and events of the day beat me there. I climbed the ladder to the lofted bed hoping to return to my interrupted dream.

4

TWELVE HOURS PASSED in a breath and I awakened with a bursting bladder. In South Carolina, I would be eating lunch. O'ahu awaited the sun. Memories of the bliss of watching the sun rise from the Pacific played while I made a smoothie with milk, banana, and raspberries.

I pulled a swimsuit and T-shirt from my suitcase and stripped naked. Trees shielded the windows, so I stood there, arms beside my skinny body, small paunch at the waistline, considering my past and my response to it. I could loaf, or I could get my shit together. Now was the time to decide. Drinking did not make me happy. It only sent the seemingly incurable sadness shopping for a few hours a day. Today was the day.

I turned and pulled on my fish-pattern swim trunks. Marlins. When I turned back to face the entrance, a slender woman, who looked to be sixty-five or seventy, stood at my door. She appeared to have been doing something athletic or a geriatric vitamin commercial. Her gray hair, pulled back in a ponytail, dropped over the shoulder of her form-fitting purple sun shirt. Her expressive face, with a faint tan, showed no sign of photoaging common to her generation. She waved as I approached the door.

"Don't worry, when I arrived the closing credits were playing."

This lady, unlike me, was sophisticated. I wondered if she had been an actress, but I couldn't place her face. "Ah. Yes. You must be Jane. We rented downstairs before."

"Yes. I'm glad you found your way in. I heard footsteps and wanted to see if you needed anything."

"I'm pleased to be settled and enjoyed my sleep. Stan stocked me well."

"So, what's your connection with Stan?"

"He called, I gather."

"Yes, he insisted I allow the delivery men from Whole Foods and the wine store access."

"It's not complicated or anything untoward, but he should share the story with you."

"Well, I must ask him on Tuesday. I'll see you then. Knock if you need anything. Soap and shampoo in the outdoor shower."

"Great. Listen, they delivered some items I won't be using." I packed the bottles of liquor and white wine into a doubled paper grocery bag.

"What have you there?"

"Stan was quite generous." I presented the bag.

She peered into it like there might be a live animal. "This wine will be nice. I'll keep the others around for guests. Thank you for thinking of me."

Someone more crass, my golfing buddies for instance, would inquire why I chose not to imbibe. Mormon? Muslim? Ulcer? Trying to lose weight?

The thermometer read seventy, but I felt a chill, so I retrieved my Gamecocks pullover and carried a folding chair in one hand, smoothie in the other.

———

Sunrise viewing on Kailua is a communal affair. Friends drank coffee wordlessly, lovers intertwined fingers, and all faced the Mokes as the margin of our star burned between the islands. After settling in my chair on an unattended spot, I enjoyed my smoothie and the celestial show. I leaned forward, elbows on knees, thinking of nothing while surf kept its rhythm. A dimension void of time lived until full sun rested on the sea casting long shadows from men and mountains.

Her braided strawberry blonde hair tossed as she turned toward me. Her buxom yet thin frame suggested an age of thirty-five, but crow's feet framing verdant eyes, betrayed age of mid-forties. The symmetry of her face, petite nose, and full lips enhanced her essential beauty. Freckles for character. In the motion of a dancer, she descended to the sand cross-legged, just out of reach.

"You're new to Kailua."

"Ah, yeah. Quite observant of you. Is it my pallor that tipped you off?"

I'm a ginger and I don't tan well even when I'm in the sun.

"No. I know everyone here but you." She extended her slender hand. Long digits. Flawless nails. "I'm Kayla."

We held hands a moment longer than comfortable for me. "I'm Sam. Just landed yesterday."

"Welcome, Sam. And how long will you be with us?" I detected a hint of accent from the old country. Subtle. Most wouldn't place it.

"Three months."

"Visitors stay a week or two. Then back to the world, and all. Retired?"

"Extended vacation."

Her eyes brightened. "I'll take a wild guess—you're some kind of doc."

"Spot on." A hint of suspicion. "What makes you say that?"

"A doctor says pallor. Everyone else says pale."

"You should be a detective." Less suspicious now. "I'll take a stab you're from Ireland, but not recently."

"Well done. I came here to work in a hotel in my early twenties and here I am." She spread her toned arms then pointed at my shirt. "Is that a school in New Orleans?" She said it the proper way, not "Orleeens."

She noticed the South Carolina Gamecock logo. A block C with a feisty chicken inside. Most people don't recognize it. I never mentioned New Orleans, so it seemed odd she would guess the school was there. Her infectious smile was endearing, but I smelled a rat and his name was Stan. Limo drivers and groceries don't fall from the ether and neither did Kayla. Attractive women never approach me. I give off that boring married guy vibe.

"Will you be having dinner at Stan's on Tuesday?" I said.

She smiled again with a hint of a blush. "Oh, it's you, sir, who should be the detective."

"Well, I am a medical detective of sorts. What mission did Stan concoct?"

"Don't be cross. He just asked me to make you welcome. Left the details to me." Brief wink.

"And what did he tell you?"

She leaned toward me. "JoJo says God put you there to save Stan's life."

I stood to stretch and offered a hand up to Kayla. "Yeah, I'd say that's up for debate."

"Walk with me. Your chair won't go anywhere," she said.

We turned our backs to the sun and walked the firm sand of low tide. I admired the multimillion-dollar homes surrounded by dense grass and high palms.

"So, you're a full-time resident?"

"My husband and I were neighbors of Stan and JoJo. He died of a stroke last year."

"I'm sorry to hear that." A chill traveled down the back of my neck. "How long have you been neighbors with Stan and JoJo?"

"Ten years now. I miss them when they go away to

the mainland. Don't say *the states* or they'll peg you for a tourist."

"Right."

We stopped at a sweeping one-story home with a Spanish-tile roof. Three sets of wooden sliding glass doors opened to a covered patio with a kitchen. An outdoor sitting area and kidney-shaped pool framed the one end and a croquet court the other.

"This is me. It's too big for me now. I use about three of the rooms."

Kayla stepped inside and emerged with tall glasses of orange juice. We relaxed in oversized wicker chairs. Potted flowers accented the deck and candles of various diameters and heights populated the tables.

"I love this time of day. When they are in bloom, the gardenias make a heavenly aroma, and it lingers until the wind kicks up," Kayla said.

"I had this dream yesterday. Just pieces now. I smelled gardenias."

"What happened?"

"Stan."

"He was in your dream?" She turned to me, eyes wide.

"No, interrupted my dream."

"Ah. Ha ha. I shouldn't laugh. That was a close one." She took a drink. "Tell me something important about what you do."

I liked her already. Sophisticated yet not snobby. She didn't ask my specialty or about the worst trauma I ever saw. Kayla showed interest in what I found important in my work. That meant she wanted to know about me more than my work.

"Emergency docs do what few doctors do. See anybody for any reason at any time. We are the medical safety net."

"Wow. No idea."

"Now, a lot of folks game the system and take advantage of their unfettered access. So, if you are cynical, we are the bottom of the birdcage."

"What do you say?"

"Some of both. Really satisfying to diagnose a pulmonary embolism in a twenty-eight-year-old mother of two. That gets you through the toothaches and drunk fools."

"Such a fascinating world. I could ask you questions all day. Vacation is to escape that, so I'll stop."

"You've seen TV shows about the ER, right?"

"I don't own a TV." Hands on hips.

"Have ya indoor plumbing, lassie?" in my best Irish accent.

"You're a card." She nudged my elbow.

"Do you miss the Emerald Isle?" I said.

Quiet now. I could tell I had stirred an emotion. Not a pleasant one. She nodded her head and eyes glistened. "My mother died when I was seventeen. I left to escape my father. He never touched me now, but he was a verbally abusive, insufferable curmudgeon."

"After your mother died?"

"No. No. He was born that way, I think." A mournful laugh. "I tell very few people this story."

I placed my hand over my heart. "You've seen some loss."

"The one enduring thing he taught me was how to be tough." She touched my forearm. "Spend the day with me."

"Oh, that would be splendid, but I'll take a rain check." She made a pouty, sexy face. "I'm here through Christmas and I'm looking forward to spending time with you. You'll think I'm strange, but I need time to myself."

She pecked me on the cheek. "Nice to meet you, Sam Buchanan. See you tomorrow night."

5

HAT, SUNGLASSES, SUNSCREEN, backpack, lunch, water, and camera. Check. One of my favorite hikes on O'ahu is the Ka'iwa Ridge pillbox trail. This steep trail leads to concrete bunkers used during WWII for coastal defense. I hiked two miles to the trailhead. No sweat. There are no signs until you arrive, so having been there before was a bonus.

I swigged water and navigated the abrupt rocky terrain. One thousand feet in and my thighs burned. Stairmaster from hell. I stopped often to catch my breath. A rugged dude who looked Army waved as he ran past. For most, this hike is strenuous. Running it proves killer aerobic fitness, which I did not have. I trekked the tight trail, surrounded by tall brush, to the first pill box.

Thoughts of young men carrying hefty packs during the war put my sense of accomplishment into perspective. The six-hundred-foot elevation provided a splendid view of the Mokes and a perfect way, at least in the 1940s, to watch for an invading Navy or Air Force.

I scaled the concrete wall of the pillbox and sat

with my legs dangling over the front. The clouds, that made for an eerie purple sunrise, had burned and now the water reflected a rare, intense aquamarine. To my left lay the expanse of Kailua Beach. I found the edge of Stan's property. Trees covered my place. Nobody in the world knew or cared about my location. For two decades, either the hospital or my wife could always find me. At work, the clerk knew when I took a dump in case a catastrophe happened. I realized that I could just check out. Not kill myself, but move to a remote place, live off my savings, and disappear. I would depend on nobody, and nobody would depend on me. It doesn't get any simpler than that. No worries, no hassles.

The sound of someone climbing up the back of the pillbox startled me. A skinny, but muscular, guy in his mid-twenties, jaw like Sparty, Greek nose, sat beside me and extended his hand. Grip like a gorilla. Michael, from Ohio, with fine sandy hair tied in the back, arrived the same day as me, except his jet came from the other direction. Beijing. He recounted his travels through the east coast of America, Europe, the Middle East, Africa, and Asia.

"When did you start?"

"Nine months ago," he said. Midwestern accent.

Funny how people from the Midwest think they don't speak with an accent.

"Don't answer if I'm prying, but that's a long time to travel. How do you support yourself?"

"I camp and stay in hostels. Live on thirty dollars a day once I get someplace."

"So, you have savings."

"Yeah. I'm a minimalist. Everything I own, except my tools, is in this pack." He pointed his thumb over his shoulder. "I'm a licensed plumber. I saved a hundred grand in four years. Alls I want to do is travel and hike. I pick up work when I want."

"I'm not criticizing. I'm envious. Most guys in my generation started college, then work, wife, house, cars, kids. You are the antithesis of my life until now."

"Yeah, my dad and I had this talk. He understands what I'm about now." Michael slipped off his pack and pulled out a protein bar and offered me one. I declined.

"You say *until now*."

"Recently I learned what you already figured out. I worked twenty years and accumulated a load of shit. I sold or gave away most of it."

"Did you quit your job?"

"Yes and no. I'm leaving everything behind in Columbia, South Carolina, and taking a job in New Orleans."

"Dude. I'll be in New Orleans next year. After I do the west coast and the Rockies, I'm there. I wanna fish the Mississippi Delta."

I pulled a card from my wallet and handed it to him. He took a picture with his phone, handed it back and took a shot of me.

"You call me when you get to New Orleans. Stay with me," I said.

"I'll do that." He smiled and laughed as he placed his phone in his pocket.

"What?"

"Most people assume I'm a psych case loser since I'm drifting across the planet with no plan. You don't even know me."

I could tell this was a sore spot for him and he did not enjoy being judged. "Listen, I'm an emergency doc, and I get a private glimpse into the lives of all sorts. I can tell you're a good soul."

"Thanks." We bumped fists.

"Few of your generation want to work with their hands."

"Yeah, I'm not much of a 'pie are square' kinda guy."

I smiled and looked at him. "I don't follow."

"It's an old joke in my family. Farm boy comes home from college to a family gathering and his uncle says, 'So college boy, whadya learn?' Kid says, 'I learned pi R squared.' Uncle says, 'What the hell. Everybody know pie are round and cornbread are square.'"

I laughed and nodded. "Was it odd when your friends left for college and you to trade school?"

"Ha. Like I was joining the communist party or something." He pulled out binoculars to check out the birds nesting on the islands. "Thing is, I was making more money than most of them two years after they graduated college."

Michael handed me the binoculars. Wedge-tailed Shearwaters flew in and out of burrows high on the islands.

"Man, those birds are fast." I handed them back. "There's a freedom in having no debt."

"Fa' sure. My high school friends are swimming in it. None of 'em happy."

That was it. Not happy. We try to live up to expectations of careers, cars, homes, schools and we get on the treadmill. This guy never got on it. He owns little, yet he is cash wealthy and more importantly content with his life. A life, not for everyone, I'll admit, but who says only one path exists?

I regretted, not the path I took, but the way I traveled it. As years passed, I found no joy or satisfaction in experiences that should have teemed with both. I cringe to think how a more caring, empathic demeanor on my part would have lessened suffering of my patients. I wasn't outright mean to people, but from the patient's perspective, a wide gulf exists between being pleasant and truly giving a crap. This holding of the mirror was necessary and productive, but painful. I could take only one or two whacks at a time.

"Do you get lonely?"

"Dude, I made friends in like a dozen countries. I meet someone new every day."

He showed me faces he had collected in his phone. A guy he biked with in France, this smoking hot girl in Israel, and a farmer in China. I was adrift in his stories.

"What about enduring relationships? Again, not criticizing. I'm the guy getting the divorce here."

"Ya. I understand. That will come in its own time. When I'm not looking."

6

I WALKED SHOELESS TO Kayla's wearing the only dressy shirt and shorts I packed. We made no plans to meet but figured I could sit on the deck and watch waves crash. An off-shore storm kicked up the bay and the six-foot surf pounded the sand releasing rhythmic thunder. Palms rustled above me while my chat with Michael replayed. I considered the collision of generational cultures. Some might say Michael is precociously wise, and others might say he is lazy. I decided neither label is needed. He is happy, and he depends on nobody. I smiled. My thoughts returned to how I might have lived more happily. There was no question I chose poorly at many junctures but looking back helped little. Along with abstinence, my new companion goal became forward vision. Why not buy a two-bedroom place four back from the shore? The only formal relationship needed would be with the electric and water companies.

Kayla stepped on the patio, life in her eyes.

"Sam. I'm so glad you stopped by early." A smart,

flowery knee-length dress flowed about her lithe limbs. She sat on the footstool with her back to me. "Zip please."

I wanted to run my hands over her muscular, but feminine, back. She was adept at arousing me without impersonating a hooker. There's something the younger generation could learn. She turned to face me and wriggled her shoulders to position her dress.

"I'll make drinks."

I leaned forward and held my hands flat as if in prayer. "I hoped we might talk before going next door."

She nodded.

"I fear that everyone has an augmented, yet unfounded, positive opinion of me. There are volumes to tell you but now I want you to understand that I'm an alcoholic, and I don't drink anymore."

This was the first time I said it out loud. Like getting a cast cut off your leg, I felt a freedom but also trepidation of walking without crutches. Telling myself the drinking was not a problem was the biggest lie of my life. This was an important baby step.

She placed her hand, gold bracelets dangling, on my knee. "Good to know. The way JoJo talks, you walked on water over here, not the beach."

I exhaled, like I'd been passing a graveyard as a kid. I barely knew Kayla but an intense desire for acceptance welled. I gathered her response as an undeserved gift.

"Enjoying your time alone?" she said. She remained close, with no uneasiness as before on the beach. I thought of her being alone. No one to zip her dress or share a meal or a story.

"Yes. Interesting. Do you have kids?"

"No."

"Do you know many people in their twenties and thirties?"

"Sure. Mostly from work."

"Do you notice a meaningful generational divide?" I said.

"Oh, yes. I'm involved with a foundation, and we have a young staff. On one side, few want to work more than a forty-hour week. That's good and bad, I suppose. What I love is their devotion to a larger goal. This group wants to be part of something big, and they enjoy the collaboration."

"Well, I talked with a guy at the pillbox today who is traveling the world. I have no kids, so I'm clueless about this generation. We spoke of happiness. To answer your question, it was a superb day."

She bumped my knee with the back of her hand and smiled. "So, enlighten me."

"This guy, Michael, reaffirmed a decision I made. He is happy carrying most of his possessions in a backpack."

"You're not going to be one of these guys that hikes across country, are you?" She tilted her head and gazed from the corners of her eyes.

"No, ma'am, but I jettisoned most of my belongings. Cars, clothes, gadgets, golf clubs. None of them brought me joy. I want to live simply."

"Minimalist," she said.

"I guess. I'm not going off the grid in a tiny house and let my beard grow three feet. I'm getting off the treadmill."

Kayla looked past me at the tumultuous sea. I lost her for a few breaths and she returned. "Where will you find it? The joy."

I took her hand and we smiled and held each other's eyes. Most of my recent smiles had been the forced smile of social convention that get you through the day or the absent smile of inebriation. The ease of my organic smile brought a flush to my face. "I traveled the ocean to answer that question."

"Now that's something. I hope you find it." She looked at my wrists. "No watch. Island life already. Where's your phone?"

"No phone."

"At all?"

"Plugged in. I check messages once a day."

"Okay, then. It must be after six, so we should go."

She led me through a narrow passage between the properties. Ample thick leaves, foreign to me, encroached and we cleared the way with our hands.

Stan, tall, heavy set, with a weathered face, stood by the outdoor bar mixing a drink for Jane, the landlord. JoJo jumped from her seat and came to greet us. I recognized the design trend. Outdoor kitchen, eating area, and pool, dotted with tall palms in lush turf. Stan's was a step up from Kayla's. A lighted coy pond with blooming lily pads and a bridge served as the focal point.

"Look what washed up on my shore." Kayla laughed.

Booming Georgia voice. "There they are. I was thinkin' about coming over there and throwing water on y'all."

Kayla and I cocked our heads and looked at each other, eyebrows high. Hugs all around.

"Never mind him." JoJo winked.

We gabbed for a few minutes and the ladies left Stan and me to attend to preparations in the kitchen. My anticipation for the evening surprised me. Possibly it was a meal with a billionaire. Everyone is curious about the lives of the uber-wealthy. Just a peak in the window for me.

"I'm happy you're here. What are you drinking?"

"Taking a break from it." I expected cajoling from Stan, but he let it go.

"Say no more."

"Hey. Thank you for the groceries. I hate going to the store the first day of vacation. And the limo. I'm sure that was yours."

"You know I can never repay you. I am eternally grateful."

"Right. So, do nothing else for me. Your happiness in this stunning place, is sufficient." We sat on lounges by the pool with a mosaic tile dolphin on the bottom. "Hey, I received a call today from the Chief Scout Executive at the Boy Scouts. He wanted to acknowledge the one-hundred-thousand-dollar anonymous donation in my honor."

"More than most donations, that gave me a real thrill."

"Do you make all your donations anonymously?"

"Yeah. I fly under the radar. Beyond a few circles, I am not well known in Georgia and I want to keep it that way."

"You don't want your name lit up on a hospital?"

"Hell, no. I matched funds for a couple. They tried every which way to publicize the donation, but I declined."

Jane swished over in a knee-length coral dress, tied at the waist, shoulders exposed. She slipped next to me on the lounge and looked half over her shoulder. "Kayla is perfectly intoxicated over there, and she has barely touched her wine." Then a stern face. "Don't hurt my friend, Sam." She poked me in the chest and smiled.

"Last thing on my mind."

Jane's phone dinged, and her smile faded while she read and enlarged a photo.

"Everything okay, dear? Stan said.

She handed me the phone. "Sam. I prefer not to put people on the spot, but I'm worried about my three-year-old grandson in Houston. He's been punky today and now has this rash and a fever of 103."

I peered at the picture expecting a simple viral appearing rash. Head-to-toe red rash. Might be serious. Maybe not. I turned and planted my dusty feet on the deck. "I need a better one than this. Better focus, closer."

Jane texted back and forth with her daughter and more pictures appeared. Focus was better but not helpful.

"What other symptoms?"

"Vomiting and lethargic."

"Did they vaccinate?"

"No. I stopped bugging her. She and her husband think it will give him autism."

The anti-vaccination crowd grew after a flawed study, later proven false, regarding a link between vaccinations and autism. The myth lives. Convincing people otherwise, once they set their mind, is a swim upstream.

"Ask them to lay him on his back and flex his neck forward."

I had decided that he needed care but wanted confirmation before sending them on a potential wild goose chase.

"High-pitched scream."

"I don't want to cause a stir here, but this could be meningitis. Call, don't text, your daughter and tell her they need to drop what they are doing and go to the children's hospital. It might be something less serious, but this boy needs an examination now."

She walked toward the coast to make the call. I looked at Stan and held my arms out to the side.

"She asked," he said.

JoJo and Kayla arrived with appetizers. Kayla sat next to me and fed me a bacon-wrapped shrimp.

"JoJo." I said with a serious expression on my face. "Is it you or Stan who is friendly with the Obamas?"

"Oh, please." She has the full Georgia accent. "We

are not political and don't know them. Stan needed to work something out for the GFA with the head of the Democratic Party in Georgia. As part of the horse trading, they got to use the house a few times."

"GFA?" Kayla says.

"The forestry association."

"How did you and Stan meet?" I asked. That's a good question to ask when trying to understand people. How they share it reveals as much as the story itself. Much better than coming right out and asking how Stan made a billion dollars.

"You wanna tell it, dear?"

Stan walked to the bar to fetch the wine. "Yes. 'Cuz I don't sound like as much of a doofus when I tell it."

He filled glasses and sat across from Kayla and me as Jane rejoined the group. She gave me the thumbs up sign.

"I had never been married and wasn't lookin' to either." He held up a finger. "And I wasn't particularly wealthy."

"He always starts it that way," says JoJo. "But he forgot to say I was never married too."

"Am I tellin' this?" He smiled and winked at JoJo. "Anyway, mutual friends introduced us. Lots of people there, and I had … over-served myself."

"Nice way to put it," says JoJo, elbowing Stan in the side.

"Well, I did not remember her. Fast-forward two months and I'm taking a rare vacation with the same couple on Jekyll Island. They invited JoJo for the same weekend, and I introduced myself as a stranger."

"Smooth sailor," JoJo says sliding her hand through the air.

"Yeah, well you got over it and stayed the whole week, as I remember. Twenty years, one month from now, we married on the sand in front of the Westin on Hilton Head."

"Who did the ceremony?" I asked.

"Dan. Childhood friend. He's a minister at a big church in Atlanta now."

JoJo served swordfish, sweet potatoes, and kale salad. A simple, but elegant, meal followed by chocolate mousse with raspberries atop. I wondered how I might feel not drinking, but I needed nothing more from the evening. After we cleared the table, JoJo shooed everyone from the kitchen. I circled back.

"When's the last time you surprised Stan?"

"He's a tough one. I can't get much past him," she said.

"He's been a step ahead of me since we landed, and I can't let that stand."

She rubbed her hands together. "Tell me."

"Would Stan go for renewing your vows?"

"Oh, he'd love that, and it will kill him he didn't think of it."

"So, plenty of time to plan. Can Minister Dan come to officiate?"

7

KAYLA AND I stole to her place at midnight. Long past my east coast and my Hawai'i bedtime, I longed to become horizontal. Sans the opulent setting, I might have been dining with family. A billion dollars did not alter JoJo and Stan's outlook on life. There was a lesson for me. I was guilty of being a pretentious rich bastard. What was my damn excuse?

Kayla led me by the hand to an oversize sectional sofa and promised to return with waters.

My next conscious moment, in the morning, I lay sprawled on the couch covered by a USS Chafee blanket. A hint of her perfume lingered. I would remember if we had sex, but I wondered if she stayed with me for a while stroking my forehead, wondering what went on inside. In the bathroom, I found toothpaste under the sink and brushed with my finger.

My desire to spend more time with Kayla caused me to stand on the pool deck and consider my options. The gray pre-dawn sky offered no glimpse into the weather for the coming day, but I took the calm seas to be a good omen. Omens aside, I needed more time alone to work through the debris of my life. I felt good about that, but anxiety arrived like a gull landing near your picnic. This reminded me of being in the MRI machine when my shoulder troubled me. I didn't need a pill to do it, but certain relief arrived when the MRI ended. I did not enjoy the coffin-like quarters. Standing there made my skin crawl. Maybe the circumstances of being the only one awake at her home put me on edge. I walked the beach back to Tree Tops.

I toasted a bagel, topped it with cream cheese, and poured a short glass of OJ. *Back in the MRI.* Two bites in and sweat formed on my brow. Lightheadedness, not that of pleasant intoxication but the sour swimming head of illness, landed like a vulture at road kill. Then the nausea. I counted back. This was my third day of sobriety. I counted my pulse. One hundred ten. Pulse like a hammer. Alcohol withdrawal. What the hell. A novel experience, but I did drink with gusto for a few weeks before leaving Carolina. Two choices. I could drink whiskey until my symptoms resolved or find treatment. Many patients came to me in a similar predicament. A helpless puppy dumped into a snow-bank, I stared at the kitchen drain knowing my survival depended on the help of others. This was a pinch. I wish I treated every alcoholic as I desired for myself.

The one person in the world who heard my confession was my logical avenue to treatment. I grabbed my wallet and phone and returned to the beach. Half the sun looked over the horizon illuminating a cloudless sky.

Low waves lumbered ashore while nausea intensified. Legs heavy in the soft sand, I returned to Kayla, with words of the song Willy Nelson wrote about heaven swimming in my head. *Oh, they tell me of a home where no storm clouds rise, oh, they tell me of an unclouded day.* I needed treatment, or I would have a seizure, meet the Lord, and see heaven firsthand. Or not.

Kayla approached from her place and waved. I stopped and put my hands on my knees, trying to breathe through it, but the nausea charged. The sound of someone vomiting is universally despised. Fingernails on the blackboard. I'm always quick to give medicine for nausea in the ER. More than hearing it, I hate being the one who is vomiting. Especially in public. Sweat dripped from my forehead. The diarrhea train approached the station. High-speed rail. Just shoot me now. I dropped to my knees and regurgitated a foul-smelling bilious blend strong enough to take the chrome off a trailer hitch. I pushed sand around it as Kayla approached.

"Sam. I was worried about you. Is it something you ate?"

I sat back in the sand and wiped the mucus from my nose. "Kayla. Thank you for coming. I'm embarrassed to say I need your help."

"No. No. Don't ever be embarrassed. What can I do?"

"I told you I don't drink anymore. What I didn't tell you was my last drink was three days ago."

She kneeled by me and rubbed my back. "Come with me. I'll take you to a place. They'll help you."

"Do you understand I'm in alcohol withdrawal?"

"Sam, I'm Irish." Full accent. "Ya' think you're the first person I ever helped dry out?"

"Okay, then," I said. I struggled to my feet.

—

On the way to the rehab facility in Kāne'ohe, Kayla talked nonstop, save for a call to the director. I suppose she imagined if she dominated the conversation, I wouldn't ask her to drop me at the nearest liquor store. She assured me that a fellow, Steven, would take excellent care and she would return in five or six days to retrieve me. The modest cinder block building rested in the shadow of the Waiāhole Forest Reserve near to the Marine Corps base. Dense foliage blanketed the hills in the background. Kayla pulled into a handicap spot in front of the entrance and Steven, a fit-appearing bald man in his forties, opened the door to greet us. I pointed at the handicap sign like I was mute.

"I'm not staying. This part belongs to you," she said.

"Okay." I held her hand and considered what she had done for me. "Thank you. You are my one true friend in the world right now." I wanted to kiss her cheek, but my mouth tasted like fire. I walked to Steven, my hand a fish tail behind me.

8

SIX DAYS PASSED in a blur dominated by incomprehensible dreams swollen with fleeting vibrant visions. Steven kept me hydrated and free of withdrawal symptoms. They laundered my sweaty clothing, and I dressed after the nurse removed my IV. He led me to a covered alcove at the back of the building and Steven, three days growth of dense beard, greeted me with a genuine smile. Like when you see a dear friend after prolonged separation. We sat in padded white chairs with tall backs, rocking on uneven bricks, looking up to lush mountains. My clothes smelled of rain. He offered me water.

"How do you feel?" he said.

"I'm weak like after a cold, but mentally..." I searched for the words. "I'm ready. I'm motivated."

"Good. Good. Because this was the easy part. You should prepare yourself for difficult times."

I nodded. I spoke those words to many patients before they departed for detox, but I needed to hear them. When I stopped drinking, I assumed success would come with ease. Just as an outsider might assume my financial success translated to my entire life, I made the same false assumption and it gave false confidence. I did not want to be the guy driving around for two hours, too proud to ask for directions.

"Don't take this the wrong way, but you doctors are the worst," he said.

I smiled knowing docs are bad rehab patients and fall because they want to skip what works for *regular* patients. What Steven asked, I would do. Throwing up on the beach, drenched in sweat, is a humbling event. Like a kid warned to avoid the ice, running home, soaked and freezing, I had no standing to claim I knew a whiff about the weight capacity of thin ice.

"Normally I recommend three months of residential treatment here. I spoke with Kayla and she plans to look after you. If anyone other than Kayla made this commitment, I would not agree. She helped me with three other people and she bats a thousand."

"Thank you, Steven. Your work here is life-saving and life-changing. You have my eternal gratitude. When do I see you again?"

"If it's okay with you, I'll work that out with Kayla. I'll give you a few days to regain your stamina."

"Sure. One more thing," I said. "Nobody has asked me for any payment."

"Kayla pre-paid your treatment. I'll let you work that out with her."

Mid-morning glare flooded my eyes causing me to make a visor with my hand. Kayla leaned against her vintage Ford Mustang convertible in the shade of a soapberry tree, arms crossed, teeth gleaming. A statue for a moment, I wondered why this undeserved blessing had fallen at my feet. I doubted it was payback for saving Stan. I've never thought God graced our lives in such a concrete fashion. I might have been contemplating the volume of the universe. I hustled to her, and we embraced. I rested my chin on her shoulder and her hair fell on my cheek. Jasmine.

"I deserve none of this," I said in her ear. "But, I'll take it."

She pushed me away and put her hands on my hips. "I talked to Jane yesterday. Her grandson has some kind of meningitis. Starts with H."

"Haemophilus Influenzae B. HIB. I was afraid of that."

"Right. Well, he's doing fine. The infectious disease doctor said you saved his life." She pointed right at me. Serious now. "That's why God brought you here. Stan was the side show."

That chill down my neck again. "Really. Most fourth-year med students know this stuff."

She flipped her hand at me. "Whatever you say, Dr. Sam. Get in."

I clicked my seat belt. "The clinic bill. Thank you. But I'm paying you back."

She pulled out of the lot, not looking at me. "Really, it's pocket change. We'll work it out later."

—

I stretched getting out of the Ford. It looked like it came off the line the week before. Kayla's black-and-white checked garage floor shined better than most kitchen floors. Racing red cabinets surrounded a tidy tool bench and above it hung shiny implements for automotive maintenance and repair. In the middle bay sat the boring, compared to the pristine '65 Mustang, Mercedes GLE Coupe. I think my wife and I had that one. Or maybe it was the GLC. I can't keep the models straight.

"I'm guessing Gordy was a car guy."

"Oh, yeah. Like saying Pavarotti could hum a few bars. He also had a 1955 cream Mercedes 190 SL convertible with red interior. It was not a driver, as he called it, so I sold it."

I spent enough time at the Mercedes dealer to appreciate the value of that car. I guessed $175,000.

"Why don't you put on beach clothes? Let's take a walk," she said.

"Sure. Back in fifteen."

"No. I moved your stuff to the guest room."

"Really. Kayla. I can't impose on you any more than I have. You have…"

"Ah, ah, ah." She raised a slender index. "What did Steven tell you?"

"That you have experience, and he trusts you."

"Okay then." She twirled her finger. "If you please."

Kayla had folded and organized my limited wardrobe in a mahogany dresser. Coral terry-cloth towels and a navy-blue robe, Gordy's I guessed, rested on a white and blue-striped king-size bedspread. I hung my shorts and shirt in the closet and emerged in my fish-covered swim trunks and Gamecocks T-shirt. Kayla, in white shorts and a form-fitting electric orange long-sleeve shirt, handed me a bottled water and my sunglasses. She insisted I apply sunscreen.

We turned right at water's edge. High wispy clouds did little to filter the intense solar radiation. I welcomed the heat on my face.

"Fatigue will hound you for a few days. You need to stay active."

She speed-walked, and my heart rate kicked up. This was no romantic stroll. As we approached the palm tree log on the beach near my place, my chest tightened, and the air hung one step ahead of me.

"Uncle," I said. "Let's sit." We did, and she patted my knee. "You made your point well."

"And what point was that?" she said.

"I'm a pale, weakling, recovering drunk, mainlander who has no clue."

"Good. You made it farther than I thought, *and* you have good insight. Most Irishmen require a mule kick or a wide plank across the head. And don't cross me now." Full Irish accent. "I have no mule but there's lumber in the garage and I'm not afraid to use it." She put her arm around my shoulder and touched her head to mine.

The intimacy of that moment excavated untilled dirt bringing forth a massive serotonin rush.

In the truck with my dad. Too young to drive, I rode with my dad to a volunteer thing at church. Must have been ninety degrees, and my legs stuck to the seat. She and I had been hanging out together with friends that summer. We both loved music and sang make-shift duets. The music brought us together. She kissed me on the cheek the previous time we parted. I expected her to be there, and I had the same whole-body tingling then.

Tears darkened the sand. "There's been a few turns where I did spin a bit," I said.

She took my hand and sang with voice soulful and mellow. *'Til I Gain Control Again.* She sang a verse and on the next I came in with the harmony. Since I was a teenager, I could sing the harmony without thinking. Together we said, "I love that song."

She leaned into my ear, her breath soft. "I can be that lighthouse."

We strolled back to Kayla's. "Rodney Crowell," I said with authority.

"What."

"Rodney Crowell wrote ''Til I Gain Control Again.'"

"Really. I thought it was Emmylou Harris."

"Yeah. No. Several recorded it. I know it from Willy Nelson and Kimmie Rhodes."

We walked in silence and settled on lounge chairs by her pool. I considered napping.

"Do you want to tell me why you are running?"

Man, this girl could squeeze a confession out of a three-time felon. Why not? I pondered, and thoughts rushed forward settling into order. I looked back on the life built with my wife and realized I was an ass. Being an ass is generally not a self-administered label. Now, when you spend most of your time with other asses, the realization you are a gigantic, rotund horse's ass can come like mail on Sunday. And that was the case with me.

"My soon-to-be ex-wife and I are multi-million-aires. As you know, being wealthy does not make you a jerk, but I'd be less pompous if I made eighty K a year. I made ten times that as a partner. We owned several contracts in central South Carolina and employed thirty docs. Not everyone made partner. Only eight of us. We enticed docs with the potential for partner-ship, but we never saw fit to tap them with the sword. The partners lived high, and we were all shits. Then, and this is a whopper, we sold the group to one of the national ER companies and a huge windfall rained. Millions. That's when we bought the house in Kiawah."

"Did you enjoy being there?"

"Sure. I'm a better person at the water. Not a rousing character endorsement, is it? My soon-to-be ex-wife, who is a partner in her law firm, earned more than me. We own an immodest house in a gated commu-nity with a golf course and country club. I drove the biggest Mercedes available and she drove the convert-ible, plus we had the SUV." I sat up and turned toward Kayla. "Did we pause to contemplate our degree of satisfaction and wonder if our desires, perfectly saturated, could be pronounced quenched? Hell, no. This is what digs at me." I paused to swallow. "We never allowed the younger docs in on the success. I recruited this guy from Ohio and promised him a partnership at one year. He moved his whole friggin' family, and we backed out. That makes me the flipping flaming ass of the year."

"Tell me about your wife."

"Soon-to-be ex-wife."

"Right. Got it."

"She is driven. I say that like I lived in a monastery for the past twenty years. We were both driven. Work hard, play hard. Own the nicest car, house, watch, jewelry, swimming pool, and yard. Grounded is not the word to describe her. The only time she was near being down-to-earth was when she bitched out the landscaper."

"She can't be that bad."

I crossed my legs and rubbed my hands as if washing. "No. I'm being snarky. Let's say I'm still touchy about how our marriage ended. Life wasn't terrible, but we were not close. To casual observers, it appeared we spent time together. Physical presence concealed a lack of emotional intimacy. On vacation, we read at the ocean and barely exchanged a glance. We might be random strangers on the bus. A really nice bus."

"Did you golf together?"

"We both golfed but not together. I mean never ever. I think that says a lot."

She nodded in agreement.

"As you might guess, things weren't the greatest between us. We lived our detached lives in the same house with no fighting. What's to fight about when the banker calls to say you have too much money in your checking account? I was content to work and play golf and go to parties. Until last May. Three of my golfing and drinking buddies and I were ready to tee off on a blustery Saturday morning. A thunderstorm hurtled over the ridge at the southwest corner of the course. Lightning split open an ancient oak on the ninth fairway. Like a bomb." I tossed my arms. "The sirens started soon after and that ended our golf for the day. The usual agenda was to play eighteen holes, eat a leisurely lunch, drink, and tell lies to each other until three in the afternoon. My buddies headed to the clubhouse to drink, but I begged off. Fatigue from working nights earlier in the week hit me, so I went home. I found my wife in her robe and one of her partners in *my* frickin' robe. No explanation required. I drove out to Camden to horse country and checked into a bed-and-breakfast for the night."

"Did you try to work things out?"

"I considered it, but she was done with me and asked for the divorce. I had nobody to talk to. Every one of my golfing buddies had cheated on his wife. I'd be asking the fox if he should be forgiven for stealing eggs."

"Did you?" she said.

"What?"

"Steal eggs."

"Never."

"Not even close?"

"Tempted, but never."

She made a wistful face.

"Don't feel sorry for me, now. I realized that I still loved her, but I didn't enjoy her company anymore. I could understand if I was not available to meet her sexual needs, but she had resisted my attempts to initiate intimacy many times. And this is it. The take-home message. Still stings she didn't lose interest in sex but in me. Like lightning splitting that tree open, I realized that I too was unlikable. At that moment, I decided that to get over being one of the top horse's asses in Columbia, South Carolina, I needed to do something drastic."

"I assume there is more than living here for three months." She winked.

"I sat in a green wooden rocker on the second-floor veranda of the Camden House and sketched my future."

"What did you draw?"

"Stop drinking, sell my shit, move to New Orleans, and learn how to be a proper human again."

"This is random, but is New Orleans the best place to stop drinking?"

"Yeah. No. That part might not be well-planned. Thing is, I'm setting that life down. I need to prove that I can be a person someone wants to love."

9

FOR THE NEXT two weeks, I followed Kayla's program. Up with the sun, big breakfast, speed walking on the beach, weight training, light lunch, afternoon nap, swim laps, light dinner, evening conversation, and early bedtime. My stamina returned, and I stored the emotional energy of a sage. Monday morning, Kayla made eggs Benedict, and I ate like an Olympic swimmer. Still, I'd look back at my crappy life with regret for squandering those years. Pavlov's dog. Little things might trigger an unhappy journey to the past. This morning, Patsy Cline sang "Crazy" on the radio. My parents collected albums from the country stars of the '50s through the '70s. Singing was a staple of life in our home. During meals we took turns deciding what song to sing while doing dishes. We were bound by it. My wife showed no interest. I could clear the room if I played Hank Williams. I turned it loose. Those memories cascaded into thoughts of disappointing my parents.

"Hey. Still with me?" she said.

"Yeah. Just engaging in a bit of self-loathing."

"Can you change what happened before today?"

"No." Her toughness showed. No sliding back. She turned our barstools to face each other, and we intertwined legs.

"And does dwelling on it make the pill any easier to swallow, *doctor*?" She emphasized doctor.

"No. I am finding it tough to keep my failures out of my head." Except for my parents and my wife, Rachel, I never had a stronger desire to please someone. I could feel Jane poking my chest.

"I got that. Some things you need to release." She took my hands in hers and opened her arms. "Regret, doubt, fear, anger, grief. You can leave them at your feet."

"I had similar thoughts standing at water's edge the day I arrived. Those emotions are tricky bastards."

"Yes. Definitely. Be right back." She returned wearing a basic one-piece red bathing suit like the lifeguards wear on *Baywatch*. Those chicks had nothing on her. My bathing trunks dangled from her long finger. "Pants off, please."

I returned from my bedroom in proper attire. We hauled yellow sea kayaks to the coastline and Kayla barked the lesson, over the din of crashing surf, on how to paddle through the breakers. I mounted the craft but couldn't get forward momentum before the next wave. She offered encouragement but no assistance. Success came on my third try and she followed like crossing a millpond. Despite recent weight training, my upper body strength sucked, and my arms ached already. We paddled fifty yards out to smoothly rolling sea, leaving behind the sound of the raucous rollers.

"See that flat spit of land before the Mokes?" she said.

"The one ten miles from here?"

"Quit whining. It's a three-mile round trip. I could swim that. Popoia Island. We'll kayak around it. No thinking. Just paddling."

We sculled for a few minutes and she let me catch up. As I reached her, she took off again and yapped a sports cliché. Her encouragement helped, but my failure to keep up embarrassed me. Golf had been my only physical activity if you could call it that. Pathetic. I looked trim and fit, but I had softened. Body and mind. I made a goal to one day beat her on this trek. As we reached Popoia, my thoughts centered on not vomiting.

"I take a minute to look for birds and return."

I glided next to her in opposing directions. Only a few stray Bulwer's petrels stood watch since breeding season was past. "You're not out of breath. Killing me, you are."

"I normally cut between the Mokes. Add another two miles."

"Not helping. How long have you been at this?"

She looked up and her lips quivered. "Four times a week for fourteen months. Now when I'm in the mood."

Since her husband died. Now I understood why she

was driving me. Casual observers might say she was too hard on me, blind to my feelings. The opposite.

"Why did you stop?"

"There was no more to carry," she said.

"What?"

"Grief. Those negative emotions. I loaded them up each day and cast them between the islands."

"Simple as that?"

She gripped my wrist. Hard. Serious now. "Not simple. Next to leaving Ireland, hardest thing I've done. At first, I hated it. I cried dragging this thing to the bay." She set her chin and looked to Lanikai. "First time I traversed high surf, took me eight times. We'll talk more at home."

She pushed off and paddled twice as fast. Didn't turn back. Didn't stray from her course. The advantage of seeing success before me and having a guide was mine. Like the guy who ran the first four-minute mile, doubt might have been her heaviest burden. She landed fifteen minutes ahead and waited on the sand as I approached. A wave caught me sideways as I entered the breakers. Too much angle. A six-footer drilled me into a flat rock, forcing the wind from my chest, and dumping the kayak and paddle twenty yards along the shore. My hat and sunglasses vanished. Kayla ran to find me fighting to draw a breath. On hands and knees now, I sputtered and coughed. Water rushed under me. She kneeled, and I raised a hand to signal my desire to deal with my mess. I stood and shuffled around, hoping to find my glasses.

"Lost to Poseidon. A hip dolphin will wear those by nightfall," Kayla said.

Funny. When I was young and pouting, my parents would tell me my face was cracking and I laughed. My face wasn't cracking. I jogged to my kayak, now twice as far, towed it clear, and ran another twenty yards to the paddle. The voluptuous veteran, steadfast at the high tide mark, surveyed the rookie floundering. I considered returning to the water to float the kayak back but wanted to avoid another beating. Alternating arms, I trudged through forgiving sand forfeiting one step for every three.

"I'm sorry. I should have warned you." She prodded my abraded ribs. "You think you broke one?"

"Did anybody warn you?"

"No."

"Okay then. That will never happen again."

She turned my kayak on its side next to the other. "Please don't be cross."

I stepped nose to nose and rested my hands on her shapely hips. "How could I be cross with you? I love you." The words left my mouth like a breeze turning the pages of a novel on a park bench. Unplanned and unrehearsed. I forgot what page I was reading.

Then the tears. She fell into my arms. I sensed the last of her consignment of sorrow sift through eternal sand. I knew my silent presence was enough for now. There was only the moment. We held a long sensuous kiss and sat on the sand.

"Grief was my unwelcome companion and when

I was freed of it, the solitude was nearly as painful. Thank you for finding me."

"I believe it was you who found *me* sitting on the beach. And it was you who saved me from a thorny problem. That's a most unselfish act. It is you, Miss Kayla, who deserves the thanks."

We walked to the house. The tenderness of that moment made me realize my sketchy plans demanded reconsideration. A year in New Orleans now seemed like a decade and a solitary life void of personal attachments a naïve farce.

"When you said, 'That will never happen again.' Meaning, you're not going out there again?"

"Hell no. That's the last beat down I take from the damn Pacific Ocean. I'm splitting the Mokes tomorrow."

"Why don't you take a day tomorrow? Give those ribs a rest. Come to work with me. We'll get you sunglasses and a strap on the way home."

I stopped her at the pool and we faced each other.

"Do you feel the anticipation?" We held hands, almost exchanging vows. "I remember leaving for prom with my date. The wonder and the freedom."

She smiled and nodded. "The hope. Excitement." Her smile widened. "Tell me about your prom."

"Well. I enjoyed a tight gang of friends but with girls, words like awkward and klutzy applied. My date and I shared secrets but never intimacy. The only date we had. We partied until breakfast. Great fun."

"And you?"

"End of my final year of school in Ireland. I dated a boy for three years. That week I decided to come to America. Slow dancing to some tune I can't recall, and I told him." Her smile waned. "He walked away. Full of myself. I should have thought of him more."

"I didn't mean to stir up an unhappy memory," I said.

"No worries. I started it."

I pulled her close. Nose to nose. "Listen. On the beach. I know that came out of nowhere. I meant it, but I don't want you to be uncomfortable."

"I like that your feelings were spontaneous. More genuine that way." Another long kiss. "So, I'm off to work, then dinner with potential donors. Not sure when I'll be back. We have hours and hours to talk."

While she dressed, I found shrimp in the freezer and a variety of veggies. I peeled a dozen twenty-count crustaceans and tossed them in boiling water. I put the shrimp on ice and arranged a vibrant mix of sliced green and yellow peppers, carrots, and tomatoes on *poco piatti*. Ranch dressing in one bowl and cocktail sauce in the other. As I placed napkins and ice waters, I wondered if my avowal of love was premature. She didn't say *I love you* back. Although I was married twenty years, I considered myself to be an amateur regarding relationships and was not versed in the social convention of the first *I love you* interaction. I dated a few women in college but nothing serious. Medical school may as well have been a monastery until I met my wife at the end of my last year. There was no getting around it. I sucked at relationships. Of my wide circle of friends, I shared no close relationships. I never offered feelings of success, failure, frustration, to even my best friend and rarely to my wife. This avoided the highs and lows that accompany intimacy. And then you vomit on the beach.

Nurses admired me for my even-temperedness. There is a happy ground between clinical detachment and crying everyone's tears. Doctors need to keep patients at arm's length or self-destruct from emotional fatigue. I leaned toward clinical detachment but found turning this off for my personal life challenging. Work often required the emotional stoicism of Spock.

> It's four a.m., my eyelids weigh five pounds, and a pill addict, emaciated, half-toothless, face like a dirt road, soiled Clemson T-shirt, with chronic pain, wants a shot of morphine. The rest of the medical staff, along with most of the city, is at slumber and this guy, who I'm seeing for free, is bitching me out. *You don't give a shit about me, asshole. I wasted my freaking time coming in here 'cuz you ain't doin' nothin' for me.* I stand there and take it while the guy storms out. An hour later, EMS brings in a skinny fifteen-year-old girl. Cardiac arrest from a house fire. Smoke inhalation and cyanide poisoning. They found her in the bathtub clutching her dead schnauzer mix.

He looked like Toto. We devote an hour to saving her but after that she lay motionless on the white vinyl body bag, fake pearl earrings, barrette in her blonde hair, purple nightgown. The dad burned dead at the scene. I hold mom's hand and say, marble faced, her daughter died too.

I can't flip the emotional switch when I get in my car after a night like that. Whiskey helped. Until it didn't.

I didn't hear her coming. Kayla put her arms around my belly. "You were looking to California there. Everything okay?"

"Sure. I'm here with you and little else matters right now."

10

THE FOLLOWING DAY I showered and stood before the mirror drying my beard. Save for trimming it, I hadn't considered it more than one considers their nose or ears. It was there for thirty years. My wife, neighbors, friends, coworkers only knew me with a beard. It sprouted a few weeks after completing high school. Eager to become independent, the whiskers, according to my underdeveloped frontal lobes, were the physical manifestation of adulthood. Mom and Dad razzed me for weeks until it matured. No desire existed to return to young adulthood. I sucked at it. I hoped to recapture some of the guy with the clean face, though. I could grow it back any time. What's the difference between a good haircut and a bad one? Three weeks. I opened and closed three drawers trying to locate razors and shaving cream.

I wrapped a towel around me and walked toward her bedroom. "Kay. I'm looking for a razor."

She stuck her head around the door. "Did you call me Kay?"

"Uh, yeah. I won't do it again if you don't want."

"No. No. The last time someone called me Kay was when I was seventeen. My mother. She was the only one. I love that you called me Kay."

I dulled three razors shaving it off my round cheeks and considered, but vetoed, a solitary mustache. All or nothing. The cool feeling on my face, foreign, like the first time you wear glasses, would take some getting used to, but the result pleased me. I walked to the kitchen where Kayla rinsed a breakfast dish and she performed the mother of all double takes.

"Who is this strange, beardless man in my house?" She came to me and rubbed the back of her hand on my cheek. "I love it. But why?"

"Samuel Buchanan with the beard no longer exists. Like witness protection."

She held my face in her hands and then a passionate kiss. I wondered if we might be headed to her bed. "Okay, then. Off we go," she said.

———

I started toward the passenger side of her Mercedes.

"Uh uh." She tossed me the keys to the Mustang.

"Oh, no. If I crash this thing, I'll go to automotive hell."

"Come on. Don't be a pussy."

I backed out. Strange to drive a car without a backup camera. We rolled to the end of the weedless pea-gravel driveway, and I put it in park. This was not a gnawing question for me. The guy was dead, not a crazy ex-husband, but I needed to understand Gordy as much for me as for Kayla. Just like shaving, today was a good day.

"Tell me about Gordy."

"Six months ago, this conversation brought tears," she said. "Couldn't do it."

Gordy retired from the Navy as an O-6. A Captain. Air is getting thin at that rank. Kayla called him wicked smart. He learned computers and software, early days, on his own and wrote an important program for the Navy. He built a software company that dealt with classified navigation systems.

"So, he was older."

"By ten years."

They would have welcomed children, but Gordy was infertile because of treatment of leukemia as a child. She knew it going in. She held her love for him above any desire for a family.

"Did you pick him up on the beach like me?"

Thwack. Right across the chest. "This story is not as romantic but still sweet. I was cutting hair in Kāne'ohe. He drove from Ewa every three weeks for two months, giving me excellent tips, before he mustered the courage to ask me on a date. He told me he was an introverted nerd, and he was, but he had a heart of gold. Drive, please."

I could have passed a driver's test. Like driving with a goldfish bowl on the front seat. "Tell me more about the foundation," I said.

"Before Gordy died, we discussed forming a foundation to help create programs to assist Polynesian teens. When he died, I used half of the windfall from insurance and the sale of his business to create the Leilani Foundation. Ten million."

"Wow. Why Leilani?"

"Leilani translates to *royal child of heaven*."

"Enjoying it?"

"Yes, but I'm building a house I've yet to live in, planting a tree that has not bloomed. We'll make our first grants soon."

"I understand. Could be years before you see tangible results." I pulled into the lot at the foundation office.

"Right. I'll be patient." She rested her hand on my thigh. "Sam, I've been thinking about your job. How do you cope with the chaos and the death?"

"First, I did not cope. I drank too much, and I shut out my wife. Forgot the reason for being there. My light went out."

"Can you rekindle the flame?"

"Yes. Lots of work to do there."

"You say you forgot. Have you remembered?"

"Partially. I need patients to show me again, so it's part of me again. As emergency docs, we have this colossal gift and responsibility. Some say privilege. I say gift because we have no right to care for people unless they grant it. People invite us into their lives when they are most vulnerable. Pain, bleeding, trouble breathing, stroke symptoms, suicidal thoughts, fever, vomiting."

"How do you know all this stuff?"

"The lost decade."

"You lost me too."

"College, Medical school, three years of residency, devoted to this gift."

"Long time."

"Yes. And I've been squandering my skills. I need to show up each day to give my very best. When patients offer this gift, I owe them nothing less."

11

COOL RAIN PELTED that early November day as I entered mild surf at low tide. I set a goal to reach the Mokes. I paced myself and rested often. Peace lived within the rhythm of the paddle strokes. I forgot the rain and left my unhappy past alone for a time. Despite my issues, my father and I remained close until his death. My mother died a year after him. After his funeral I sat alone on the time-worn front pew of the church. There was the grief but also a serenity, a quietness of mind, which I found reassuring. Being the only one in the bay allowed that feeling to visit me again and even though the sky was full of mist, I could see past the horizon. The smell from an extinguished candle filled my head as I stroked.

I reached the shallows between the Mokes and Lanikai. As I caught my breath, the rain abated, and the clouds dispersed. I smiled because my skin appeared to be an orange peel fresh from the fridge. I wondered as I approached the bald man, clean shaven today, in the neon green kayak. Three more strokes and I recognized Steven.

"You'll miss it unless you turn around," he said.

I dug the paddle, pushed forward, and came about. A double rainbow arched above Kailua, lost in the mountains at either end. Postcard perfect. I eased next to him and extended my hand.

"Thanks for that. I might have missed it. Figured I was the only one crazy enough to start out in crappy weather."

"You can't see rainbows if you don't go out in the rain. This double rainbow is fortuitous because it's a symbol of transformation."

"For me?"

"Yes, indeed. I share these waters with all sorts. Lazy paddlers, eco-tourists, and athletes. I can tell when someone is paddling through a crisis. It's the look on the face. Resolute tears are the dead giveaway."

"Is this a coincidence or were you expecting me?" I said.

"I'm out here most mornings. Figured I'd see you eventually. I hear you are doing well."

"Kayla." I smiled.

"Sure. Part of the deal. Would you like to talk?"

"Yes. Very much so."

"We could discuss anything, but I'm interested in what you enjoy most at work," he said.

I tucked my paddle along my feet. "Making the diagnosis." I didn't need to think.

"Go on."

"Everyone goes into medicine so they can help people. I can hold someone's hand or get them a turkey sandwich or fluff their pillow and they will feel better, but I'm not helping them. In the ER, it's the diagnosis. They come with fever and chest pain and I find pneumonia. They come with abdominal pain and I find appendicitis or diverticulitis. Or a sixty-five-year-old man coughs up blood and he can't sleep for three nights thinking he has cancer. I do a CAT scan and tell him it's only bronchitis, not cancer or a blood clot."

"I see how that's rewarding."

"Yes. It is."

Steven paddled to the other side of me, face to face now. "There's always a *but*."

"I don't follow."

"My job is rewarding, *but...*" he said.

Now I understood and the memory crashed forward in a blink.

My last shift in Carolina. The Tuesday after Labor Day. The first weekday after a holiday sucks. I guess I felt guilty for leaving and agreed to work through the holiday. Bad decision. When I arrived, the unmistakable stench of an upper GI bleed assaulted me. I smelled it the rest of the night. Every other bed in the place was full of admitted patients and the others housed people in various stages of their workup. Plus, ten pissed-off patients crammed the lobby. The stress was thick as toothpaste. I could do it without fear because I had done it before. At my order, the nurses moved stable patients from their rooms to the hallway. They gave me the look a teenager gives when told to cut the yard on Saturday morning. The first guy back from the lobby, a forty-year-old guy with indigestion, was having a heart attack. What the hell. Just as I asked the clerk to call the cardiologist, EMS called in with a double trauma. CPR in progress on one. We called a Trauma Alert and between the cardiology team and the trauma team, a dozen outsiders barked orders at my nurses, already overwhelmed. The cardiologist, a year out of training, had the balls to bitch me out for letting the guy with the heart attack sit in the lobby for forty minutes. I let it go then but before I said goodbye to the nurses, I found that pissant cardiologist. I had nothing to lose, so I ripped him a new one in the middle of the ICU. Then I went home and drank whiskey.

"We handle a lot of shit in the ER. You need to wear waders," I said.

"And."

"And it sucks the flipping life out of you." I rarely show anger. That jumped out between the cars. "There are so many obstacles and distractions at the hospital you would think they are trying to *keep* you from making the diagnosis. The damn electronic medical record designed by total fools, endless interruptions, slow lab, slow X-ray, grumpy consultants, and hospital administrators less useful than tits on a bull."

Steven grabbed the edge of my kayak as a rogue swell passed beneath us. "I see why you are frustrated."

"No. It's flipping frustrating when they screw up your order at Panera. It's downright maddening when you are working your ass off trying to help sick people, some near death, and the rest of the hospital doesn't step up. Our door *never* shuts, and we can't turn people away, but the hospital floors and the ICU take patients at their leisure while our new patients pile up like derailed boxcars, and administrators hide in their offices. Few people work in that kind of chaos."

"You have little control over what happens in your work, yet you must take full responsibility. Am I right?" he said.

"Yes, and what makes you want to drink heavily, which I did, is when people who never get their hands dirty and know next to nothing of medicine try to tell you how to do your job. They have no clue how damn useless they are."

I was gripping the edge of the kayak, riding a twenty-foot wave. Steven touched my hand and I released. I shut work out of my mind since arriving on the island and I found no joy in kicking that door open.

"You plan to start work in January in New Orleans. Do you suppose these things will be a problem there as well?"

I wrung my hands and studied them. This was pissing me off because he showed me the holes in my plan without being direct like my wife. The chess match in my head was progressing well. Then he knocked over my queen. "Yes."

"Okay. We are making progress here, but we don't need to rush. Let me say this before we part, and we'll see each other soon." He placed his hand on my arm. "Your work is incredibly challenging and often out of control. *But.* You will always have control of the most important thing. How you react. How you view the situation. Consider that and we'll talk soon."

I paddled home in a fury at first, and then a comfortable rhythm. Quiet mind. Just the rhythm. When I reached Kayla's yard, mental and physical fatigue caused me to collapse into a sunbathed lounge. Ten minutes or ten hours might have passed. I awakened to the sound of water. Not the ocean. Splashing. I turned to view Kayla flow naked from the water and reach for a towel. She wrapped it above her upturned breasts and another around her head like a sexy swami. I had never been so aroused.

"You were out on the ocean, right?" She smiled and gave a wet kiss then sat facing me on the adjacent chair.

"Ha. Forget the water. When I opened my eyes, I had to consider what continent I was on. I was really out."

"Hawai'i is not a continent."

"My point exactly."

"How was your paddle?" she said.

"I talked to Steven, but you probably knew that."

"Actually not. He knows you paddle." She placed her hands together as if in prayer, eyes on me. "We are not conspiring, Sam."

"Yes. I'm sorry. I'm touchy because we discussed my work and it stirred me up."

"Did it piss you off?" She pushed my shoulder. Like a cat jumped out from a dark alley.

I sat up and faced her. "Damn right."

"Good." She stood, and the towel slipped to the ground. Kayla left it in a heap and strolled to her bedroom.

I sat there pouting for a minute and then ran after her. I caught her from behind and wrapped my arms around her waist.

"If we don't make love soon, I might go mad," she said.

She pulled off the bedspread as if it were afire and we fell into bed in a tangle. Our emotional and physical release might have been heard on Maui.

"Last to the pool makes lunch."

She pushed me back on the bed and fled naturally. I followed knowing I gave up the race before it started. June Carter and Merle Kilgore wrote the song "Ring of Fire" and it was in my head now. I fell all right. To say this was a departure from my intentions would be like saying Elvis enjoyed modest success in the music business. I found her floating on her back, Mokes on full display. The cannonball I landed flooded the islands and we held a long embrace. And the fire got hotter.

We pulled close. "My prom didn't end like this," she said.

"Right. Me neither." I wanted to joke about hiding from her father but reconsidered.

"What? You're smiling."

"Nothing."

"I can tell when you want to make a wise crack, Dr. Buchanan." Full Irish.

I kissed her forehead. "A long time has passed since I've been this happy."

She drew in resting her chin on my shoulder. A whisper. "I know why you were on that plane."

In my best Johnny Cash singing voice, I sang the refrain for "Ring of Fire."

Kayla joined with the harmony.

Foliage rustled between the properties, so we kicked to the edge, chin level, against the wall. JoJo wore a simple red sundress. She crossed the yard, engrossed in something happening near the shore, and almost missed us as she passed.

"Oh, Lord." She stopped and started several times but couldn't control her laughter. "I was coming over to chat. There you go. Look at you two. I'll leave you be."

"No. No," Kayla said. "Sit and talk a while."

"Was that Johnny Cash on the radio? They never play him here."

"That was us."

The way Kayla cocked her head when she said it, ushered a closeness absent from my life for so long

I stopped yearning for it. The serotonin rush came again, and I shivered.

"JoJo, thank you again for a splendid evening. You and Stan made me feel so welcome here."

Kayla looked at me and pushed my head away. "And this is what?"

"This is an entirely new dimension of welcome."

"Good answer."

"I'll leave you nudists alone now," JoJo said.

"Wait, wait. Tell me what the minister said."

Kayla cocked her head and furrowed her brow. I explained.

"Oh, right. You naked folks are distracting me. He can do the ceremony. We'll make a nice party of it. Your job, Sam, is to get my husband out of the house for four hours that day."

"No worries," I said.

"Take him fishing," Kayla said.

"Fishing stinks this time of year, and I'll just get sick. Happens every time."

"You'll think of something. I'm going. Enjoy yourselves now."

Kayla planted a sloppy smooch. "You heard her. Let's get back in there."

———

Kayla invited Stan and JoJo to dinner that night. She introduced me to sous vide cooking and we made tender and moist tuna steaks fit for a five-star restaurant. We let them rest in their warm bath while tending to Caesar salad, rosemary redskin potatoes, and brownies. Brownies baking is to food what the smell of gardenias is to flowers. I told her that only my love for her exceeded my love of chocolate.

Stan and I seared the tuna on the stainless-steel Viking outdoor grill. He swigged his Kona Longboard, and I sampled the nonalcoholic beer he summoned from Whole Foods. I sensed Stan wanted to say something, so we drank, and seared, and viewed a freighter pass in the distance.

"After Jo was over here, she ushered me into the bedroom, and we had the most energetic sex in years. Skip the stress test. If I didn't get chest pain, I know my heart is good."

I laughed so hard St. Pauli N.A. came out my nose.

"What the hell did ya'll talk about over here?"

I recounted the skinny dipping. She didn't see much, but sometimes it's just the thought. The memory of it made my face, and other parts, flush. Stan offered to come over and lifeguard any time. If someone told me, as I boarded in Atlanta, in a few days I'd be having this chat with a billionaire, I would have suggested they missed a dose of their antipsychotic medication.

"What did you think of Gordy?" I said.

"Solid as they come. I'm just a country boy and only understood half the stuff he said. We were not buddies. Jo, Jane, and Kayla? Sisters. In the mafia. I call 'em the Tropical Tribe. Jo stayed with her for a month after he bought it."

After our meal, JoJo and I cleared the last of the dishes and found ourselves alone in the indoor kitchen. As with Stan, I perceived she had something to say.

"Samuel." Like my mother called me. "I see you use the diminutive, Kay."

"Uh, yeah." Not sure where this was going.

"Six months passed before Stan called me Jo. This is getting serious isn't it?"

Our cascade into adoration, and unforgettable sex, was hasty. I wrestled with my post-Kailua plans. I committed to myself, Touro Infirmary in New Orleans, and my landlord, for a year. These were promises I would not break. The idea of separating from Kayla made me nauseated. I explained the commitments I had made and my shortcomings as a human, like a kid trying to convince his mother of his capacity to care for a puppy. Kayla stepped into the kitchen. JoJo raised her palm and flipped her hand as if shooing the dog off the furniture. Kayla retreated. I was figuring things out as I spoke. Words were leaves stirred by a passing car. Visits back and forth, Skype, time speeding by, etcetera...

"This is an uncharted sea." I held my hands together beneath my lips. "I promise I will make this work."

JoJo stepped to me putting one foot between mine. I expected the finger in the chest. Like in the airplane galley, on her toes, her mouth at my earlobe. "Recent times have been a mystery to me. You are a mystery to me. Maybe this is why you were on that plane." She placed her hands on my cheeks. "No beard. I like it."

12

I AWAKENED WITH KAY behind me spooning. Rain, same as the previous day, pattered on the tile roof, only harder. The soundtrack for sleeping in. I used the bath and returned to find my love with the covers tucked under her. I tugged against firm resistance while she tried to suppress that million-dollar smile.

"You promised to kayak today," she said.

I stood there naked trying to figure a way back into bed. "But I paddled yesterday in the rain. Plus, I checked the Weather Channel and they issued a three-hour rain delay."

"Nice try. I went fifty times in the rain." She gave me the JoJo flip of the hand shooing me. "You'll thank me one day. Plus, I'll be your reward when you return." She flashed me and, in an instant, covered again. "No shortcuts."

—

Kayla found the paddling to be therapeutic and I understood. I meditated with the rhythm of the strokes. The mindfulness allowed my brain time for renewal. Muscles ached, and the rain nipped but I worked through it. I stopped in the shallows and dismounted. No Steven. Because of the cool air and pelting rain, the water warmed me. I rested with my chin at water's edge and ran my hands over the surface, alive from the minute aquatic explosions. *On the pew again, I could smell the candles.* The lights of the homes on Lanikai leaked through the mist. I sat on the ocean floor, invisible to the world, and considered my discussion with Steven. He was telling me to let it go. Forget the obstacles and just take care of people. So, what if something sucks or someone is an asshole? Don't give a shit about anything but the sick patients. Everything else is just bullshit. Do I care if someone with a damn zit on their butt waits for three hours? No. Because I can't fix that. Let a worthless shiny-shoed administrator waste her time. Let her worry about the stupid patient satisfaction scores.

Yes, they are stupid. Do they ask the guy with heart failure, who I saw thirty seconds after he arrived, and saved, if he is satisfied with his ER experience? No. Because he gets admitted. Do they ask the guy with back pain for four weeks, who I declined to prescribe an opiate, about his experience? You bet. It's like grading a detective on how many jaywalkers she catches. I decided to value only the stuff that mattered. Anything else, who gives a crap? I'd be outwardly pleasant. Some administrator drones on about this or that statistic—on the inside I'll be thinking *blah, blah, blah*. I laughed out loud, looked up at the sky, and let rain fill my mouth. The comfort of solitude arrived. My mind quieted and I felt the sand, the motion of the water, the rain on my face, the joy in my heart.

A following wind eased my journey home, but the deluge persisted. Who cares? I was wet anyway, and I didn't need to shovel it. As I reached the pool deck, the shivers came. I sprinted to the pool and landed a world-class cannonball. Until the applause, I missed Steven and Kayla sitting under cover drinking coffee.

"Unhappy people don't fling themselves into the pool," Steven said.

The pool felt like bathwater. "Despite your absence, I made a fruitful excursion."

"Nobody else is foolish enough to kayak in a downpour," Kayla said.

"Funny." I splashed in her direction. I considered continuing the banter but was unsure if Steven knew of our sleeping arrangements.

After a brief shower, I returned in warmer attire with a mug of hot tea. Kayla left us to talk. I told him of my morning's revelation borne of cold rain and warm ocean.

"Good. I can't help you with the nuts and bolts of functioning in your workplace. You'll make that work. What I might say to an accountant will have little application for you." He drank his coffee and studied the rain. "Do you have any empathy left?"

"Am I so burnt out that I can't appreciate the feelings of others?" I said.

"Yes. Can you understand the life circumstances of a poor mother of four unruly children who brings them in at eleven p.m. for something more appropriately seen by her pediatrician?"

"Yes, I can do that. I need to break some bad habits. I've been cynical and have ignored the patient's perspective. Sometimes I view patients as the enemy, a potential threat."

"Tell me more."

I hate to think about it and never want to talk. I would give up chocolate to erase it from memory. "I lost a terrible lawsuit. Still invades my sleep. Like damn termites in my head."

"Sam, I sense this will be difficult for you. We can save it for another time."

I shook my head. "Ten years ago. I worked this ER only two shifts each year. Healthy five-year-old vomited for two days. Mom brought him to one of our small rural ERs. He was dry as a chip. Sunken eyes, tongue a dirt road. I hydrated with IV fluids because he looked like hell. I transferred him to Charleston because he was a new onset diabetic and had ketoacidosis. Very serious. He ended up with swelling of his brain, and he died two days later."

"Seems to me you provided good care."

"Yeah. When a kid dies, people search for someone to blame. They found a damn rent-an-expert to say I gave him too much fluid. That was crap. Cerebral edema happens with ketoacidosis and sometimes there is nothing to do."

"You did your best and the people you helped lashed out at you."

"Right. And it's hard to not let that infect your life. The case dragged on for five ugly, tedious years. They tried to make me look like an itinerant imbecile. And the judge was biased. She should have recused herself. She had a fifteen-year-old daughter with diabetes. I hate that the kid died, hate being skewered in court, and hate, hate, hate that the boy's parents think I injured him."

"I'm chilled. Let's sit inside," Steven said.

We sat on the sofa. I leaned forward and rubbed my face with my hands. "It's better with time, but I drag that around. Some days it's a thick old log."

"I understand. Sometimes it helps if you can recall another serious case where things went well. To remind you things are not always unhappy."

It came immediately. "This will seem strange to you because it involves another child that died. Christmas morning 2014. First patient of the day, my stethoscope was still cold. EMS brought a six-week-old girl. Mom found her in the crib not breathing. SIDS. I placed a breathing tube, and we did CPR and gave epinephrine. After forty-five minutes of resuscitation, I place my hand on her perfectly shaped head with fine black hair and decided to stop. I told the nurses and respiratory therapist to keep working. I explained to the mom, a tall brunette, alone in the family room, winter coat over her nightgown, and offered she could come in before we stopped. We walked toward the room and she grasped my hand as a child would before crossing the street. *Lizzy has not been baptized. Can I do that before you stop?* In the storage room I filled a stainless-steel bowl with sterile water and found a white towel. I placed the towel under Lizzy's head and held the bowl. Mom dribbled water on Lizzy's forehead and made the sign of the cross. *'Mary Elizabeth Lee. My dear child of God. I baptize you in the name of the Father, Son, and Holy Spirit. Amen.'*

We couldn't save Lizzy, but we did something for the mom that will bring her comfort for the rest of her days."

Tears traversed Steven's cheeks. That was enough for the day.

13

BETWEEN KAYAKING, HIKING, and evening time with Kayla, I familiarized myself with the surfing scene. For this to work, I needed to convince Stan that I loved surfing and needed him to go with me to the North Shore to view the surfing competition. I scoured websites and social media and, after a few hours, I realized I enjoyed it. Stan offered his car but after JoJo aimed the evil eye of guilt, he agreed to go with the stipulation that we stop for lunch at his favorite place up there. Sure. Easier to kill the time.

On the big day, I showed up twenty minutes early. JoJo and I sipped tea and reviewed the plans for the day. An hour up, an hour to view the surfing, an hour to eat, and an hour home. *And don't let him drink more than one beer.* She reminded me of my key role in keeping the element of surprise. She, out of the side of her mouth, admonished me to not *screw the pooch*. No pressure. Not long after our departure, the tent company, caterer, musicians, and florist, descended and transformed their home. Hairdressers for the tribe came later. I surprised JoJo by asking about her dress. Evidently men, in general, overlook the meaning of the dress for such an occasion. Go figure. She revealed the many factors they considered. This was much more information than desired. I was just making small talk. After hours of discussion among the Tropical Tribe, they settled on a dress and Jane found it in downtown Honolulu. Off white, three-quarters-length linen dress, open shoulders, medium straps, and a hint of cleavage. They spent an afternoon finding new pants and coordinating shirt for Stan. Kisses all around, except Stan and me, and we were on our way. *Enjoy your day. Take your time.*

Stan's garage had four bays, and like Kayla's, was nicer than most people's homes. Georgia Bull Dog theme. Red and black. Centered on the floor in the solitary open bay was a generous Georgia G. In the next bay, an E-Class Mercedes. A modest choice for someone who could buy the whole dealership. Next slot, a Honda CR-V Touring. That was for the ever-practical JoJo. The 1928 Ford Model A Roadster Convertible, cream with red wheels, was clearly a driver. There were scuffs on the fenders, the spoked wheels suffered chips, and tires showed wear. Stan gave me a choice figuring I would choose the Benz. I checked the weather app on my phone. A marvelous sunny day awaited. I pointed at the Ford.

"This make it up there?"

"Hell yeah. I drive this baby all over the island."

I lied and told him I hadn't driven a manual car in thirty years, so he would need to drive. That solved the problem of restricting alcohol. Also, I knew it would take me a while to learn to double clutch, and I wanted to avoid grinding his transmission. Stan drove like a stunt man. The top speed surprised me. He advised that a high compression head, added last year, gave it another five miles per hour. We navigated the narrow coastal byway, getting occasional glimpses of the ocean. I marveled at Mokoli'i, the Chinaman's Hat, lonesome off the coast, erupting from the sea. We slipped past small groups of homes, some well-kept and others near collapse, past the Polynesian Cultural Center, the Mormons, and Turtle Bay Resort.

We arrived at the Banzai Pipeline to find cars scattered as if a tsunami happened. Stan pulled up to a gate, spotted with warning signs, where two linebacker-sized policemen stood. NO ADMITTANCE. TOURNAMENT STAFF ONLY. He stepped out and shook hands with each. They talked with heads bobbing and arms moving followed by laughing, back slapping and another round of handshakes. The officers opened the gate and Stan drove through and parked next to a low metal building where surfers loitered.

"They speak the universal language," Stan said.

"Love?" I elbowed him.

He chuckled. "Dinero. A hundred clams each solved that problem."

Several surfers came to admire the Ford. The old girl was growing on me. The patina, the distinctive low voice of the muffler, the click of the transmission, and the simplicity of the machine attracted me.

These surfers were skinny guys, but they looked strong enough to pick up the car and carry it away. In my studies I learned names and faces. I recognized one of the top contenders, a short blonde dude.

"J.C. Collins, right?"

He smiled, we shook hands, and I wished him luck. As we walked away, I saw Stan left the key, and I mentioned it. He kept on walking.

"I could leave it running. These jokers couldn't drive a stick shift to get to the two-for-one special at the whore house."

We walked to the sand and stood among scruffy-looking kids in their twenties. After my time with Michael, I had a much better appreciation for this crowd. We, in the parlance of Stan, stood out like two hookers in the confession line. Just to set the hook, I fed Stan the high points of competitive surfing. Wave scoring, maneuvers, combos. He showed more interested in the hot chick in the white thong. The short-board surfers, waiting for the primo wave, bobbed like toy ducks. Once caught, they carved the twenty-foot wall, accelerating upward only to reverse course, making moves like a blues man works the neck of a guitar. When the required hour passed, we returned to the Ford.

Stan blasted the *aoogah* horn and waved at the cops as we cleared the gate. For a few miles we continued the same direction as our initial route and turned up a slim dirt road marked by a weathered wooden sign. The classic traversed the holes and ruts better than I expected. We would all need a wash at home. In a mile and a half, we gained a thousand feet of elevation. My ears popped, and my thoughts flashed to the flight from Atlanta. I wondered if Stan flashed back, but I suspected not. He didn't devote much attention to life's rearview mirror.

In a flat clearing, a wooden and metal building, freed of paint for ages, listed. The rusted corrugated roof hung over a stretched-out window where a clique of brown men with flat faces lingered. A hastily painted piece of plywood leaned against the wall. *The Kahale Grill.* As we climbed, Stan had warned me we would be the only *haole* there, and the menu contained one item. Wild boar sandwich. The only questions were how many and what to drink. Kona, iced tea, or water. I could smell the sweet barbecue sauce before we opened our doors. Like Norm on *Cheers,* Stan's exit from our trusty Ford brought a chorus of "Mr. Stan!" He glad-handed like he was running for governor and called each man by his name. Stan dropped a Franklin on the counter and egged the owner to serve the men whatever they wanted. He flashed the victory sign, and I raised an index. On paper plates, they served a generous portion of meat on a sesame seed bun dripping sauce plus coleslaw and chips. We both drank tea.

A row of picnic tables, aging no better than the building, pointed toward the coast so all could enjoy the panorama. If I didn't enjoy the food, I would still return for the 180-degree view of the north coast of O'ahu. Seabirds, with effort no more than breathing, soared and danced as they had been doing eons before man thought to ride the surf. We lost perspective of the size of the waves but gained the prospect of the girth and mass of the island.

"How are you doing?" Stan said.

This was more than polite conversation. "Kayla told you I visited the rehab place."

"She told Jo and you know how it goes."

"I don't mind. I'm well and I'm happy. In Carolina, I had the job, the money, the cars, the house, the country club, the beautiful wife, and I did not appreciate my blessings or find joy in them." I ticked them off on my fingers. "I'm embarrassed to say it. Like a spoiled kid."

"Yeah, you know what they say about money. Why don't you stay here? Get a Hawai'i license and open one of those urgent care deals. I think Kayla would like that."

"Maybe later. I made commitments to be in New Orleans for a year. I have something to prove to myself."

"Sure. JoJo and I are here for you."

I answered my phone because the ID showed an 808-area code. Kayla. I walked to the edge of the clearing. We had never talked on the phone. Disposal clogged and there was a sink full of stuff. Plumber says three hours. What to do? I promised a text back.

I thought of my new friend from my hike to the pillbox.

"Michael. Sam, from the pillbox. Where are you?"

"Lanikai, man. I'm with this awesome woman. She's like thirty-eight, but who cares, right?"

"Right. I need a huge favor. Tell your friend you'll be back in an hour and you're gonna take her to any restaurant she chooses tonight. I don't care if it's on Maui. My treat."

I explained the situation. Uber to Stan's, ask for Kayla, fix the disposal. Any tool needed will be at Kayla's.

I texted Kayla.

Plumber on way. JJ gives $500 cash. Love you.

"Everything okay?"

"Dinner plans. Kayla wants us to stop at the market and get shrimp."

"Hell, they can just call for delivery."

Whatever. Stan called and two, no three, pounds of twenty-count shrimp, plus six bottles of white wine, would beat us there. We enjoyed another cup of tea, sun on our faces, and discussion with the owner. He and Stan reviewed potential businesses in need of seed money. Stan wanted to create jobs for native islanders. It's not that he couldn't just give a bunch of money away. A gift was a short-term fix and did nothing to allow islanders to be productive, independent, and happy.

Stan paused before he started the car. "I thought ya'll were setting me up for something. Then you droned on about wave scoring and I knew you were into this stuff."

———

A quick shower was in order, so I asked Stan to drop me at Kayla's drive first. He questioned the cars on the street, and I shrugged my shoulders. On her bed, arranged in a circle, I found cotton khaki pants, a floral Hawaiian shirt, leather sandals, weaved leather belt, a variety of underwear choices, and a maile and orchid lei. In the center, a card embossed with a pineapple.

My dearest Samuel,
Two moons past, adrift in my boat of solitude, yearning,
You came in a fever,
Casting us into brimming river,
Aware quiet will come as waters widen.
Lift one oar, I the other,
And row to an orphaned lighthouse with me.
Kay

I read it thrice, finding nuance in succession. I dropped to the edge of the bed and wondered why an undeserving cuss, like me, received this bounty. In medicine we are humbled often. Diagnoses elude our grasp, patients die, taming our hubris with the blister of a whip. That is to be humbled before man. I was humbled before God, not asking why I was punished, but why I was blessed. Volume of the universe.

I dressed in time to spare and used it to refresh lyrics in my mind. Kayla and I agreed to sing a duet. JoJo suggested "The Wedding Song" but Kayla and I both thought we could do better. For several days we tossed around possibilities and I won out with "You and I Again." A favorite James Taylor song. She sang the harmony and I the melody. This was a well-cho-reographed affair, and we were to enter from either side of the tent, as if we were the ones getting married, to begin the ceremony. I felt confident because of practice sessions with the musicians.

I found Stan and Dan, the minister, talking on his patterned brick driveway. Stan put his arm around my shoulders and introduced Dan. He expressed his wonder at how easily I fooled him and joked that I might have been a confidence man previously.

"I'm a difficult person to buy for, according to my wife. This is one of the most thoughtful and heartfelt gifts. But, hey, I'm the one that owes you."

"Stan, we saved each other's life. You brought Kayla to me and I am reborn."

———

Sun glistened off the white tent, fixed to the sand with steel spikes, adorned with flower arrangements in stands and attached to the supports. Like a maypole, streams of tropical flowers flowed from high. Stan and JoJo stood with Pastor Dan at the front and the gathering of thirty witnesses sat in linen-wrapped chairs. We approached, out of view from all but Stan, JoJo, and Dan. The musicians playing piano, French horn, drums, and violin gathered on the patio. After their intro, I began. The congregants stood and turned toward us. Not expected. I sang the first verse solo with Kayla bringing in high notes sporadically. The second verse carried the full symphony of voice and with it came the same rush as our first day together.

The horn and violin carried us to the end and eyes, not all dry, looked to Stan and JoJo.

Kay and I remained in place and held hands. I placed my hand over my heart, turned toward her, and bowed. I wish I had a picture of her face at that moment. The smile of peace, joy, and love. Stan and Jo pledged the same vows as twenty years prior. Dan led us in the Lord's Prayer and added the part of the passage I had forgotten. He talked about not expecting forgiveness from God until you grant it to others.

"We fall in life. We say regrettable things. We act selfishly, or arrogantly, forgetting to put others before ourselves. We hold grudges. These actions fill up a sack we carry, and the burden can become oppressive unless we unload it at the feet of our Lord." Then the verse about faith, hope, and love. And the greatest of these is love.

I think his eyes never left me. Like a homing signal to find the biggest sinner present. I didn't need to ask why this guy was on the plane. Sweat formed on my brow and I must have looked green because Kayla asked if I was all right. I considered my wife's transgression. Even though I was an inadequate husband and a drunk, I kept my vow, the promise we made before God and four hundred witnesses. Her personal failure started me on the path to Kayla but that secondary benefit did not excuse the primary offense. Her infraction seemed unforgivable. I needed to paddle to consider it more. We waited while Stan and JoJo walked the aisle to our embrace.

As the group surrounded the couple, I took Kay by the hand and to the water. Later, JoJo shared that half the party was watching. After a long embrace I placed my hands on her hips and we reflected smiles. The sun cast a short shadow in wet sand where, body and spirit, we melded to one.

"Thank you for everything. The new clothes, the flowers, and your note. I will prize that note when I am ancient and weathered as much as I do today." I pressed her forehead to my lips.

"Yes."

"What?"

"Yes, I will row. Wherever we go."

—

Later that afternoon I found Pastor Dan, a short man, round face, bushy eyebrows, perpetual smile, at the margin of the yard, eyes on the horizon, sun reflecting shades of jade and turquoise off the water.

"I understand what you said about forgiveness. Putting that into practice is troublesome."

"Someone has broken your trust," he said.

"My wife cheated and then asked for a divorce."

"Let's walk," he said. We found firm sand and turned to the Mokes. "Betrayal is a deep cut. Hard to heal that."

"Yes. Still stings." I thought of my friend Roy. We were tight until thirteen. Friday and Saturday nights spent at each other's homes, mothers nearly interchangeable, but we were not alike. His extroversion held my introverted hand through childhood. I might have spent the better part of seven years in my room. Summer before junior high he found a new set of friends and I lost my way. Took me years to heal it.

"Can you think of someone else who suffered a terrible betrayal?"

"Sure. And my betrayal is a paper cut in comparison."

"No. No. That's not my point. What did Jesus say as he suffered on the cross?"

"Forgive them, Father," I said, looking at the sand.

"Yes. When we cling to bitterness we pick at that wound, harming ourselves, never healing. Do you suppose you are blameless?"

"No, sir. I have failed on many levels in my life. In God's eyes I'm a miserable lout."

"Sam don't assume God sees you through that lens. Understanding forgiveness is important but believing in its gift is paramount. When you ask forgiveness, God sees you as an innocent child, fresh to the world." He rested his hand on my shoulder.

"I find it odd that God forgives me when I can't forgive myself."

"Put your hand into God's, Sam. Look from the other side. If you believe and you ask His forgiveness, grace will flow to you. If God forgives you, how can you withhold this gift and not forgive yourself and others?"

We stopped and sat on the log in front of the path to my place.

"Forgiving my wife doesn't erase her actions," I said.

"No. Forgiveness dwells aside from the consequences. God may forgive a car thief, but the consequences of a jail sentence remain. God wants us to adopt a posture of grace and set free of the bitterness in our lives. She will find peace of her own. You can't give her that, but you can offer her grace."

"You know, Dan, since I left Carolina, friends have tried to explain God's role in my presence here. I saved Stan, gave life-saving advice to parents of a toddler, stopped drinking, and tumbled into a magnificent relationship with Kayla. I asked for none of this and still question why I have been so blessed."

"That is a question for the ages. What's crucial is your recognition of His presence. God is omnipresent, but you will be blind to Him if your heart is closed."

I nodded and grasped Dan's hand. Forgiving myself might take time, but that instant I forgave my wife. I thought of those shearwaters soaring above the sea, untethered, sight beyond the horizon. All those years and I didn't realize I could fly.

"I'm sure you are tired," I said. "Let's start back."

"Since you recently traveled, you remember how it feels the first day."

"Yes, I'm still getting up with the sun. I kayak most mornings. Very peaceful out there at that hour."

"It's been a few years. Would it be an intrusion for me to come?"

"No, no. I'm thrilled to have you join me. I'll be on the beach in front of Kayla's at sunrise."

———

Out-of-town guests lingered as most of the other guests took their leave. Kayla and I toed through the path avoiding more questions we could not answer. We scooted across her grass, like we had TP'd someone's house, and disrobed in silence poolside. I rested on the bottom step, chin on the surface, and she on my lap facing away from me.

"So. How did you find a plumber so quickly? And a buff one at that."

"Stan's not the only connected one on this island."

She jabbed with an elbow. "Get lost. You do not know a plumber on O'ahu."

Things were so chaotic she asked no questions and didn't wonder why a plumber wanted to borrow a wrench. He was in and out in twenty minutes and left with William McKinley in his pocket. I reminded her that I met Michael at the pillbox.

"He seems like a solid young man, Samuel. If he were my son, I'd be very proud of him."

As she said the words, I could feel her muscles tense. I let it go and held her. Another day.

"Can I ask about your father?" I said.

"Ah, sure."

"He's gone now, right?"

"Five years."

"Did you forgive him for being so difficult and angry?"

"I suppose. I didn't hold a grudge. Years passed,

and I stopped thinking of it. What has you thinking about forgiveness?"

"Dan."

"I thought you disappeared."

"He opened my heart. I've been carrying this bitterness and he showed me how to put it to rest. I can't go forward dragging it around."

Kayla turned toward me and kissed my nose. "I love you, Samuel."

After drying we fell into bed and she nestled her head on my shoulder. Sleep came to Kay in five breaths. I watched the wooden fan blades above and replayed my conversation with Dan. For the first time since vomiting on the beach I felt confident success and happiness would come. More than ever, I felt the urgent desire to return to work in the ER and share my precious gift.

14

I STOOD ON THE beach, cool moist sand, a mug of Constant Comment tea, watching wispy gray clouds at the horizon reflect the first light of day off crimson edges. This moment of peace at land's end, at juncture of horizon and heavens, transition of night to day, ushered me each day one step farther along my path of transformation. I gave thanks for the day, the people in my life, strength, peace, and grace.

"I see why you come here now," Dan said. He rubbed his forearms.

"Yes, I have Kayla to thank for this. You'll warm up as we paddle."

We dragged the kayaks to the water. Low surf made for an easy entry to flat surface and we pulled in parallel, talking little, toward Lanikai. The daily transition from monochrome to color reminded me of Dorothy's entrance to Oz. From dull shades to vibrant sky, water, sand, and foliage. This was not Carolina, or Kansas, and I was not the man that left the mainland. My father liked to awaken with the sun and I thought of him often as I paddled. I missed him because that day I could shake his hand, hold his gaze, and he would be proud of me. It saddened me he died before seeing this. We coasted as we entered the shallows, and I recalled my conversations with Steven.

"Dan, I encounter difficult people in my work. I suppose you do as well. Many of these folks have burned bridges in their lives. Often the paramedics, nurses and I are the last people on earth willing to help them. Yet they lash out at us, spit, fight, call us horrific names. I find it difficult to..."

"Not want to strangle them?" he said, smiling.

"Yeah. More or less."

"You and I are called. This is where we are tested. I'm sure you find joy in stitching the hand of an upstanding father of three who cut his hand at work. The challenge is in keeping the same posture for a foul-mouthed drunk who won't hold still for an X-ray."

"Definitely."

"It's human nature to retreat from this behavior. Your calling draws you to it and it requires a strong will to serve people who live at the edge of humanity. Here's the thing: When I ask God for help in assisting people who are difficult and needy, he sends me more people who are difficult and needy."

I nodded and smiled.

"You chose this work, so you might as well be the best at it. If you look, you will see God in your work, but he won't appear in a two-thousand-dollar suit."

"Right. I understand."

We dismounted between the islands, full sun on our faces, flat water, soft sand.

"You were baptized as a child, Sam?"

"Yes."

"This is not required. I don't offer this often because I've encountered few people willing to reconstruct their lives as you are doing. If you like, I will baptize you now in the tradition of John the Baptizer."

I looked at the water, the offset reflection of my feet wavering, sand floating at my toes. "Please do."

Dan faced my side and I the horizon holding my hands clasped. I felt that total body rush again.

"What middle name was given to you?"

"Morgan."

"In baptism, God promises by grace alone to forgive our sins, to renew and cleanse us, and to resurrect us to eternal life."

He placed his hand on my head.

"Samuel Morgan Buchanan, do you ask God for forgiveness and affirm your acceptance of Jesus as your Lord and savior?"

"I do."

He placed his hand behind my neck, and I leaned backward into the sea and submerged. No sound or light, only water. Warm now. The weight of my transgressions and failures lifted. I understood my past would never change. I could make the diagnosis well but left my patients wanting. I lived with my wife but was not present. I put my interests above those of my younger colleagues. I received an undeserved bounty and did not appreciate the gifts or their origin. At my next breath I knew I controlled the past no more than celestial movement, but my attitude, my posture, my reaction, my behavior, my presence with God belonged only to me. I stood. *Gardenias.*

"If anyone is in Christ, the new creation has come. The old has gone. The new is here."

And we said the Lord's Prayer together. "Go in peace and serve the Lord."

Upon return I found Kayla curled in a lounge by the pool in my Gamecocks pullover, coffee beside her, novel in hand, blanket over her legs.

"What happened?" she asked.

"What?"

"Well, your hair is wet, and you have that won-the-lottery look on your face. Did you fall in?"

"Sort of." I jumped in the pool to warm and glided to her side. I spit water at her missing on purpose.

"Quite a mood you're in."

"Yes." A memory appeared. On the shelf for a score, hidden by the clutter of unhappy outcomes and regrets. Now tangible. A blink after finishing training, a blistering day in central South Carolina, EMS delivered a six-week-old infant, limp, pulse of a mouse. Older brother had fed him grapes. EMS removed one grape yet breath, still wanting, left baby Anderson gray as winter sky. I steadied my hand on his head to conceal the tremor of fear and exposed his larynx with the smallest instrument at hand. After piercing the grape with one half of a hemostat, I closed carefully to avoid ripping the edge off. I dropped it and delivered breaths through a special mask. Pink skin returned, and he wriggled and cried. I found the parents huddled in the family room. The mother enveloped my hand in hers and tears of happiness and relief streamed over her cheeks. This was the first person I saved with no help from other doctors. Her joy flowed into me. Long forgotten. "Hardly anyone knows the feeling of being baptized, right?"

"Right. Babies."

"Now I know."

"What are you saying?" She set her coffee on the table and sat up straight.

"Dan baptized me off Lanikai just now."

"You weren't baptized?"

"Yes, as a baby. This was the second."

"Really. Is that a thing?"

"Yeah. Like John at the river. Full immersion."

"Wow. Did you ask him to do it?"

"No. His idea. My reconstruction, as he called it, is a rare event, and he offered a second baptism."

"Sam. I know you want to be a better person, but this is stunning. You surprise me daily with your commitment."

"Thank you." I held out my hand and she took it. "You are my best friend, and always will be. I love you."

"And I you." She blew a kiss.

I pulled up onto the ledge of the pool and rested my arms on the cool tile. "I would be a lonely drunk without you."

"Not so sure about that," she said.

"Believe it."

"Okay, I will."

15

M<small>Y ENDURANCE, TECHNIQUE,</small> and strength improved with each trip between the mountains. Kay was right. At first, the loneliness and physical pain felt like I dragged an old boot behind me. That mid-December day I entered the water with no more thought than turning into light traffic. I pulled through cake-icing ripples with full strokes—muscle memory now—fresh sun and a breath of headwind in my face. Kayla refused to join me citing the prerequisite of solitude.

Two hundred yards off the public beach I spied it. Twenty yards ahead. On earlier trips I wondered, but the sun, water, and shadows play tricks. I rested my paddle on my lap, coasting. Wavelets licked the sides of my craft. Rhythmic clapping. You could fall asleep to it. The head of a green sea turtle poked from the inky blue facing away from me. The ridge of his shell just broke the surface. The head resembled a thumb. In a wink it vanished. I moved only eyes and neck scanning 250 degrees. Five minutes passed.

Mindful of water only. Off to port the water broke. Had I extended my paddle its full length, I could have touched it. Eyes of a bandit, elliptical, dark, arched by crinkled lids. Irregular green shapes separated by pale yellow lines made a hood for head and neck. A giraffe's markings came to mind, but the nose seemed more birdlike. What a gift. She was off to her own adventure.

The small beach at Moku Nui, a modest triangle of sand pushed from the ocean floor by an ancient volcano, brown and black rock and scattered vegetation the backdrop, held an elderly man, late seventies, wispy white hair haphazard on his scalp, short, stocky but not obese, kind eyes, standing by his blue kayak. Another unclouded morning, the sun above the top of the Mokes just reached the edge of the sand from over his shoulder. I recall seeing his canary yellow life vest with the block M. He waved at me and I raised a blade of my paddle. I pulled several strokes avoiding the social unease of unguarded introduction.

Smell of cotton candy hung in the air. The stickiness could not be licked off. Ten, at the county fair, riding without a parent for the first time, I shuffled in line for the Ferris wheel with my friend, Roy. With each clanging rotation, I watched people enter and exit. All smiled. Nobody died or vomited yet my fear of falling lived. Roy bounded on and I followed. The clack of the smooth metal safety bar startled me, and I shook it for reassurance. As we rose, Roy rocked the cab, and I gripped tighter.

The only way to overcome my shyness was to get on the big wheel. I dug three times on the right and beached near him. I breathed the earthiness of the shaded side of the mountain.

"Good morning." I stepped out and pulled my craft up the shallow incline. "I'm Sam."

"My pleasure. Peter." We shook hands. "At first I figured you were on vacation. I've seen you for two months now."

"Extended vacation." I gave him the thumbnail sketch.

"You're no lazy paddler. I see you come from the end of Kailua. I'm just across the water." He pointed to a robin's-egg blue bungalow beachside Lanikai. "Just enough exercise for me."

"I'm new to it. My friend, Kayla, started me and now I can't stop."

"Oh, I've met Kayla out here. She's a beauty."

"Sure is," I said. "I'm assuming you're retired."

"Yes. I owned a trucking firm near Detroit."

"Ah. The M on your vest is University of Michigan."

"Go Blue." He invited me to sit on the sand and we did.

"You a U of M grad?"

"No. No. Couldn't be farther away. Night business school when I was driving for a produce company."

"I love to hear stories of people who pulled themselves up to success," I said.

"That's the story of my father. Emigrated from Germany as a teen after the First World War. No friends, a few bucks in his pocket, with a handful of English phrases in his head. He worked auto manufacturing and retired as a line supervisor. He and my mom lived a modest life, but nobody was happier than those two."

"As I paddle, I think about happiness lately. What brought them happiness?"

He didn't hesitate. "Faith, family, function, and friends. My parents always thought of the other guy. What could they do to help someone out or make their day a happy one. They genuinely appreciated the gifts offered to them through the years."

I remembered the sign at the mess hall at the YMCA summer camp Roy and I attended. "I'M THIRD". His parents lived it. I did not. "Did you enjoy running your business?"

"Yes. Yes, I started with a few trucks, local routes, and after years of work covered most of the Midwest. I made a good living for my family but the thing that gave me the most satisfaction is the kids who had a nice home and food on the table because one or both of their parents worked for me."

"I understand. That's a great legacy." A couple beached a double kayak at the edge of the triangle and waved. I gave a half-salute. "What do your kids do?"

"Two sons. Both docs on the west coast. Family medicine and oncology."

"Those specialties both require someone willing to give a lot of themselves," I said.

"You're right. I see their grandfather in both. And you?" he said.

"Emergency medicine. I start fresh in New Orleans at the new year."

"I'm sorry to hear you are splitting from your wife. Sam, you can end your marriage, but your emotional and spiritual connection never dies. No matter what vows were broken, what was said in anger, your link to that person, good or bad, is everlasting."

"Are you saying you can never truly be divorced?" I asked.

"Well, you can separate legally and physically and make peace with it, but with any past event or action you can't erase your common history and the bond you once held. When you married, I bet you didn't think of it as a legal contract. It was much more than that."

———

Kayla sat at the kitchen counter, in my favorite PJs. I liked the royal blue color and the tailored fit, but the silky feel made them my favorite. She spoke to someone on the phone in Hawai'ian. The degree of her fluency was unclear, but it sounded good. She turned on her stool as she completed her call.

"I was getting worried. Figured you tried to circle Chinaman's Hat."

"Tell me the reward I would get for that."

"One track mind."

"Yeah. No. I talked with this guy in a blue kayak a while."

"Old guy, white hair?"

"Yeah."

"Peter, right?"

"It is you, Miss Kay, who is the connected one on O'ahu."

She flipped her hand at me. "Great guy. He is a big donor to the foundation."

"Well. We discussed happiness."

"Any conclusions?"

As a medical student, the first time I identified pneumonia on an X-ray, there was this sense of the stars and the moon aligning. Anatomy, physiology, microbiology, pharmacology. I knew what it was, and what to do for it. After diagnosing pneumonia a thousand times, I do it with such ease I'm surprised that anyone would marvel at it. A revelation came over me as I paddled, but it embarrassed me to see something anew that is bred into others.

"Journey rather than destination. Focus on others, not self."

"Very good," she said.

"Can you say it so it doesn't sound like I fetched something?"

She held me close. A hint of coconut on her skin. I smoothed my hands over her back.

"Don't take it that way. We make our own way. I didn't understand that, I mean truly carry it with me, until I was married for a while."

We sat on the couch and I pulled a blanket over us.

"He said something about marriage. Whatever happens to end a marriage, you are connected forever."

"Sam, people talk to you on a different plane," she said. She held my chin in her hand. "You have this knack for drawing people into almost spiritual conversations."

"I don't know about that. I'm not much of a conversationalist."

"Yeah, small talk is overrated. This is different."

"Okay," I said. "What do you think?"

"I agree, but it's not just marriage. We connect with family, friends, workmates. Physical and emotional separation doesn't change it. You can ignore it, but like the weather or cockroaches under kitchen cabinets, ignoring them does not make them go away."

"I was looking forward to completely severing ties with my wife."

"No can do," she said.

She straddled my lap, facing me, nipples tenting through my favorite pj's. I slipped my hands under her shirt and we shared a long, wet kiss.

"Cockroaches, huh?"

"What can you do? It's the tropics," she said.

We stole to the bed.

16

A WEEK BEFORE CHRISTMAS, I donned a Santa hat and paddled. Dark when I started, only a full moon guided me from over my shoulder. My muted shadow darkened silvery sea, the calmest water in three months. Usually I paddled near shore, but I sensed, like Kayla, there was nothing left to unload. I made an outside path for my last trip and paddled a mile off shore. I didn't sum the miles traveled. The physical distance mattered little. I crossed an emotional ocean, content that few watched me do it. When first light broke the horizon, I turned right and dug hard, not out of anger or frustration, but out of joy. I thought back to my breathless first feeble strokes and my lack of emotional direction or strength. Mozart played in my head and I crossed to the Mokes lost in the color and texture. I turned between them and approached Steven from his back.

"I took a different path," I said.

"And that has made all the difference."

"Happy Christmas to you. I bet you thought I wouldn't catch the Frost reference."

"One never knows. Merry Christmas to you." We shook hands. "You'll be leaving us soon."

"Yes. I have mixed feelings. I also believe that I'll return."

"That will be a grand day. So, Sam. We haven't discussed how you will keep your sobriety. You've been sheltered here with us. Soon you will return to work and enter new relationships that will complicate your life. You will be thrilled, disappointed, sometimes injured. You can't avoid it, nor should you want to. Your sobriety is like a garden. You must protect it and tend it every day."

"Okay. I'm with you. Do I go to AA?"

"I always say to go with what works. There's a group just a few blocks from where you'll be living. Kayla did the research. You will find a kinship and camaraderie that will lift you through difficult times. I know you feel on top of things now. It won't always be that way."

"You're making me a bit nervous, now," I said.

"I don't mean to be discouraging, but you have changes ahead of you. I rarely recommend such a change this early in recovery. I understand your commitments. I just want you to beware. A lapse will sneak up like a pickpocket on the train."

"Sure. I'll take care. Listen, thank you for your presence with me. I'd hug you, but I fear flipping us," I said.

We shook hands, and I returned to deep water. Others may disappoint me, but I vowed to not disappoint anyone, especially Kayla. And my own expectations for attitude and behavior. I knew I needed to balance setting a high bar and not being overly critical of myself. I paddled leisurely stopping as I liked to absorb Kailua. From a mile out, I viewed the full panorama of beach and palm trees kneeling at the alter of the mountains. At the point I planned to turn toward the beach the water churned twenty yards ahead. I dug my paddle and stopped. Swells of water rose from below and small fish fluttered near the surface, sliver scales reflecting the light. The water calmed, and the fluke of a dolphin's tail flashed, and fish boiled to the surface again. A brown booby saw the opportunity. He hovered then crashed his long narrow beak into the mix. Upon emerging he looked skyward, swallowing fish breakfast I supposed. He was a handsome boy with a white face and a blush of blue around his eyes, brown coat of feathers and a white belly. He lifted clumsily from the water and none of the participants left any remnant of their dance.

Kayla met me on the beach, hands on hips, wide smile. "You took the long route."

"Yes, and I got a show for my trouble. Brown booby."

"Oh, I'm so glad you got to see that."

"I know how you felt now."

"What?"

"When you had nothing to unload. You can't explain that peace if you didn't endure the pain and the loneliness yourself."

She nodded, and we stowed the kayak. She put her arm around my waist, and we walked to the wicker chairs by the pool.

"Kay. We have been putting off the discussion neither

of us wants to have. The last time I tried to bring this up you tricked me into having sex and made me forget it."

"That's not quite the way I remember it but go ahead." She whacked me with the back of her hand.

"I never want to leave here. But I'm not done fixing me. Not even close. There's still part of the guy with the beard in here. For you to want me for the long term, I need to go away for a while and keep the commitments I made. Plus, I want to prove something to myself and I can't do it here."

"I agree. This is important stuff and there will be no mission creep."

"Not familiar with that term."

"Military thing. Gordy said it. Make your goals and stick to them. I'll come visit. I love New Orleans. You need to go four months alone. No visits, no phone calls."

"Four months, huh?"

"Yes sir. You need to make a life for yourself without me to lean on."

I explained to her I intended to settle into my house and be a monk. I'll find a hobby and I'll avoid social commitments and attachments. She nodded as I spoke, her grin enlarging.

"That was the plan here, right?"

"Ah, yeah. But this is different. You made me fall in love with you."

She counted with her fingers. "Jane, JoJo, Stan, Michael, Steven, Dan, Peter. You are a magnetic person. Allow people into your life. That's the way to be a better human."

17

ONE BLOCK TOWARD the river, two blocks toward the city. That's what Maria said. I was walking to Breaux Mart. The pantry and the ice box sat empty except for a six-pack of Coke, left by Maria. She's my new landlord. Everything smelled new in the house. Born a hundred years ago, this shotgun house dearly needed Maria's restoration. Kitchen and bathrooms were new, but she preserved everything else. The restored wooden floors glistened like new yet revealed their age. The meticulously crafted woodwork and twelve-foot ceilings made it a historic gem. I'm her first renter. And I brought no food with me. There's just a fruit basket, also from Maria, sitting on the kitchen counter. So, I walked to Breaux Mart to stock up. One block toward the river, two blocks toward the city. This will be a project since I can't carry many bags.

New Orleans was novel and mysterious. Names like Guidry, Melancon, and Thibodaux. Breaux is pronounced Bro, like *Hey bro, Can I bum a smoke?* There is no east, west, north, or south. In Uptown New

Orleans, *you either goin' toward the river or toward the lake*. Or *you goin' toward the city or toward the park*. Audubon Park, a wondrous place where you can run, or ride a bike, or plan a picnic, or play golf. No golfing for me anymore. Ancient Live Oaks spread their knobby arms over what seems an acre per tree. Tulane and Loyola sit at one end of the park and the zoo is at the other. If you keep going through the zoo, you hit the Mississippi.

I know this stuff now but this day, when I walked to Breaux Mart for the first time, I could barely find my way to St. Charles Avenue, where the trolley runs. Toward the park or toward the city. For a buck and a quarter, you can arrive at the finest restaurants on earth or you can find yourself in a world of trouble on Bourbon Street. Rider's choice.

They rebuilt Louisiana Avenue. I cross the boulevard to reach Breaux Mart. Lots of road construction here after Katrina. These side streets were down the list. I'm glad I missed Katrina. You must truly love a city to stay after a biblical class disaster. Lots of folks love New Orleans. I never saw that level of devotion. Living in Columbia was pleasant enough, but I don't hold a deep affection or experience this visceral attachment that New Orleanians enjoy.

People love Uptown like an older sister who gets shit-faced, falls at the tavern, and calls you for a ride at two a.m. so you can haul your butt out of bed and pour your sister into hers. You take the roses with the manure. Only the best houses in Uptown sport a garage or even private parking. And by best, I mean seven hundred-fifty thousand. A lot of these places go for five hundred and you need to scope out a spot on a street with potholes and no curbs. This is mystifying since my $600,000 house in Columbia dressed up in a four-car garage. I guess life is what you are accustomed to. I don't care either way now since I sold my car.

Breaux Mart is one of the few businesses on Magazine Street that has its own parking. The small box sits back while the other stores crowd the street like betters at the rail. Breaux Mart doesn't fit in, but same as the parking I don't care so much since I can walk there.

I found a well-used cart sitting lonely and asymmetrically parked near the front entrance and wheeled it through the automatic door. Few shoppers graced the intimate aisles. People enjoy a nap at two in the afternoon. That's when I go to the bank or the store, when I'm not napping. I welcomed the quiet because I wanted to learn the local geography without having to negotiate around my new neighbors. Until that day I did not go to the grocery store or as they say in New Orleans, "make groceries." My soon-to-be ex-wife and I used servants to do the menial chores of life. I guess servant is not the PC term. She called them personal assistants. Made no matter. The work was the same. Buy stuff or do chores for us that we were too busy or lazy to do for ourselves.

A well-fed man, mutt face, crooked nose, Marine-style haircut, stood behind a long metal-and-glass case that held a variety of meats, cheeses, and prepared foods such as coleslaw and potato salad. A blood-stained white apron, I assumed from the butchering of cloven-hoofed animals, hung around his ample neck. Either that or he cut his hand badly. I didn't mind his interest in me when he took a double take but wondered when the cashier gave me the same treatment. I thought maybe a chive clung to my tooth or toilet paper trailed from my shoe.

The store reminded me of the Piggly Wiggly we frequented when I was a kid in Beaufort, South Carolina, pronounced *Bew*-fort. Another Beaufort, pronounced *Bow*-fort, is in North Carolina. By the looks of the place, it might have been 1972 in Breaux Mart except for the life-size cardboard cutout of Peyton Manning in his Broncos uniform next to the frozen food aisle. He grew up in Uptown and attended Newman School, on the other side of St. Charles. Also, Peyton joined the world in 1976. I wonder if his mom shopped at Breaux Mart. Maybe Langenstein's.

I made a dry run around the store before filling my cart. That gave me time to prioritize. Halfway through the aisles the cashier caught my eye. She noticed my lack of commitment toward any grocery items. She may have thought I was summoning the courage to rob the place. Now, I speak with what people describe as a genteel low country accent. A New Orleans accent is much different especially if you come from the Ninth Ward where this clerk is from. The best I can describe this unique accent is New Orleans with a bit of Brooklyn. People from the Ninth Ward display a natural sassiness. Not in a bad way. It's an upbeat, confident, forward-leaning personality with a hint of *don't mess with me* thrown in.

As I made the turn to the next aisle, she stepped from behind the register looking to be sixteen or seventeen. To notice her standing sideways, she would need to stick out her tongue. A long mane of brunette hair hung from a ponytail that flowed from the back of an emerald Breaux Mart cap that captured the green in her eyes. She flashed a broad smile. Cute nose on an oval face.

"Excuse me sir, but you seem to be looking for something and not succeeding. My name's Billy, by the way. I stocked shelves before I graduated to cashier, so I can tell you where anything is."

"My pleasure. Sam Buchanan." We shook hands, and she held my gaze longer than the average teenager would. "I believe that you will be a good person to know."

"How so?" she said with hands on hips and inquisitive grin.

"I just moved here…"

"There ya go." She slapped her leg. "I shoulda bet Mr. Breaux. I've never seen you before, and you don't look like a tourist."

"Yeah, I'll take that as a compliment. So, here's my situation. I own nothing. Not even salt. I'd buy it all now, but I don't want or need a car."

I heard myself saying this and thought my planning skills were lacking. Maria would have loaned me her truck. This comes from twenty years of having other people do things you can very well do yourself. It makes you lazy and dull-witted. Billy, who came from different circumstances, responded at once and without reservation.

"No worries. Fill two carts. I'm off in thirty minutes. I'll check you out, and we will drive those carts to your house. How far?"

Now that's service. Most teenagers can't make change. I felt bad about being helpless but not enough to reject the offer.

"Camp and Delachaise. So how do you return the carts?"

"They nest." As she glided her palm through the air, she spoke not quite condescendingly but close enough to make me feel like half a dope.

"Right. Thanks for the expert advice."

"Start on your left. That way you reach the cold stuff last."

The nuances of making groceries baffled me. I can say that in a bona fide fashion now. The canned food aisle looked promising. Soup is easy. I suppose a true dope might burn soup, but since I only qualified as a half-dope, I could handle myself. The frozen food aisle was a stockpile of easy meals. I wove my way through the corridors of culinary possibilities gaining confidence with each step. By the end my cart brimmed, and I presented myself to Billy like a toddler who pooped in the pot for the first time.

"I made it with one, so you are free."

"You get butter?" No expression on her face.

"No."

"Aluminum foil?"

"No." *This chick will make one hell of a mom.*

"Plastic containers, kitchen gadgets, eggs?"

"No, no, and yes."

She made a twirly motion with her long slender index finger. "You put that cart over by the best quarterback ever in the NFL, and I'll find an empty one."

"I thought Aaron Rodgers..."

"Nah, ah, ah," she scolded. "It goes Peyton, then Drew Brees, and then the rest of those jokers are back-benchers."

Okay then. So, we started over. I missed numerous necessary items. *Two or one carton of eggs? Two, they're on sale. No Tabasco sauce? What's wrong with you? You gotta get red beans and rice. Monday is wash day. You make red beans and rice on Mondays.* By the last row the second cart was full. While Billy rang me up for $258.73, Mr. Breaux, the guy in the apron, approached and extended his big mitt with a satisfied smile on his round and weathered face. We exchanged pleasantries, and he welcomed me to the neighborhood.

"Buchanan," Rex Breaux said rubbing his chin. "My wife, Renée, is a Buchanan. You may be distant relatives. Her family has been here more than a hundred—he said it 'hunnert'—years, but they started in Carolina. I think North."

"Fascinating. My father owned a construction business in the Lowcountry of South Carolina. His parents spent their entire lives in the Fayetteville area. Beyond that, it's sketchy. Did Renée ever make a family tree?"

"Oh, Lord. Like asking if they got beer on Bourbon Street. She's got relatives traced back to Ireland. She's also got a bunch buried in Lafayette No. 1. She'll talk your ear off. What's your father's name?"

A warm sensation came over me. Not hot and sweaty like when you left to do errands and forgot the job your wife asked you to do. This was a comfortable, familiar sensation. I imagined I had been shopping at Breaux Mart my whole life and grew up next door to Rex.

"Samuel Morgan Buchanan. He's number two. I'm number three."

"Yeah. You'll be in there. Renée will check it out. Ask (he said it 'aks') me next time."

"Lafayette number one?" I said.

"Cemetery in the Garden District."

We shook hands again, and Billy and I rolled our carts out to Magazine Street. I thought about my father. He told me stories from his childhood, but I never made notes. All that history and those stories lost.

"So, what's your deal, Mr. Sam?"

We were a block over by the time Billy drew me back from my thoughts. In the south children tradi- tionally call their elders mister or miss, followed by their first name. Since Billy could be my daughter, I more than qualified to be an elder. Plus, coming from South Carolina I was used to this display of respect. I figured that I'd run into Billy at least twice a week at

Breaux Mart, so I told her to just say Sam. In a year, that would save her a couple hundred misters.

"Since we are only walking three blocks, I'll give you the abbreviated version."

I knew someone besides Maria, my landlord, would ask me my story. I didn't expect it the day after I arrived. My soon-to-be ex-wife says I planned this whole adventure like a teenager. I disagree. Plus, she was no longer the boss of me, so I could plan poorly at my sole peril.

"I came to the Crescent City to start my life over."

"Oh, I did that once too."

I didn't intend to, but there I was with the opener in one hand and a wormy can in the other.

"How so?"

"When I was seventeen, my mom died in an accident on I-10."

"I'm sorry to hear that."

"Thank you. She was all I had. My dad's in prison and I never met him anyway, so I started over."

"That's how you came to Rex and Renée?"

"Right. Our families have been friends for generations. Rex said I could live with them if I stayed out of trouble, didn't get pregnant, worked in the store for spending money, and finished my GED."

"Must have been an adjustment."

"Yes. I had a rough time at first and missed most of my senior year. Renée made me stop crying in my soup."

"You realize you fell off a shit truck into a feather bed, don't you?"

"Yes, Sam. I tell them I love them every day."

18

BILLY AND I argued about her need to help me put away my new purchases. She, of course, won, and we hauled the load into the kitchen. She started on the refrigerator and I put dry goods into the closest cabinet.

"What's your plan with your cupboards?" she said without looking.

"Ah..."

"Right. Why don't you hand me the cold things, then we'll get to those cupboards?"

I saw no sense in resisting any more. She expertly arranged the freezer and then the refrigerator. Every time I said there were no more cold items she told me to find the cream cheese or the salad dressing. Billy gave me a crash course in kitchen organization. Twenty minutes later we completed the job, and Billy made a pitcher of lemonade.

I invited her to sit out back. Sun filtered through an old magnolia to the uneven stone patio, soothing the back of my neck. We sat at a round wrought-iron table spattered with just enough rust to make it look vintage. I rested my feet on the adjacent chair and took a deep breath. Funny how talk can start on one topic and be dominated by something else. She asked about me and I kept asking questions about her and never answered her question.

"Do you enjoy living in Uptown?"

"Sure. Not like I have many choices. I miss my friends. They're off to college now."

"I think you have adapted to your circumstances well. Just because you missed the train doesn't mean you should abandon the tracks."

I palmed a folded Franklin and extended my hand. We shook hands, she revealed a half-smile, and her eyes glistened when she examined the bill.

"Oh, thank you. This is too much, and Mr. Rex says no tips."

"For the hassle you saved me I'm getting off easy at a hundred. We'll keep this classified."

"I believe you will be a good person to know," she said, trying to mimic my voice.

She gave me a hug and a peck on the cheek, and she skipped through the side gate. She sang and her voice faded as she pushed the carts down Delachaise. Something about being "All About That Bass." I smiled and felt something against my right leg. A faint vibration. A well-built orange and white tabby, with a head the size of a grapefruit, weaved between my legs. His ears sported multiple healed splits at the margins. He had likely been mixing it up with the other cats and I suspect he proved to be top feline. I kneeled to pet him, and he pushed his head against my hand and then rolled over to expose his ample belly. While I searched for a tag, a voice came from the side yard.

"His name is Floyd."

I scanned across the yard to find a balding, middle-aged man, inspiration for the Pillsbury Doughboy, with a blonde chevron mustache.

"Excuse me?" I held a hand to my ear.

I heard the man, but I lost words. My awkwardness regarding meeting new people persisted, particularly in the unstructured setting of an unsolicited feline introduction. Maria warned me a few of the neighbors where a bit odd, and one randomly retrieved his morning paper in the nude. I deemed this guy to be a strong candidate for both. I stood and walked to the fence. He received my extended hand with a dead fish handshake leaving me with a great desire to wipe my hand on the side of my trousers, but refined southern manners kept me from doing so.

"Maximillian Dupuis. Call me Max."

"My pleasure. Sam Buchanan. Just moved from South Carolina. Did you say Floyd?"

"More precisely, Prince Floyd de Delachaise."

Why not King? He said this in a French accent, making me believe that Floyd belonged to him, and Max held the impression that Floyd cared a lick about his human name. Floyd loitered at my feet again, so I hoisted him and offered to pass him back over the aging wrought-iron fence. Max held up his hands and chuckled the laugh of someone on the knowledgeable edge of an inside joke. After a moment, I dropped Floyd at my feet.

"Did Maria explain you are living in the home once occupied by Vivian Broussard?"

"She did not."

"Well, Miss. Vivian lived her entire ninety-five years as a spinster who never ventured beyond the boundaries of the river, Carrollton, Claiborne, and Esplanade."

"You'll need to help me with the geography, Max."

"That's Uptown, the Garden District, the Central Business District, and the French Quarter. Quite a small area to spend ninety-five years."

"Indeed."

"Miss. Vivian's mother died during childbirth in the back bedroom," hushed voice. "She passed in the same spot nine months ago."

I nodded and narrowed my brow. I assume he believed such a revelation shocked me. Though I did not reveal this to him, I had no qualms living in a home where someone died, since I see dead people at work at least weekly. I'm sure someone entered this world, and someone expired in most homes in Uptown. Birth and death at the hospital is a modern phenomenon. If I did not need to feed or clean up after them, ghosts could loiter as they please. Cats too.

Max explained Floyd sort of *comes with the house*. Interesting how Maria left out that piece of information. I planned to stick with the blueprint. I did not intend to clutter my life with unnecessary belongings or pets. The last thing I desired was attachment to a fat feline who requires feeding, grooming, vet care, and worst, a litter box. By the looks of him, Floyd excelled as an outdoor puss, plus he rid the streets of rats and other vermin. As I crossed the back threshold, he tried to enter with me. A gentle launch to the grass with my foot ended that notion.

19

TWO BLOCKS TOWARD the lake. That's a top reason I chose Maria's place. Living near the market, a few restaurants, the trolley, and most of all Touro Infirmary, was a bonus for me. Touro is two blocks from my house. Away from the river, that is. I made a quick and pleasant walk on most days. Many days, rain falls copiously. An inch can fall in an hour. The pumps don't keep up after an inch. Then the walk is not so pleasant. I brought my Gamecocks golf umbrella just for such occasions.

In Columbia I golfed about twice a week. Eight of us played well and drank even better. We lived in a golfing community, so I walked home when I was too drunk to drive, which was most times. When too drunk to walk, my soon-to-be ex-wife collected me and delivered me into bed. The old Sam played an eight handicap. Not anymore. And so, I marched to Touro to restart my career. I used my umbrella as a walking stick and stashed my middle-of-the-night snack along with my stethoscope and reflex hammer in a small pack slung over my shoulder.

From a block away, I spied the illuminated rectangular EMERGENCY sign off Delachaise. A beacon for the troubled. This sign elicits no more emotion in me than the one at the filling station. Unless I've had to pee for thirty minutes, then the sign at the filling station brings boundless joy. For many, the EMERGENCY sign provokes anxiety and dread. What painful or demeaning event will follow when they cross the threshold? What dreaded diagnosis might be revealed inside the impersonal edifice? Heart attack? Cancer? Herpes? Easy to forget what a trying experience a visit to the ER can be.

A crescent moon shone on the chilly New Year's Day night and the brick four-story structure of Touro Infirmary. Live Oaks, and other trees I could not identify in the dark, reached over the unbalanced sidewalk creating a canopy I came to appreciate in the sun and the rain. The football games ended and, even in New Orleans, the Big Easy, the party must expire, and folks needed to return to work. I expected a quiet night for my first shift in the Touro Infirmary emergency department.

The ambulance doors *whooshed* open as I passed my ID near the reader. I encountered a wary-eyed security guard. A diminutive man in his thirties, body of a fifteen-year-old nerd, with greased-back thin brown hair and a rat-like face, appraised me. I caught his eye, extended my hand, and addressed him in my best Irish accent. That accent always works because by my appearance I might have visited Ellis Island. My ginger hair, thick eyebrows, and bright hazel eyes draw the map of Ireland on my face.

"Aye, laddy, I'm Dr. Buchanan. I'm the new G and O. Someone dispatched me to rescue goldfish from a woman's lady parts."

"G and O?" he said.

"I'm sorry. You Americans say OB-GYN."

"Right. I'm Gabriel Broussard. Call me Gabe. Let me find who's consulting you. Goldfish. Did I hear right?"

I could hold a straight face no longer and broke into a loud hoot. "Sorry, Gabe, I'm just tugging your leg. I'm the new night ER doc. Call me Sam."

"Oh, you're a slippery rascal. You had me goin' there."

"Is that your best insult?"

He seemed confused for a beat. "I guess so."

I surmised he carried suspicions of this crazy red-head masquerading as a doctor. "Well, think on it and lay one on me the next time we meet." I walked a few feet and turned. "Hey, are you related to Miss Vivian Broussard?"

"Shirt tail."

Nobody else noticed me walk into the doctor's room where I placed my snack in the small refrigerator. Nurses, clerks, and techs toiled quietly among cardiac monitors and computers. Possibly they were hung over. My crisp white 40" long lab coat, with the

Touro logo on the pocket, dangled in my locker. I stood there staring into the steel abyss.

For twenty years, my work had a routine. ERs run around the clock, but my standard approach varied little between shifts. I knew the nurses, clerks, techs, doctors, housekeepers, administrators, and paramedics. I could recite the hospital policies like my birth date. You know these things when you serve as chief of staff of the hospital for two years. At Touro, the minute and the complex chores would be a challenge. I found my way to the bathroom, and I learned to use the electronic medical record during my orientation, but for everything else I was a neophyte. The medicine was the same, but I needed to earn the respect of everyone. Now came my moment of buyer's remorse. I recalled signing a lease contract for a thousand dollars per month for a car I didn't need. Brief remorse was forgotten as I drove from the dealership. This deal gave me a knot in my gut. Daily difficult work lay ahead. I expected months to pass for people to know me well enough to toss me a mulligan when something went awry. Things would go awry. No matter how lucky or good you are, things go awry.

"You're Dr. Buchanan, right? I'm sorry to trouble you before you settle in but Dr. Deno hoped you could handle this full arrest coming." Kathy Wilson's deep musical voice stirred me from my contemplations. She stood with her hand on the door frame, a knee bent, and one white clog resting on the toe. She smiled with her hazel eyes. Late twenties, auburn hair, held back with a braid, lay across her clavicle. Crooked smile. Dried plaster dotted the legs of her green Touro scrubs. Young enough to be my daughter.

"Yeah, I can do that. No worries. Call me Sam. Dr. Sam if you must."

A jump in the deep water is the fastest way to find your routine and get to the business of starting over. Cardiac arrest is a cardinal reason I show up to work. Toothaches, back pain, and upper respiratory infections are what I do while I'm waiting for the sick patients to arrive. I jammed my stethoscope in the pocket of my coat and donned it. Tight. I must have put two inches on my chest paddling. I removed the coat and carried on. Kathy led me to an expansive bay where six workers sporting various colored scrubs and quizzical looks awaited our nearly dead patient.

"Hey everybody, this is Dr. Buchanan. This is his first night so be gentle. He says to call him Sam."

They all said, "Hi Sam!" I felt like a drunk at an AA meeting. I should have been. No coffee and doughnuts though. *Hi, I'm Sam, and I'm a perfect asshole.* We made quick introductions and Kathy gave me the report. These rooms appeared the same everywhere. Two-thirds of the way back, a long narrow rectangular box containing electricity, oxygen, suction, and an arm to attach a cardiac monitor extended from the ceiling. An adjustable and uncomfortable wheeled stretcher rested in front. At one corner of the bed a nurse stood by the crash cart, a lockable multi-drawer cart full of drugs and supplies of limited help for cardiac arrest. I ran hundreds of resuscitations over the years. I would always begin with the goal of a successful resuscitation tempered by two realities. Few will survive, and resuscitation of certain people does nobody any favors. Some people need to die, and there is no pleasant way to say it. Just like there is no way to handle a turd by the sterile end. But I rarely involve myself in those decisions unless family tells me to stop. I do my job and let God and the ICU sort out the rest.

I made a few memorable saves. A six-year-old drowning, a twenty-five-year-old shot in the chest, and a father of six who collapsed at my feet were notches on my belt. Nursing home patients waiting in God's alcove played the biggest role in the resuscitation game. Unlike TV, where almost everyone survives cardiac arrest, few survive on Real Street.

Our task at hand was a sixty-something man found down on Magazine Street. That's three blocks toward the river. EMS didn't have much more. At first, he had a pulse, and then they lost it rolling in. EMS has a crappy job. People call them, at every odd hour, to impossible situations with limited information and equipment. Supremely fat people on the third floor, half-dead people wedged in small bathrooms, and people entrapped in vehicles after a crash are common scenarios. They inserted a breathing tube in the man and placed an IV. They started chest compressions when the pulse stopped. I figured this might last the duration of a cup of coffee, pronounce him dead, and then proceed to the next live patient.

EMS wheeled into the room and moved the patient to the cart. Ray, a thin and frail, sparsely bearded man, well-known to the emergency nurses and the respiratory therapists, lay motionless. He was homeless, and he visited the ER every two weeks. Had he been a customer of Touro airlines, he could go to Tahiti free by first class. He suffered from emphysema and alcoholism, occasionally took his medications, and smoked unfiltered Camels. A restaurant owner welcomes someone who visits every two weeks and encourages them to return soon. This is not the case in the ER. Everybody receives proper care, but you roll your eyes when you see a patient more often than your in-town relatives. Wires attached to various spots on his chest transmitted a heart rhythm on the monitor but no pulse. This is akin to *lights are on, but nobody is home* for the heart. The respiratory therapist forced air into the tube with a ventilation bag attached to oxygen.

"I got nothing here," I said as I listened to his chest.

"He's difficult to bag," the RT said, straining to force another breath.

I spied the paramedic, a middle-aged heavy-set guy who appeared to have done this a few times. He held his hands out to the sides.

"I looked that tube past his vocal cords," the EMT said.

This told me he did his job well. I placed my hand on his barrel chest and thumped the back of a finger with my other middle finger. Hollow as a drum. Same on the other side.

"Stop bagging. Quick now, I need two long six-teen-gauge angiocaths, betadine, and four-by-fours. Somebody else set me up for two chest tubes."

I grabbed two gloves out of a box on the wall, poured the iodine solution across his chest and scrubbed with gauze. As I dropped the gauze the nurse arrived with the catheters. I found my landmark and jabbed the IV needle through his chest wall. Like deflating a tire, the air hissed while I repeated the procedure on the other side. I removed each needle and left the flex-ible catheter in the chest wall. The nurses started chest compressions again, and the RT smiled as the air moved in and out, easier with each breath. The lungs re-expanded, allowing air to return and blood to flow to the heart. Bilateral tension pneumothorax is uniformly fatal if not treated. I placed my hand at the artery running through his groin. I could feel the pulse, and with each chest compression it became stronger.

"Stop compressions. Keep bagging." The pulse bounded, and his lips turned from gray to pink. I did not expect him to awaken right away. Maybe never. "Family here?"

"This is Ray. We know him well. No family," Kathy said with a stern look.

"Primary doctor?"

"Spell your last name."

"You're cute." I carried on.

20

I DROPPED INTO ONE of the leather easy chairs in the doctors' room. The television sat idle, various memos tilted on a bulletin board, and the smell of stale coffee drifted from the machine. One benefit of working nights is the usual downtime between five and seven a.m. A kid with an ear infection received his first dose of antibiotics and the tracking board cleared. In Carolina I preferred not to work nights if I could avoid it, because working nights cut into family and social activities, a common source of friction with my soon-to-be ex-wife. Plus, when you work a few nights you need to convert back to a day schedule. It's jet lag on crack. Now that I carried no family or social commitments, being a permanent night guy appealed to me. Our director back home commented that no doctor could have a personality disorder so egregious to prevent him from hiring for full-time nights. My personality works well enough, but still I appreciate how they give night guys more slack because of the difficult circumstances. On nights, you are invisible.

To hospital administrators, you are like a fart. Your presence is certain, but they never see you.

Because of my administrative duties at the hospital back home, I had my fill of the silk suit and shiny shoe crowd. Like the sensation on Thanksgiving when you ate everything and then wolfed down a piece of pumpkin pie with whipped cream. A few bites too many.

My attire has always been white athletic shoes and scrubs. I understood what the suits did. They appreciated little of the challenges of taking care of multiple ill undifferentiated patients. An enormous disconnect existed in understanding what needed to happen between arrival at the triage desk or through the ambulance doors and admission to an inpatient bed. An especially obtuse administrator back home named Denny carried this affliction. He preferred Dennis. Everyone called him Denny or D-bag behind his invertebrate carcass. He imagined patients arriving with the diagnosis taped to their foreheads. Forget the fact that some patients (and some administrators) can be simpleminded, demented, intoxicated, delirious, or blatant liars. You need to tease diagnoses from a tangled fabric.

At night, half the patients are drunk, crazy, or both, so they tend not to complain much to administration. At night, you can say, *Look, Roscoe, dude, stop giving the nurses such a hard time or I'll call the cops to come check for outstanding warrants and then they'll haul your fat ass off to central lockup.* Say that to someone during the day and there might be some 'splaining to do to the patient advocate. The night crew is a grounded and forgiving bunch. You won't find them pointing fingers or bitching out people like the day queens. I use that term with affection. If you don't mind sleeping during the day, it's a grand gig for a guy who is sailing with no anchor in the boat. At ten nights per month, I rode fair seas with following winds. As I opened the cover on my iPad to search for a new novel to read, Kathy stuck her head in the door. "Hey," she said.

I sensed an invisible force field at the threshold. An electric shock might be delivered if she stepped one more centimeter. In another time, Kathy was a drop-dead traffic stopper. Recall the pre-Barbie era before beauty was a firm butt, tiny waist, and pregnant breasts. This is a rare anatomic combination. Less rare if you visit the plastic surgeon. She sported a full figure and a full personality to match. I sensed no self-consciousness of her weight, nor in displaying her ample cleavage.

"Hey," I said.

I can be sociable, but I am dull as a drumstick when meeting new people. When a person walks away, five clever bits of social tasters come to me. Instead, I say *Hey* or worse, give a nod of the head. *'Sup?*

"I didn't have time to tell you that first patient was amazing. Plus, the nurses appreciated your compliments afterward."

"I have a confession to make."

Her eyebrows narrowed. I'm sure she was thinking, *Oh, Lord, is this guy going to tell me he's an imposter and stayed at the Holiday Inn Express last night, loser?*

"Actually...I met that guy when I was walking over and paid him for that performance." Blank expression. Three, two, one. Belly laugh.

"Oh, I'll never know when you are teasing. You'll fit in with this group like beer and bratwurst."

What satisfaction. Like a pregnant belch after too many hospital administrators. Or flatulence. I felt for Ray, but for me, it was fortuitous to arrive ten minutes early.

"Yo, I don't bite. Take a load off." I extended my palm toward the other easy chair.

"You sure?"

According to Kathy, this room belonged to the lions. What remained was the kingdom. Watch *Lion King* and you'll understand. Doctors are lions, nurses are hyenas. Only one hyena had to have her head bit off for the rest to fall in line.

"Not my rule. So, when I'm king, you may roam."

She took the other easy chair and crossed her legs on the ottoman. She let out a sigh and laid her head back. I spied a stain on her right scrub leg, the source of which I did not want to know. "I could fall asleep right here. This is awesome. If we had these in the nurses' lounge, I'd be collecting food stamps. Ha."

I sensed she came in search of information and I understood. Nurses are a social group. Besides patient care, they gain much of their satisfaction at work from their relationship with coworkers. Because I was busy, I had offered no personal information to the staff, and I doubted that Wales, the medical director, had either. I had nothing to hide. Well, I had one or two things to hide, but nobody, not even Wales, knew of my booze problem. I intended to keep it that way. The EMS phone squawked. We would talk again.

21

THE MOON, NOW half, offered enough light to avoid stumbling and becoming my own patient. A sense of belonging and rhythm ushered a hint of ease long missing from my life. I anticipated another night of caring for those with limited options and unfortunate circumstances. Gabe sat on a tall stool near the edge of the nurses' area. A toothy grin appeared on his muroid face. "Hey, doc. The pharmacist called to say your Viagra prescription is ready."

A few heads tilted in our direction and I didn't breathe. In my best Irish accent: "Wonderful. Your sister will be pleased." I let him explain it to the nurses.

My first patient, Danelle, a blonde sprite of twenty years of age, fidgeted on the gurney as I entered. A smartphone protected by a multicolored case rested near her leg. Bad sign. For most young ladies, the phone is an appendage, relinquished sparingly. Her lack of interest in the latest pop star wedding or cat video signaled trouble. After an exchange of pleasantries I learned of her right lower abdominal pain. As

I examined her, the list of possible diagnoses, what we docs call the differential, collected in my well-used but high-functioning cerebral cortex. Appendicitis, ovarian cyst, ectopic pregnancy, kidney stone, gonorrhea, and the monotonous and mundane condition of constipation topped the list. Urine, urine pregnancy test and a blood count made for a thorough initial evaluation. The utility of the blood count lived in the red blood cell count, not the white. The overrated white count offered limited help in the diagnosis of appendicitis.

A sprained ankle, a sixty-year-old with chest pain, and a urinary tract infection occupied my time until the tests returned. A nurse, whose name I had yet to learn, sailed a slip of paper across my desk. The lab called a low hemoglobin, which is odd for an otherwise fit twenty-year-old. Urine and the urine pregnancy test proved negative. Now, she may have hemorrhaged from a ruptured ovarian cyst, but she could have chronic anemia and appendicitis as a bonus prize. Off to CAT scan for her. Because of the radiation, I am reticent to CAT scan young people. Dannie, as she preferred, qualified. My conversation with Steven came to mind. This was it. The diagnosis. The heart of the lost decade. The reason for my presence there. I felt the spark, the anticipation of the result of the CAT scan.

Kathy pulled me to room seven, where a forty-five-year-old man rested upright on the cart, perspiring like a politician in confessional, and supporting his elbow with the opposite hand. A portrait of pain, he was, so I breezed through the history and learned he previously dislocated this shoulder, and it happened again just before arrival. A reach above and behind him caused the arm bone to move forward out of socket again. He appeared to be a rugged sort, and I believed he could tolerate reduction of the dislocation without sedation. He agreed. When in severe pain, you'll agree to eat dirt. I grasped his right elbow with my left hand and his wrist in the other and rotated his arm away from his body. While doing this I wiggled his arm to relax the muscles. He grimaced as we chatted about his son, who pitched for the Brother Martin High baseball team. He told me he stopped catching for his son when the velocity reached eighty miles per hour. Too many tips off the glove into his face mask. This conversation, or Kathy's cleavage, provided adequate distraction to allow full rotation and a lift of the arm above his head. A satisfying clunk ensued accompanied by a child-birth quality yell. He expressed his appreciation with an offer to join him at a baseball game and after a quick X-ray and sling application, Kathy discharged him. That beats the Martin Riggs method.

"Dr. Sam, radiologist on eighty-eight," said the clerk.

The radiologist never calls to tell you the test is normal. It was Melvin. I hated this guy. Not a bona fide hatred, but an extreme envy. Melvin lived in a condo, on the beach, on the west coast of O'ahu. He enjoyed days of fishing or kayaking and worked evenings reading CAT scans, MRI scans, and ultra-sounds from his damn living room, which rested close enough to the Pacific to hear the waves crashing in the distance. The magic of the Internet. Why I am doing a rectal exam on a guy the size of a steer while this guy sits on his well-tanned ass looking at high-resolution pictures?

"Mel. How's the smartest man this side of the international date line?"

"Nursing a shoulder strain from casting, but otherwise top shelf."

"You need an in-person consultation from a real doctor."

"Ha. You are welcome to come any time. So, Danelle Washington. What's her quant?"

He wanted to know the pregnancy test number. There is a yes or no test, the qualitative. The quantitative provides a number.

"Not ordered. Urine is negative."

"Get the quant. Could be an ectopic with rupture. Lot of blood in her pelvis."

I added the lab and reconsidered the differential.

Kathy stuck her head out of room three and summoned me with her index finger. Dannie's blood pressure read eighty over forty, and she looked gray and diaphoretic. She was one hundred and twenty over eighty before. I lowered the head of her bed and tilted the cart to put her feet higher. She vomited, and the pressure dropped to seventy over thirty. Now I was sweating as I peered into her dull and pleading eyes. The nurses placed a second IV and used the rapid infuser to give two liters of saline. I asked for type and crossmatch of blood and dispatched a call to the OB. This scenario is the portrait of death twenty minutes before the real thing.

A somnolent and cantankerous OB chastised me for the call and told me to call back when the quant returned. Her lack of concern for my patient, who appeared to be bleeding out internally, was troublesome. Kathy reported improved blood pressure and skin color, making my pulse return to normal. Blood would be available soon.

I spoke to the hospital charge nurse, someone who wouldn't break a rule to save the pope, and suggested she call out the OR team. Unless I had a surgeon ready to cut, this song was not on the playlist. Saving people from dying at night can be a challenge.

Thirty minutes of frequent bedside assessment passed until both the blood and the quant were available. The number was twenty. What the hell. Twenty is low enough to miss on the urine test, yet not zero. She was pregnant, but not in the correct location. I expected another stiff arm from the OB because of the number. She agreed to come in to see the patient with the admonishment it would piss her off if I was wrong. I too would be angry if this young lady kicked off in my department, so we were even.

By five a.m., Dannie dreamed under anesthesia while the OB wielded her laparoscope. Sleep did not beckon, but I welcomed the chance to put up my feet in the doctors' room. Kathy soon took her place beside me.

"Still on a reconnaissance mission?" I said.

"Yeah, they're chicken. So, who asked for the divorce?"

"Why does it have to be divorce?"

"Come on. Guy your age uproots, divorce until proven otherwise."

"Actually, my wife perished in a climbing accident on Kilimanjaro."

"Nice try." She whacked my shoulder with the back of her hand. "Wales told me you are getting a divorce. I am onto you."

"Okay. It was her."

She smiled and wagged her finger at me. "Were you a bad boy, Sam?"

"No. I can't say I'm blameless, but it was her playing hide the sausage with her law partner. I'm here to start my life over."

"Ah. Never heard it put that way." Devious laugh. "And you're here for how long?"

"I signed for a year. Then we'll see."

"So, you moved your stuff from Columbia?"

"I sold or gave away almost everything I own. What fit in my two suitcases and what I purchased at Breaux Mart comprises my material possessions."

"Wow, you're not just whistling Dixie."

"Go big or go home," I said.

"Speaking of going home, we have breakfast and a shot or two at the place across Prytania. You should come."

The night charge nurse craned her neck in the door.

She glanced at Kathy and made a sly smile with the right side of her mouth.

"EMS is five minutes out."

She handed me the field transmitted EKG. Heart attack. The big one.

"Get me the on-call cardiologist and call out the cath lab."

22

THE OTHER NURSES begged off the liquid breakfast. Kathy and I crossed to the Prytania Bar and
settled in a booth with threadbare cushions. Typical drinking establishment with a long wooden bar,
a few booths and tables, pool table, dart boards, and
jukebox. "Night Moves" playing. We both ordered
the special of southwest omelet, bacon, and toast. She
ordered a shot of rum and threw it back as soon as the
waitress delivered it. Didn't even make a face. Temp-
tation loitered at the door. Even when I was drinking,
I never drank breakfast.

"You have tan lines on your temples. You been
golfing?"

"No. I swore off golfing when I left Carolina.
Kayaking."

"In the bayou?" She ordered another rum and made
it disappear.

"Hawai'i."

"Cool. You look like you work out."

I had no suspicions at first but now the meter was

155

bumping the red line. I gave her the G-rated version of Hawai'i and emphasized my unwavering commitment to and love for Kayla. During this monologue, she put away two more shots. She's an adult, and I was not the booze police. Hell, at four I just started. I could tell that I had thrown water on it, in the parlance of Stan, and conversation soon reminded me of being on a blind date. As we finished, she had a buzz going and was not fit to drive. WWKD. What would Kayla do?

"Listen. Carefully now. I live three blocks from here. You're coming with me. Sleep in my bed. I'll take the couch. Nothing else happens."

She bobbed her drunk head, and we made a refreshing stroll to Camp and Delachaise. We passed a few disinterested joggers and a tourist taking pictures of houses. In a loud voice, she expressed her regret for trying to jump my bones. I held her arm over the uneven footpath, and, as we rounded the corner, there he was, peering over the fence. Max Dupuis. Shut the front door. I couldn't give a rat's gluteus maximus for what old Max was thinking, but he is a congenital gossip, according to Maria, and by sundown the whole street would think I was bedding a nurse. I half waved and helped her to the door. As we crossed the threshold, Kathy fell back into me, her ample right breast entering my open hand. She made a rowdy, suggestive comment, which I ignored. I directed her to the bath, then the unmade bed, where I removed her shoes and covered her as if tucking in a six-year-old. If this was God sending me difficult, needy, people, I got what I asked for.

I awakened at noon from a restless nap on the couch. After making tea, I sat at the table content with beardless Sam. I enjoyed a fulfilling night of work, didn't drink my breakfast, helped a distressed drunken damsel, and didn't play sausage games even when invited. Billy knocked and entered. I forgot I asked her to help me rearrange the furniture in the bedroom.

"Hey, Sam."

I touched my index to my lips. "Do you have time for an adult conversation on the patio?"

She did, and I took her on a whirlwind tour of Columbia, Kailua, and rum for breakfast. She sat motionless as if watching a riveting movie. At the closing credits, in the parlance of Jane, she asked to meet Michael when he comes to NOLA. Really. After that story. Not *tell more about Kayla,* or *what are you going to do with this woman in your bed?*, but *I wanna meet the buff plumber.* Of course.

Kathy skulked from the back door, gave a sheepish wave, and headed to the gate. Not at her best, but not as disheveled as I expected. I motioned with my index, introduced the ladies, and reassured Kathy that Billy understood the platonic nature of our sleepover. We walked to the sidewalk. No Max in sight. Her face could have been printed next to pouty in the dictionary. I touched my index to my lips and took both of her hands in mine.

"You have nothing to be ashamed of. There is

nothing to forgive or forget." I brought her in close and kissed her forehead. "Now that you slept over, I can say we are good friends."

She started to speak and again finger to lips and I turned her toward the lake.

23

NINE BLOCKS TOWARD the city, two blocks toward the lake. According to Maria. I was walking to Lafayette Cemetery No. 1. As a teenager I made, with my dad, a hobby out of exploring the deep-rooted graveyards of Beaufort County. We traveled to Savannah for the day often and might spy a steeple on a lonely road. Gravel flew as he made a quick turn, leaving a dusty cloud in our wake. He told me this or that church was a Negro church, and we were likely to find the burial place of freed slaves in the churchyard. Back then it amazed me he knew this stuff before we even left the truck. Unlike today, tombstones often told a story. The engraving might tell what the person did for a living, or if they served in the military, and sometimes how they died. I found it captivating to read the tombstones in a family plot and figure out how they were related. We learned death can tell an engrossing and enduring story.

This graveyard, which rests across from Commander's Palace, is a city of seven thousand quiescent souls descended from numerous nations and all walks and stations of life. The bulk emigrated from Germany and Ireland to settle in the areas known as Lafayette and the Irish Channel. They have their unique stories, but a collective story permeates the rows of above-ground tombs of varying architecture. Because I am a physician, I find this to be a most compelling story. The narrative told is that of the summers of the mid 1800s, in a time of immense prosperity and growth, when an epidemic of yellow fever, which made Katrina appear to be a brief rain shower, overwhelmed New Orleans. The viral scourge started slowly, as in earlier years, but like a tornado upon the plains, blew to every corner of the city. More than seven thousand perished the summer of '53, taxing the capacity of every burial ground in the city and the faith of its citizens.

I walked the orderly rows of crypts scanning names and dates. The history hung weightless like the aroma of warm pumpkin pie. I ran my fingertips over the letters in the moist stone. On older tombs, the faded engravings proved difficult to read, sometimes nearly absent. The engravings on a few recalled entire families taken in a matter of weeks. I imagined a suffering mother of three who buried her husband and later her children in succession only to find peace in her own death weeks later. And who remained to bury her?

Many vaults held youngsters. Throughout the generations, children often died before their fifth birthday, perishing from illnesses we don't give a second thought to in modern times. The line in the child's prayer, *If I die before I wake,* as tangible as a tattered blanket clutched at the bedside, revealed the fears of every parent. A toddler put to bed with a fever on a sweltering windless evening, a lock of hair pasted with sweat to her forehead, could be found cold and lifeless the next day.

So, in these tombs the grieving placed the casketed remains of loved ones lost to infection or trauma and less often to cancer or heart disease. After a year and a day, the casket may be removed, the remains swept to a bag, and then placed in the caveau, the space below, to await the next family member to die. Most of these sepulchers are brick and mortar covered by stucco. On a ninety-degree day, the temperature inside might bake a cake. Or hasten the decomposition of a dead body.

No generation is immune from suffering and loss. For those who practice in modern-day emergency departments, we find it easy to slide into an effortless indifference to the pain of our patients. Guilty. I just stopped giving a shit. I stopped remembering my purpose in showing up to work each day. Maintaining the enthusiasm to give a crap can be difficult; but we are not excused because of it. There is a sweet spot to find between crying everyone's tears and callousness. I found patient care much easier if I shrugged off the misfortune of others rather than confront the emotion and channel it to help the patients and their families. My energy for empathy waned, and I hastened this with rye whiskey.

I found a weathered stone bench at the main crossroads and rested. For late January, the day was warm.

I removed my garnet Gamecocks sweatshirt and absorbed the sun. The weight, the burden of a life poorly lived, began to lift from my shoulders. That was, when I peered past the clutter, the purpose of my journey to New Orleans—a journey not ending at the corner of Camp and Delachaise but just beginning. The heft of my past transgressions was not manifest until I lightened this encumbrance in Hawai'i. Just this hint my compass read true, that I had begun a proper expedition, caused an unexpected flow of emotion. No embarrassment. I didn't fight it. Only me, God, and a few thousand dead folks enjoyed the afternoon.

Through the mist I saw, twenty yards past, my family name in bold capital letters across the top of a decaying pediment tomb. Renée's family. I stepped as if needing to beat someone to it. There was my name, but not my tomb. I spied over each shoulder like a thief. A brass plate displayed twenty members of the Buchanan clan. The family interred the last body in the 1970s. I ran my hand over the rough exposed block bared by the crumbling stucco. Through a stellate opening, the sun illuminated the corner of a rusting casket. Renée and I had something to discuss.

24

"**REX, KING OF** grocers," I hailed, entering Breaux Mart.

Virgil Rex Breaux offered a rolling salute, reminiscent of Johnny Carson, intent on the cold cuts he was packaging. I strolled to the produce section. Since leaving Carolina, I experienced a significant uptick in my mental and physical capacity. Because of the multiple variables, I could not prove the cause. Carefree lifestyle, increased physical activity, new job, abstinence from alcohol, lack of a nagging wife, and improved diet might explain the favorable change. Or just Kayla. I cut back to one red meat meal a week. Fish, nuts, whole grains, fruits, and vegetables replaced most of the crap I ate. I lost five more pounds without a craving. I spied Billy as she emerged from the stockroom.

"Hey Sam, where y'at?" she said as she adjusted her apron.

I looked around my feet and held my arms out. "Uh, Breaux Mart?"

"No. It's a greeting. Then you might say *I'm chillin'* or *What it is.*"

"Ah...fine. Settling in. I'm looking for fresh produce."

She filled my cart. *The satsumas came the day before. Let these bananas sit a day. Buy two raspberries but eat them this week.*

"Easy now. Remember, I live alone."

We proceeded to the front where she tried to interest me in the twenty-count shrimp, but I passed. The freezer still overflowed from my last visit. Setbacks aside, I surmised Billy was on her way to success. She had a natural enthusiasm. It was organic, and nobody could hold her back.

"You need one of those collapsible carts on wheels," she said. "You'll tire of carrying bags. Go to Wally World."

"Wally World?"

"Walmart," not quite condescendingly. "Twelve blocks toward the city, maybe eight to the river."

"Okay, I'll put on my hiking shoes. So, what's the plan for this fall?"

"Tulane if I had the money, but sixty grand a year is rich."

"Any scholarship money?"

"They offered half, but I can't come up with the rest. UNO is in my budget, and I can get scholarships and federal grants. It'll just be a pain to commute by bus every day."

"Okay, keep me posted. Hey, is Miss Renée around?"

"Oh, Lord," she said as she clapped her hands together. "I forgot. She wants to meet you. Ya'll are related. What are the chances? You should buy a lotto ticket from Mr. Rex today."

Funny how people associate a lucky or unlikely event with an increased likelihood of experiencing an even more unlikely event on the same day. A mathematician friend told me the lottery is for folks who don't understand statistics. I skipped the lotto, but I wondered how I moved seven hundred miles to land in the lap of a family member. We walked to the back of the store where Renée peered through reading glasses at a computer monitor.

After surveying the expanse of Rex, I imagined Renée to be short and stocky with a faint mustache. I imagined incorrectly. Surely, she was a knockout when she was younger. Her naturally gray hair was styled into a short bob framing her expressive face. A sleeveless white blouse revealed feminine but muscular arms, which likely came from hauling boxes. She directed a penetrating stare and a natural smile appeared.

"You have the Buchanan eyes."

Billy introduced us, and she gave me a hug like I was a brother returning from an extended trip.

"Rex probably told you I love genealogy. Having you here is such a blessing. I am the last of a long line of the Buchanan family in New Orleans." She had the full accent of a native New Orleanian.

"Well, I am happy to be here. Y'all have made me

feel welcome. Especially this one." I shot my thumb toward Billy.

"Sure, we'll keep her. Listen now." She clicked the mouse several times and turned the screen toward me. "This took a few years, but I think I made a great tree. Look here." She pointed to the name Uilliam Buchanan. "He would have gone by Liam. He married a Morgan, and they had five sons and three daughters. God bless her. Down here now. Liam was the father of Samuel Morgan Buchanan the first, your granddad, right?"

"Wow." I ran my fingers back through my thick hair. "Yes, yes."

"Liam is also the father of my grandad, Sean. We called him Pappy."

I scanned to the bottom to see the more recent names and saw she had no entries past my grandfather. That was easy to fix. I yearned to know the stories of my relatives. How did they make their living? How did they die? What kind of schooling? Why did they move or why did they stay? "I know these names," I said, intent on the screen.

"How so?"

"I stumbled across the Buchanan tomb in Lafayette Number 1."

"Oh, dear. I'm embarrassed to claim it. Decades since we buried anybody, and the family stopped maintaining it twenty years ago. I keep telling Rex we need to do something before it collapses."

25

I ARRIVED AT THE Touro ER early. I figured if patients waited, I would get started. If not, a mug of tea. Routine came quickly during my first few weeks. Most of the nurses' first names came easily but the names of the medical staff, not so much. I didn't expect to see many of them in the middle of the night, so putting names with faces might not happen. Gabe approached me, phone in hand.

"Hey, doc. What's this rash?"

"Leprosy."

"Get off."

Gabe was onto me. I looked again. Red bumpy rash on the ear lobes. "Contact dermatitis. Who's got it?"

"Wife."

"New earrings?"

"Yeah. Present from her mom."

"Sorry to say. Cheap earrings. Allergy to nickel." I reached over the counter for a prescription pad and scribbled for Triamcinalone cream. "Might get worse before it gets better."

"Thanks, Dr. Sam."

On my way to the doc's room, the charge nurse caught my elbow. She told me a man waited for me in the family room. The room in every ER in the country where you give the unhappy news. Minimum requirements are a couch, two chairs, and a coffee pot and facial tissue. You tell the parents of the fourteen-year-old, who drove his ATV into a tree, he will not be coming home. You tell the ninety-year-old man his wife of sixty-eight years died from cardiac arrest. You tell a large family that their young relative is dead from a heroin overdose. As often as you switch clocks for daylight savings time do you have positive news to share in the family room. Even rarer does someone come visit you. I was perplexed. I didn't believe I had angered anyone.

A bearded Hispanic man with a pocked face wearing an ill-fitting flannel shirt stood gingerly as I entered. Two of him could fit in the chair. "Dr. Buchanan, right?" He made a wide grin exposing a mouthful of decaying teeth.

"Yes sir. Call me Sam." I had no clue. He might be on the board of trustees.

He held my hand in both of his and then held my gaze. "I have nothing." He paused and chuckled. "And I mean nothing, but my words to thank you for saving my life."

It was Ray, Raymond T. Reyes, my first patient at Touro. People are transfigured flat on a cart with an endotracheal tube protruding from their mouth and chest tubes drooping from either side. He looked

168

fatigued, but cardiac arrest will do that to you. Otherwise he looked spry compared to the last time I gazed upon him and stuck two needles into his chest.

"Well look at you." I motioned to the chair, and we both sat. "I'll admit I didn't recognize you, but I remember you. Never forget you, man. I think of you every day since we first came together."

His rough and thick palms rested together as if holding a baby bird. These were the hands of a man who worked hard. The end of a pinky finger was missing, and several others carried scars.

"Thank you, Sam. Thank you for your skill and your manner." He let a moment pass. "You probably thinking, what do I know about your manner?"

He was right. How would he? He was essentially dead. Didn't move a muscle.

"I heard you. Not so much the words but your tone, your calm nature. You stayed cool, like everything will be okay. And I wasn't scared."

I heard of these kinds of accounts and wondered. Maybe just urban legend. Seeing Ray was both gratifying and humbling. Only one patient had ever taken the time to come thank me for saving them. A guy who nearly died of heart failure brought me a bottle of champagne. This encounter was much more meaningful. My interaction with Ray lifted me out of my earthly routine to consider what I do in a less concrete way. Like when you see an aerial view of your neighborhood the first time. Wow.

"Thank you, Raymond. How are you?"

"Get tired fast but I'm doing well."

I thought for a moment. I didn't want to pry or make him uncomfortable, but I had a genuine curiosity and Ray seemed to be someone who wouldn't mind talking. People wrote books. Adults and children alike gave accounts of talking to angels or going to heaven during near-death experiences. I never knew what to believe. Were these vivid dreams or did a messenger from God truly appear? This is very fascinating. Strange as well. Every time an angel appeared before someone in the bible the first thing said was, *don't fear.* For me the angel would ask if I prefer to change my pants before we talk. I can imagine that even for the most devout believer there comes this abrupt realization, holy Toledo, this shit is for real.

"Listen, you don't need to talk about this but I'm wondering if an angel visited when you were in cardiac arrest."

"No. No bright lights or voices from heaven. Guess it was not my time."

"Clearly not." I touched his leg. "Raymond, is there anything I can do for you?"

"No sir. You know the only folks call me Raymond are family. They gone now except for one sister. You can keep calling me Raymond. Makes me feel we been friends a while."

"I can do that. Now, the nurses told me you have no home. Right?"

"Yes and no. If I'm not drinking, I can stay with

my sister. I haven't touched it since that night I tried to die on you. So, I'm good."

"What are you doing to stay sober?"

"Winging it, I guess."

I pulled a card from my pocket. I handed him a white card with my name and cell number in simple black letters. No MD after my name or logo or fancy font. On the back I wrote an address and underneath put "7 PM Mon - Sat".

"Give this a try for a week. If it's not for you, then stop. Doing this will be thanks enough."

26

THE NIGHT PASSED without a glance at my watch. My talk with Ray filled me with energy. Much of what we do in the ER goes unnoticed or unacknowledged. Do something someone perceives to be wrong and the whole damn hospital knows. They have a parade before anybody learns the truth. The silk suit, shiny shoe crowd is adept at that. In grade school, if I wore new shoes to school the first day after Christmas break, my buddies stepped on top of them and scuffed them. They were reminding me to not get up on a high horse with my new fancy shoes. Close friends do that. As adults, we act with more tact, but still I had to resist the urge to turn the heel of my worn sneakers on the top of their fancy shoes. These people can suck the life out of you. In so many places, the ER is where healthcare worker enthusiasm goes to die. After a while, you are digging holes the first half of your shift and filling them back in the second half. So much administrative dust gets kicked up you can't see beyond the next patient or from where you came. That night I forgot all that crap. Ray reminded me of who I am supposed to be.

After a busy night, the only patients left were two drunk students who were sleeping it off until morning, so I settled into my easy chair in the break room. The magical chair. A few minutes' rest erased the stress. Kathy plopped in the adjacent chair.

"Here we are again," I said.

"Old Ray is a cat with ninety-nine lives," she said. "You gotta be pleased about what you did for him."

"Sure. I'll remember him 'til I die. Few patients on that list." I remembered a lady we shocked out of ventricular tachycardia. "Where y'at."

"Look at you, learning the local lingo."

"Yeah, I'm trying."

She touched me on the arm, hushed voice. "Thank you. For being there and not taking advantage."

I rested my hand on top of hers. "De nada."

"You speak Spanish?"

"Enough to order dinner and find the bathroom. I stopped trying to explain medical things like rectal examination. Didn't go well."

She play-punched me in the shoulder. "You're a card."

I had been enjoying my time in the Crescent City, but my time away from Kayla weighed on me. Her calling me a card transported me back to the time when Kay did the same thing and I smiled.

"Still with me?"

"Yeah. No. I'm fine."

"You would lose money at poker, doctor."

"How so?" I turned in my chair to face her.

"You make this face and I can tell the wheels are spinning." She tapped a finger on my parietal scalp. "Come on. I was naked before you. Sort of. Out with it."

"I wondered, when I left O'ahu, if my desire for Kayla would wane. Like morning dew on tall grass." I placed my hand on my heart. "I know she is here. Part of me now."

"Describe her for me."

"Not exaggerating. For a woman in her forties, she is smoking hot. Bright eyes, strawberry blonde. Way out of my league."

"Will you return to her when you finish here?"

"Yes. But I have loads to prove before I'll do that."

"I think you're our best doc. What do you have to prove?"

Kathy knew only some of my issues. The story flowed as a favorite song now.

"And you must keep this between us. I need to stay sober. If I don't, any other changes I make in my life will be a house on shifting sand."

27

TWO BLOCKS TOWARD the lake and three blocks toward the park. I didn't go every day but tried to make it five days a week. My outlook on life and other humans improved when I did. AA was my church. I enjoyed the fellowship. The contrast between my asshole golfing buddies and the recovering drunks I encountered at meetings struck me. If the choice came between the drunks and my golfing buddies, I'd hang out with the drunks. I'd been looking for Ray. At first, I wondered if showing my face at AA was a bright idea. Chances were, I treated one of these folks and they could reveal the one thing I preferred to keep secret. It was a chance worth taking. I felt a hand touch my shoulder, and the person steadied himself to sit.

"Didn't expect to see you here, Sam."

"We sinners come in many shapes, Raymond. I'm glad you came."

"Me too. Was walking to Los Caballeros to get drunk, and I fingered your card in my pocket. You give those out to all the boozers?"

"Just the rough cases like you and me." I touched his knee.

Ray smiled and nodded. The meeting started, and we both listened, lost in the stories. Neither of us talked. Hearing people talk reaffirmed the pedestrian nature of my self-centeredness and apathy for the feelings of others, making the road to forgiveness and recovery less rutted. After the meeting I introduced Ray to the regulars, and we walked out together.

"Come on, I'll walk you home."

"Afraid I'll take a detour to the bar?"

"Hey, I'm not gonna stop you. I want to talk to you about a project. A nurse told me you worked construction."

"Yeah, been a while. Mind if I smoke?"

"Well, let me ask you this. If you painted the fence in front of your house and some dude asks if you mind if his dog takes a piss on it, what would you say?"

"I say I ain't no pretty painted fence."

I stopped and turned to him. "I don't see it that way and neither does God, the way I figure it."

We walked a block in silence on a street I would avoid in daylight.

"So, what's this project?"

I explained the Buchanan tomb in Lafayette Cemetery and my family connection. The sidewalk in front of his sister's house appeared to have relented to the weeds. The bulk of the paint on the small shotgun house relented to gravity. We sat on the front porch on weathered wooden chairs. The floorboards creaked as we sat. A strong wind might collapse the place. Two termites short of condemnation.

"I'd invite you in, but my sister goes to bed early."

"Raymond, this is fine. Now, this job is stucco and brick work."

"Done plenty of that. Never done a tomb. I heard these ones from the 1800s can be rough. May have to rebuild the whole damn thing."

"You got another big job?" I said.

Ray smiled and gazed at me with his head cocked. "Okay, don't say I didn't warn you. When do we start?"

"Let's go there in two days and we'll make a plan. What's the union rate for a mason?"

"Say twenty-five dollars per hour, but you don't gotta pay me."

"Hey, this is a bona fide job, and I have no clue what I'm doing, so I'm paying."

We shook on it and I headed back toward St. Charles Avenue. There was no traffic, so I walked the pitted street. Being out in the open made me more comfortable. New Orleans could be a violent city, but I figured most problems happened away from Uptown. After making Carondelet Street, a husky man, twenty years old, hair trimmed close, emerged between two late-model parked cars. I discerned the numbers of a tattered Saints jersey. The light from a mid-February half-moon reflected off a short knife.

"Wallet and watch."

"Okay, no problem. I'm reaching into my jacket for my wallet."

I reached to my shoulder harness for my snub nose .38 revolver only to scare the crap out of him. For many years I had my concealed carry permit. Coming and going at odd hours, carrying seemed smart. I had no interest in killing anyone. I wanted to keep from getting killed myself.

"Knife," I said. He tossed the four-inch switch blade at my feet and it clattered to the choppy curb. "Where's your lookout?"

"No lookout," he said, lowering his eyes.

"What the hell. You suck at this." I still had the gun aimed at his chest.

"What's your name?"

"Buzz."

"That's a nickname. What does your mom call you?"

"James. James William when she's pissed."

I lowered the gun to my side. "You know you might get yourself killed doing this shit, James William." I emphasized the William. "What's the deal?"

"I got no money."

"No shit, James. Why aren't you working?" What a random conversation in the street at ten p.m. with a gun in my hand. I'm accustomed to bizarre conversations at night. *So, sir, a cucumber won't traverse your GI tract intact. I know you didn't swallow it. Tell me again how you got this cucumber in your rectum.*

"Got no skills."

I holstered my weapon. "Get a job as a plumber's assistant. If you enjoy the work and you save your money, you can go to trade school. Those guys live well."

"What if I don't want to be a plumber?"

There was no place to sit for a conversation. I leaned against a rusting sedan. I got the vibe that James never had this discussion with anyone before and didn't blame him for that. Private school and vacations to Disney were not likely part of his childhood.

"Well, what do you want to do?" I said.

"I like to build shit."

"Wood?"

"Yeah."

"Houses or furniture?"

"Houses." Now he leaned up against the front end of the car.

"You want to be a frame carpenter."

"How do I do that?"

Really. This guy wanted my wallet a few minutes before and now I was walking him through getting a job. I could have been doing worse things with my time. I guess I didn't see the sign on my forehead that said *Sucker*, invisible to everyone but me.

"You got a smartphone?"

"Yeah."

"Of course." The irony of this zipped right past him. "Search New Orleans carpenter union. Call in the morning and tell them you want to join and you're looking for work. Just don't tell them your last job was being a full-time dumbass."

"You're a funny guy," he said, shifting on his feet.

"Yeah, I'm a barrel of laughs. Listen, I'm not calling NOPD."

"Shit, I forgot. I'm sorry I tried to rob you."

"This is my neighborhood, man. Are you going to do this again?"

"No sir."

"Okay, who's at home?"

"Huh?"

"Who lives with you?"

"My mom and fourteen-year-old sister. Sometimes my cousin stays with us. My mom gets off work at eleven."

"All right. Go home. Get a job. Make your mother proud of you." James started to pick up the knife. "Mine now." I kicked the knife into the sewer.

He turned after taking a few steps. "What's your name?"

"Sam."

"Thanks, Mr. Sam."

I wasn't betting any of that penetrated. It made me think of the times I have counseled patients to stop drinking or stop smoking or wear seat belts or dump an abusive lover. If even one out of a hundred ("hunnert," as Rex says) takes my advice, the talk is worth having. At work I forget these conversations before seeing the next patient. This was different. I worried for this kid. I walked on autopilot and almost passed Camp Street. At the table on the back patio I second-guessed myself. Maybe I didn't do James or the neighborhood any favor by forgiving it. He could stab somebody the next time. Floyd rubbed against my leg and curled up in a ball. I thought of whiskey. First time in a long time. I knew these questions would go away after a few. Instead I stared at the moon remembering my first trip to summer camp alone on a cot, friendless, and homesick. I could smell the musty sleeping bag.

28

WHILE MOST OF the country suffered the worst of winter, spring arrived in mid-February in south Louisiana and I enjoyed a pleasant seventy-degree walk to work. As I approached the ER entrance, I could hear a man yelling, pleading almost. The sound echoed between the hospital and the parking garage across the street. EMS wheeled him in ahead of me. I found the volume of the yelling and the degree of reasonableness of the person to relate inversely. Yelling disrupts the department and raises the stress level, especially for the other patients. It also lowers the empathy level. I grabbed my stethoscope and found Gabe standing outside the room, curtain closed.

"Do you and I need to manhandle this one?" I winked at Gabe. "What's happening?"

"Old guy fell. Keeps ranting about his wife. Nurses want me here in case he gets rowdy."

"Usually it's the wife ranting about the husband," I said

"For sure."

I entered the room to find Charles Scott, an eighty-four-year-old man—broad face, wide nose, wiry body, smooth hands—in a tiff with the nurses. They were at an impasse, and voices grew louder. He didn't want to come, and he desired no testing. He was the only patient I needed to see, so I asked the nurses to give us a minute alone and they left smiling. From a laceration at the crown of his scalp a trail of blood meandered behind his right ear.

I extended my hand and shook his. "Mr. Scott, I'm Sam Buchanan. I hear you took a fall. Can you tell me what happened?" I pulled a stool on wheels over to the bed and rolled next to him.

"I'm sorry I made a fuss. Call me Charlie." He lowered his head. "I was on my way home from dinner." Tears dropped to the crisp sheet pulled to his waist.

I patted the back of his veiny hand. "Take your time, Charlie."

"Sixty years ago today I met my wife, Barb. Every year for fifty-eight years we ate dinner at Antoine's on this night. That first year, they were allowing black folks to eat in nice restaurants. You know the place?"

"No, I'm new here."

"Well, it's a great place. Anyway, I lost my wife this past autumn. No breaking the tradition. I had a steak and two glasses of wine and fell getting out of my cab on Soniat."

"Sure, I understand. Were you knocked out?"

"No. I'm fine. I guess I'm a bit tipsy and I couldn't stand."

"Anything hurt?"

"No. Really, I'm fine."

I examined him head to toe. I could fix the cut with glue. I found no other injuries.

"I understand you have AFib and take a blood thinner."

"Yes."

"So, Charlie, it's not good to hit your head when you take a blood thinner. Will you let me glue your cut and just check a quick scan of your head to be sure your noggin is okay?"

"You know, my wife and I always made love after we returned from dinner. Since that's not happening, I guess I got nothing else to do."

I saw a kid with impetigo while Charlie went to CAT scan. Locals call it Indian fire. I returned with gauze, hydrogen peroxide, and tissue adhesive. We talked as I cleaned his scalp. "How did you meet your wife?"

"Was 1960. Just out of the Navy. Scuttlebutt was there was work here, so I drove my old Crosley station wagon over from Biloxi. There was an office supply company, and they were a distributor for this new contraption called a Xerox. They were selling like hot cakes and they needed more salesmen. My boss was a retired Navy Commander. He gave me the job, but I had no place to stay. One of the other salesmen needed a roommate. Barb was his sister. He married a great gal the same year I married Barb, and we were best friends. Lost them all in the past two years."

After I glued his cut, I sat next to him again.

"You've enjoyed a marvelous life. I'm happy you continued your dinner tradition."

"Thanks for your patience with a sentimental old man."

"No worries. Charlie, for the past few months I've been asking people about happiness. Can I ask you what brought you the most happiness in your life?"

"Oh, no question. My wife. Having someone who loves you and who you can count on. That makes the low times easier and the high times better."

Why didn't I think of my wife that way? In the past I blamed her. My feelings belonged to me, not her. My appreciation, or lack of appreciation, for my blessings belonged to me, not her. At times when I missed Kayla, I questioned why I needed to be in New Orleans. Charlie answered the question for me.

His CAT scan was normal. We called a cab, and I walked with him to the ambulance bay where the driver waited. I gave a twenty to the driver and asked him to be sure Charlie made it in his house.

29

I F I WAS off the night before, I awakened by eleven a.m. A bright, crisp day. I donned a jacket and took my breakfast on the patio. Anticipating the tomb project pushed my negative thoughts aside. The key to success in my new life was staying busy.

Seven blocks toward the lake and three toward the park. The walk to the cemetery was longer than Ray tolerated so I walked to his place and we took an Uber to the tomb. A walking tour departed as we arrived. Ray crossed himself as we walked through the gate, and I led him to our project.

"This is a pediment-type tomb." Ray rubbed his hand across the stucco. "I like these the best. You can see the double-decker structure. Probably two caskets in there now." He spied the cockeyed name plate for the most recent dates. "Here's one from '72 and one from '75."

"Can we restore it?"

"Oh, no question. See this one?" He pointed to a similar tomb on the opposite row. A perfect specimen. Ray pulled a pocketknife from his shirt and picked away at the crumbling stucco. Small chunks fell at his feet.

"Stucco is bad. We should take it to the bricks. That way we can fix the mortar. He pointed to the gaps in the exposed brick. Then, new stucco and paint, and you got a tomb again."

"How much time?" I asked.

Ray smiled. "You got another project going?"

I put my hands out to the side as a gesture showing he had bested me.

"Hard to say. If the brick doesn't need too much repair and a buddy help me, we'll do this in maybe a dozen four-hour days."

I put Ray in an Uber and walked to Breaux Mart. Two blocks toward the river and five blocks toward the park. I considered my upcoming conversation with Renée as I walked. I zig-zagged to see streets I had yet to travel. The Victorian architecture grew on me. I prefer the shotgun houses. They built them long and thin. Many were side-by-side duplexes that owners converted to single homes. They kept both front doors, so you couldn't tell if it was a single or a double unless you peeked through the leggy double-hung windows. Like many things in life, first appearances are deceiving.

I wanted to restore the tomb for Renée and the memory of her family but also for myself. The value of having a hobby or a project going was a bonus and, when I die they'll cremate me and drop the bag in the caveau. They don't need to add my name to the plate. The trick was to avoid troubling Renée about not maintaining the tomb. Rex stood at his usual place as I entered the store. A clean and crisp white apron flowed over his ample belly.

"Slow day today?"

"The opposite. I'm busting my ass getting ready for Mardi Gras."

"You are wearing a clean apron."

"Yeah. That. Renée made me put on a clean one. It was nasty."

"I forgot about Mardi Gras," I said.

"Week from Tuesday. You working that night?"

I checked the calendar on my phone. "Shit. Yes. I didn't think."

"Good luck with that," Rex said with a half-smile.

"Yeah, thanks." I had no clue what was coming. "Renée in the back?"

"Usual spot."

"Okay. Hey, that thirty-count shrimp still on special?"

"How much you want?"

"A pound."

Shrimp over linguini and pesto sauce sounded appetizing for dinner. My wife would have a cardiac arrest if she saw me cook something more than toast or a frozen dinner. I waved to Billy. She was busy doing checkout. The cart brimmed with wine and liquor bottles. I heard Rex whistling "Take Me to the Mardi Gras" by Paul Simon. I know that tune. *Take your burdens to the Mardi Gras, let the music wash your soul...* in my head now.

A wisp of hair draped across her forehead and her

tight-fitting Breaux Mart T-shirt was soiled with dust. She gave me a hug and a peck on the cheek.

"I've been so busy I haven't done a thing with the family tree. Once Lent begins, I'll have more time."

"No worries, Renée. I'm here to ask a favor of you. Really more permission."

She invited me to sit by her desk and she leaned against the edge. She put her hand on my shoulder.

"What can I do?"

I explained my recent trip to the Buchanan tomb and Ray's assessment of the situation.

"This is as much for me as for y'all. It will keep me off the streets. And I'll pay for the whole thing."

"Of course. I am thrilled you want to do it. I'll get the permit from the diocese and then you can start. You know I'm not sure anybody will use that tomb again. Rex and I will go in his family tomb."

"Fine with me. Some things need doing for their own sake."

"Sure. Oh, and since you're a Buchanan, you can go there."

"Great. Hopefully not for a long time from now. Listen, while we are talking, I wanted to ask you what's going on with Billy applying to school."

"Tulane or Loyola would be so convenient but there's no money for tuition. She's got a full ride to the University of New Orleans. She's just fretting about the bus ride back and forth."

"It'll work out, I guess."

30

FAT TUESDAY. I took an afternoon nap, ate a light dinner, and headed for my shift at Touro. A feast before a shift is ill-advised. Food coma and a fast-paced patient-care environment are a poor combination. Gabe sat in his usual spot. We settled into a routine. I brought him a cup of coffee and set it next to him.

"A horse goes into a bar."

"Yeah?" he says.

"And the bartender says, 'Why the long face?'"

He looked up for a moment and smiled. "Good one."

No lobby dwellers when I arrived, but that didn't last. Why didn't those nurses warn me? I guess they figured it was obvious to everybody except a recovering drunk ass from Carolina.

By midnight, any sense of control vanished. A seemingly endless supply of ambulances brought intoxicated patients of many stripes. A middle-aged man dressed in a tuxedo cut his hand slicing a lemon for cocktails. Why this required an ambulance escaped me.

His pompous attitude won him no friends. The usual parade of problems from area nursing homes marched on regardless of the activities of the rest of the city. A psychotic man wandered the hall, sitter in tow, with his butt showing through the break in his gown. He mumbled something about the FBI following him.

The cut could wait a few hours and the nurses started testing on the others while I tended to a young ruffian on the losing side of a street fight. Another Mardi Gras reveler whacked him in the forehead with an empty liquor bottle and then flipped the light switch. I suspected extreme intoxication and a concussion. Brain injury concerned me the most. The immediate challenges came from two fronts. First, he required an immediate CAT scan of the brain. He needed to jump a long line for that. Second, I needed to protect his airway. Drunks vomit and comatose drunks aspirate. Getting vomit into your lungs is troublesome, and this could be more lethal than his head injury.

We positioned the muscular young man on the cart and the nurses placed him on a monitor while the respiratory therapist gathered items needed for intubation. A blood stain marred the Tulane logo on his T-shirt. His Rolex, stylish haircut, and straight teeth betrayed his opulence. This kid, Noah, came from money. I didn't care. My job did not change, and everyone received the same package. The newspapers and TV viewed it differently. If this were James William, who pulled a knife on me, his death would be second section, third page. Noah gets the front page. I carried on. There would be no dying.

I handled several interruptions while donning gloves and a mask and told the nurse to remind tuxedo man with the cut hand that his time would come at a break from the true emergencies. I wanted to walk into his room and tell the smug SOB and his trophy wife he was the least ill patient in the entire city and that he could zip it or get the hell out. Like a former smoker, repulsed by the smell of an ashtray, my contempt for the asses of the world was becoming more difficult to conceal. Bigger fish took precedence.

The video laryngoscope is the best invention since the pregnancy test. You slip the instrument into the mouth, barely lift the tongue, and the vocal cords appear on a screen. I slid the curved tube through the voice box and into the trachea. This protected the lungs even if he vomited. Off to CT for Noah.

The depth of stupidity, amazingly, was not reached. A Loyola student decided mooning the revelers on St. Charles from a car would be supremely funny. The plan disintegrated when he fell out the back window and rolled to the trolley tracks. The recipients of his anal exposure took no offense and pulled him off the tracks. His driver failed to notice the loss of his pre-posterous passenger until he passed two trolley stops. When the driver returned on the opposite side of the tracks, he gathered his mate, brushed him off, zipped his pants, and drove him to our doorstep before EMS or the police arrived. The driver poured his friend into a wheelchair, pounded on the ambulance doors, and then escaped to the shadows.

Californians moon the Amtrak train yearly on a certain day. The nurses confirmed that there was no such tradition of mooning the St. Charles trolley. A tradition may have begun that night.

We placed Carson, a name that suggested elevated social status, on a gurney and immobilized his neck. He received the requisite dose of radiation to his head, neck, chest, abdomen, and right hand. A broken pinky finger. That was it. I would not have been mooning, of course, but a similar mechanism might have caused me six broken ribs, two long bone fractures, and a ruptured liver. His blood alcohol read only 0.1, so we splinted his finger. He pleaded like a condemned man for me to not call his parents. I agreed knowing the insurance statements arrive a few weeks later when he could explain the ten-thousand-dollar bill for a broken finger.

By four a.m., the relentless flow of patients ceased and by five a.m., Noah went to the ICU with a first-class bruise on his brain, and tuxedo man departed with a chip on his shoulder and five sutures in his palm, and the department was as quiet as Lafayette Number 1. Nurses carry a strong superstition regarding the Q word, believing that once a patient or cop says the word *quiet*, a bus will unload soon after. I don't buy it. There is an ebb and flow and quiet periods precede busier times organically. I collapsed into my chair thinking of the Buchanan tomb restoration and could no more fend off sleep than an anvil defies gravity.

I awakened with a start from a recurrent dream where I am someplace important and don't have shoes. Kathy rested her hand on my forearm. She must have dropped into her chair after I dozed.

"You okay?"

"Yeah, stupid dream." I leaned forward and rubbed my face.

"Mine is where I'm in a crowd but I'm lost and don't know anybody."

"Well, don't ask a psychiatrist to interpret mine. Her head would explode." We locked eyes, comfortable in our platonic bliss.

"Listen, I spilled my guts to you. Time for your story."

"Do you want the full theatrical version or *Reader's Digest*?"

I looked at my wrist. "You got someplace to be for the next half-hour?"

Not fully awake, I realized that I held before me another large wormy can I opened on purpose this time.

"Okay. I grew up in rural Mississippi."

"Did ya'll have 'lectricity?"

"Sure. Telephone too." She stuck her tongue out at me.

"Sorry. Proceed."

"I lost both parents in college, so when I finished nursing school, there was no reason to return home."

I turned toward her and touched her on the arm. "Had you been here before?"

"Once with high school band. I always wanted to return, so I interviewed at Touro."

"I had you pegged for cheerleader."

"No. I was the bad girl."

"Okay. Say no more. I imagine the men line up for you here."

She cupped her breasts. "Ya think?"

"Dr. Obvious, at your service."

"Yeah. The trouble started when an anesthesiologist got me pregnant. Then he left town."

"Damn doctors. You never mentioned a child."

"June became my life. It was difficult being alone, but I loved her so much. At nine months she died of pneumonia and sepsis."

"I'm so sorry. I coaxed you into reliving that."

"No worries. Been in my head lately."

People often have trouble around events such as birthdays or holidays when they lose a loved one. I assumed that triggered it. Now the tears were flowing.

"I'm pregnant again."

I'm terrible in these situations. What do you say to that? I also congratulated myself again for not having sex with her. "You know, we figured out what causes that."

She whacked me hard against the chest with the back of her hand. She's a strong filly. "I expected that from you."

"Sorry. Low fruit." I patted her on the leg. "Are you involved with someone now?"

"No. I'm such a chump. Same damn mistake. An

on-and-off thing with a guy for a few years. Weak moment."

"No. You had a human moment, darling."

"Whatever. Misfortune knocked down my door again, and I don't know what to do."

This is like asking the guy in a cast to run a 5K. "Indulge me for a second because I can be a bollix when it comes to these things. Are you looking for fatherly advice here or am I to offer a sympathetic ear?"

"You convinced someone to marry ya', did ya'?" she said in a bad Irish accent.

"She had a weak moment."

"I see. Well, do what you think is best."

"Okay. I grew up in the sticks. Unlike you, however, we had indoor plumbing. Sorry. Sorry. I am being serious now. My father told me you should never swerve to miss an animal in the road, or you'll end up in a ditch."

"Is there more?"

"Yes. Stick with me here. You are driving on a dark and wet road with a deep ditch on either side. A dog stands fifty feet ahead. The safe thing for you is to hit the dog. The question is, can you forget the dog or is it better to risk it in the ditch?"

Wales walked in to start his day.

Wales and I discussed a new inane hospital policy, and, by the way, the staff is gossiping that Kathy and I are schtupping. He used more delicate language. I assured him my intentions were honorable and pla-tonic. He seemed satisfied, and we left it at that. Kathy slipped out.

31

THE DIOCESE GRANTED permission to begin work on the Buchanan tomb. March weather was excellent for construction. Ray recovered well and surprised me with his strength. We used our waiting time to accumulate supplies, which we stored under a blue tarp on my back patio and reviewed the steps of the procedure. Seems everybody owned, or knew somebody that owned, a blue tarp after Katrina. An aerial view of the city a few months after the storm looked like Smurf town. Now Katrina was a crappy memory.

Construction is not unlike a medical procedure. It helps to have done it before, review your plan, gather your supplies, make contingency plans, and execute the operation. We began by chipping away at the loose stucco and there was an ample supply. A dozen orange buckets filled by the end. This exposed the soft red brick, a quarter of which deteriorated from time and water exposure. This brick was made from local clay that endured poorly. The labor-intensive part of the project involved removing and then replacing the brick using new mortar. This day we knocked out the decayed brick.

"Raymond, tell me about your family."

"My parents came without papers in the seventies. I was the only one born in Mexico. My two sisters were born in Texas. Later we went to California. We worked the fields."

"What a hard life."

"Tell me 'bout it. Long days. Got tougher when my dad died. I think he had pneumonia. The time they got him to a hospital, too late."

"That made you hombre de la familia, right?"

"Sí. Was twenty then and I didn't want to do agriculture work no more. A cousin settled in New Orleans and he sent word. He taught me to be a mason. We found work, and we got the house where my sister lives."

I poured waters, and we took a break. This was sweat-through-your-shirt work.

"Are you a citizen?"

"Oh, sure. Late eighties. I always liked Ronald Reagan for doing that."

"Have you been happy here?"

"Guess so. It beat twelve-hour days picking produce."

"Did you marry?"

"Yeah. Lasted three years. She left when the drinking got bad. You married, right?"

"Getting a divorce. Same story as you. Just took her longer to tire of it."

Ray emptied another cup, refilled it and dumped it

on his head. "Look at you now. She should take you back."

"I doubt that would happen. Anyway, I fell in love in Hawai'i." I showed him a picture of Kayla on my phone.

"Aye yai mama. What the hell you doin' here wit' me?"

"Good question, buddy."

———

When I returned home, Floyd lay curled in a tight ball at the back door. He let out a feeble cry when I approached. He appeared to be down a pound or two and his coat was dull. In a human two pounds is no big deal. In a fifteen-pound animal it could mean trouble. I scratched him behind the neck and felt something moist. Inspection revealed a nasty infected cut on the back of his neck. Apparently, he met his match in a tussle. His woeful meow made me take pity. Instead of my usual launch with the foot I let him inside and he lumbered to the bed. I told myself it would be temporary. I gooped it up with triple antibiotic ointment and planned to check on him later.

32

I ASKED BILLY OVER for a late lunch the next day. Floyd lay curled at the end of the bed and did not stir when I left. My topical treatment was failing, so we were off to the vet mid-afternoon.

After a quick shower, I whipped up salads with cold shrimp and made a fruit medley. Forget my wife, I impressed myself. I put out two plastic flutes and put a bottle of sparkling grape juice on ice. Since there was no graduation ceremony, I wanted to recognize her achievement of finishing her diploma. I placed a funny card with a picture of a duck and a pig at her seat.

I never use the damn thing, yet it rang the stupid ring tone Billy chose. Nobody ever called me. Billy, Maria, Kathy, the hospital, the NSA, and my soon-to-be ex-wife are the only ones with the number. My wife. Our conversations, while civil, were best described as detached. Like with the neighbor you don't know well and need to think hard to remember their name. We had not spoken since I left Columbia.

"Preston is missing," she said in her lawyer tone.

"By Preston, I'm assuming you mean *the* Preston Matheson." Her lover.

"Yes. We broke it off a week ago. Gone for five days now."

"And?" Pregnant silence.

"And what do you know of it?"

"You are providing the breaking news, dear."

"Well, the police want to speak with you."

"Okay. Give them my number."

"In person."

"Hardly necessary." I gave her the address.

She must have sensed that lunch would be more than just lunch because she sported a dress blouse and makeup. Billy let herself in and talked before she even looked at me. "I am so happy for a day off. Rex has been killing me with hours at the store. Hey, whose car out there?"

"Whose voice is that?" Mom voice, even though she's not a mom.

"Just a friend. We...listen I have things to do and I no longer need to explain myself to you."

"Sounds young."

"Listen, we should talk but I don't have time now. I'm trying to be a good person. No booze for six months now. I don't want bitterness between us. Can I call you another time?" Only three seconds passed, but it seemed longer.

"Yes. Of course."

"I am so sorry. I didn't even see you on the phone," Billy said.

"It's nothing. You look pretty. Welcome and congrats." I tossed the keys to a dented and well-used gray Honda Civic.

"What?"

"Go check your new way to UNO." She lept over the couch like a tiger and smothered me with a three-minute hug. Then she dragged me through the front door.

"Get in," I said. "Let's go for a spin."

She put her hands on her hips the way she does. "I don't have my license."

"Sure. We can swing by your place."

"No. Sam. I don't have any license."

I didn't miss a beat. "Sure. I'll give you lessons, you study the book, and you can take the test before summer semester starts." I wasn't sure my driver's license was still valid. Why did I commit to that? That's why they invented driving school.

"Deal."

And then she danced around the car like a psychotic ballerina. Once the dancing subsided, we went over a few rules.

"Concentrate now." She nodded like an obedient spaniel. "This is my car, but I will seldom drive. When I want it, I will coordinate with you. You can use it to go back and forth to school or an errand for Rex and Renée. Otherwise park right here."

"Got it." Then another long hug.

We sat at the table and toasted new adventures. She opened the card.

Dear Billy,
You are strong and smart.
Aim high and always stand one more time than you fall.
Love, Sam

I included a check for a thousand dollars. Gas money. Then the tears.

———

One block toward the river, one toward the park. The vet on Magazine Street. I stroked his fat orange head as we walked but couldn't coax a purr out of him. I realized that I should have taken responsibility for him much sooner. They took care of cats only at the Uptown Feline Veterinary Hospital. Being a short-order cook in medicine, it would bore me to restrict my practice to one entrée.

A masculine-looking female or a feminine-looking male, I wasn't sure but bet on female, took my information. This person's gender identity concerned me little. For me, people-watching is great sport, and New Orleans is the Coliseum.

I doubted there was another Floyd in their practice, so I did not use his full name. This is the only vet in Uptown and no record of a visit for an orange tabby named Floyd or an owner named Vivian Broussard existed, so I assumed Miss Vivian took no interest in Floyd's healthcare. They weighed him on a precise looking stainless-steel scale and showed us to an exam room, which had a seventies vibe with faux wood paneling and faded linoleum floor. A tattered *Cats of the World* poster listed on one wall and cabinets with cockeyed doors hung on the other. So far, the décor did not engender feelings of confidence. I withheld judgement until meeting the vet. Strange to be on the opposite side of a medical interaction even for a cat. It was helpful for me to experience the patient's perspective.

Another person of ambiguous gender asked me a series of questions for which I held few answers. Age, previous vaccinations, neutered, et cetera. Her concerned expression grew as I failed the verbal test. A few minutes later I heard but did not discern the contents of a hushed conversation outside the door.

I petted Floyd on the stainless-steel exam table as Dr. Heidi Moreau breezed into the room. And what a sight. Electric blue hair hung to her mid neck. She tucked one side behind an ear. A short turned-up nose rested between penetrating cerulean eyes. She had a generous, but not freakishly large, mouth.

She introduced herself as Heidi and I as Sam and we shook hands. This is the time where I prefer my patients to tell me of any medical background. I don't enjoy finding out later that the person I was talking to, as if they were a grocery store cashier, is a nurse or an ultrasound tech or worse a physician. Still, I did not share my occupation, nor did she ask.

"So, how long has he been sick?"

"I think a week, but I can't be certain. I don't see him every day."

"So, he's an outdoor cat." Not an accusatory tone but communicating a bit of disapproval.

"Look, I should explain more. I guess I'm adopting him today. I moved here recently and my neighbor, Max, tells me that Floyd sort of comes with the house I am renting."

"Maximillian Dupuis?" Heidi and her tech stole a furtive glance. "Do you live in Miss Vivian's house that Maria restored?"

"I do."

They looked at each other and laughed.

"What?"

Heidi brushed a lock of hair off her forehead and said, "Oh, we've got stories for you. You should come out for drinks."

Then back to the business of Floyd. She examined him and determined that he was ill. His high temperature and neck swelling suggested an extensive abscess. She planned to hydrate with an IV, start antibiotics, and drain the abscess under anesthesia tomorrow. She warned me he might not survive. Clueless of how many lives he had used up, I accepted her warning, gave my credit card information, and left to take a nap before work.

33

GABE'S TURN. I set his coffee on the counter.
"I heard you rode the short bus to school, after
that llama kicked you in the head."

"Just a season, though," I said.

"And then you kept to the sheep after that."

"Aye, you're improving." Best accent.

I went right to work. Room four. James William.
This will be interesting. He rested on the cart, legs
with work boots dangling. His mother, who worked
in our cafeteria, sat in a chair with a furrowed brow.

"James! Great to see you, man." I winked at him.

"Hey, Mr. Sam," James said.

"You know each other?" his mother said, glancing
at James sideways.

"Yes, ma'am. James gave me directions on St. Charles
one evening. We talked for a while. A fine young man
you have here."

James studied his shoes while his mom swallowed
it whole. I started my exam before she questioned my
story. Sore throat, fever, swollen lymph nodes and no

cough. I examined him and pronounced strep throat. No test needed. I wrote a prescription for cephalexin.

"What kind of work do you do?"

He looked me square, and a toothy smile emerged. "Framer's assistant. We buildin' those apartments off Jefferson."

"Quite a project over there. Be safe now. I'm putting you off work two days."

When I emerged from the room, EMS wheeled an ancient woman into the resuscitation bay. Florence was ninety-eight and lived semi-independently until a hip fracture two months prior. Often a fatal event for someone her age. A faded yellow nightgown hung on her bony frame and her pale parchment skin fit two sizes large. Her gaping mouth revealed tall teeth surrounding a tongue coated in sticky mucus. Breathing seemed to be an afterthought.

"Code status?" I asked the medic.

"Full."

What the hell. Attempts to save Florence would be futile or only prolong her suffering and allow her to die the following week. With impeccable timing her daughter entered. Family involvement was crucial, and we needed to talk before walking an unhappy trail of inappropriate intervention. After introductions we sat in chairs near Florence. Her daughter, Patty, a spry gray-haired woman in her early seventies, held her mother's hand.

"I want to have an important conversation with you

before we proceed. I understand that her paperwork says she desires full resuscitation."

"Yes, that's what I told them when she arrived at the nursing home."

"Do you still want that?"

"I guess I should ask if you can help her."

I smoothed Florence's thin white hair over her head. "Can you tell me if she is making progress in therapy?"

"She did well the first month but since has been in bed."

"I understand she was an active and independent lady before her fall."

"Oh, yes. She was full of life. She enjoyed her garden and playing cards and listening to Atlanta Braves baseball."

"Would she want to be stuck in bed?"

"Lord, no."

"So, to answer your question I believe that any help would be temporary, and that death comes soon regardless of our intentions. There comes a time, and I think we are there, when the most loving thing you can do for someone is to allow a natural death."

Patty paused and patted her mother's hand. Tears welled.

I gave her a minute. Patty bent over so her forehead touched her mother's shoulder.

"Oh, Lord. I will miss her so. We have always been close. As we've aged, we're more like sisters. Dad's gone. My husband, too. I never felt lonely with her.

Well, she lived a full and happy life. I guess it's time to say good night."

"Do you have siblings?"

"A brother. Died in Viet Nam."

"Did your mom work?"

"Oh, yes." She smiled through her tears. "Secretary. Now they'd call her an administrative assistant. To the president of a bank. She knew how to run that place whether he was in the office or not. That man cried the day she retired."

"Well, that speaks volumes right there. I'm sure having you was a great comfort for your mom. Sounds like you are both blessed." I rested my hand on the back of hers. "Okay. If you please, you may stay with her. Timing is unpredictable. I'll check in on you later."

She stood with me and took my hand. "Thank you for guiding me through this."

I settled Florence and Patty on a mental shelf. I find it easy to do this. Lots of practice. Maybe the ability to squirrel away the suffering of others reveals a defect in my personality. Emergency physicians must do this for their own sanity and for the next patient. Grief must never follow me into the next room. I might remember Patty and her mother, but I can't mourn it. I can hope that, like an absent-minded squirrel, I'll forget where I buried the nut. Back at the desk, Kathy slipped a chart over to me.

"Ivy Greene. She comes every couple of months for something. Says she's been to two other ERs and both times they say gout. She's boo-hooing in there. I think she's drug seeking."

Nurses, especially emergency nurses, are perceptive and can tell who passed the gas. I tucked that away for reference and stepped into room eleven. I always reserve judgement. Ivy Greene. I love names like that.

After introductions I proceeded to questioning. The thin and frail fifty-year-old sat on the cart with a pleading grimace. She stroked her leg while we talked. Her gravelly voice, clubbed finger nails, and occasional raspy cough betrayed her many years of smoking.

"Where did it hurt at first?"

"Just the foot."

"And now?"

"Knee down."

"Gout in the past?"

"Never."

"What's your diet?"

"I'm vegetarian."

Another case of irony impairment. Beef will kill her but not the cigarettes. That should be an official diagnosis. "Can you walk on it?"

"About twenty feet."

"Then what happens?"

"Knives in my calf. I can't take it no more. I know this ain't no gout."

She was pissed about her other ER visits. Her twiggy leg felt cold in my hand. I found a pulse at her groin but nothing below. "How long has this sore been on your foot?"

"Months. Just won't heal."

This lady was no Rhodes Scholar, but she understood her leg more than the last two doctors. Middle-aged fat guys who eat steak and drink beer suffer from gout. The simple term for her ailment is dead leg. Little blood flowed below her thigh and any activity over-taxed the blood vessels and caused the calf pain. Her smoking and untreated high blood pressure clogged the artery.

"Okay. You are correct." That disarms people when you tell them their suspicion is right, without pointing fingers. "I'll order you something for pain and do a sound wave test on this leg." I put my hand on her shoulder. "We'll take excellent care of you, Ivy."

She rested her head back and relaxed her face.

I lifted the next chart and caught Kathy by the elbow as I passed.

"Terrible timing last shift. We'll talk later, okay?"

She nodded, and I moved on to the toddler with arm trouble in room three. I made my introductions and learned Brooks was in the other room playing with his older brother. Mom, an attractive redhead, ran after hearing the screaming. The brother took the fifth. The typical well-fed and clean, future linebacker, two-year-old sat on his mother's lap. He sported a few bruises on his forehead and shins. Usual toddler stuff. A well-used multi-colored hat with a short brim sat askew on his head. Brother pouted in the chair.

"Hold his left arm, please." I found a grape sucker in my pocket and offered it to his affected arm. He squirmed in frustration as he tried to reach with his other arm. I palpated the entire arm and found no tenderness.

"Should we X-ray?" asked the mom with the dull eyes of someone who needed several nights of uninterrupted sleep.

"This is a radial head subluxation. A nursemaid's elbow. Won't show on X-ray. His brother tugged too hard playing. Doesn't take much of a pull. If I turn his arm correctly, the bone will slip back into proper position. He'll pitch a fit for a minute."

"Okay. Hold him like this?"

"Right." I nodded reassurance. I supported his elbow with my hand and placed my thumb in the bend. With my other hand I twisted his wrist, so the palm faced the floor. I felt the satisfying click. Half-deaf people in Jefferson Parish heard the scream. I patted him on the head.

"I'll be back in ten. Call sooner if he uses it."

The clerk made an upward nod as I left the room.

"Dr. Sam, a Detective Vanderslice, line three."

That was fast. I took it in the doctors' room. I wondered if I should talk to an attorney. I wanted to spend more time with lawyers like I wanted to sleep naked at a mosquito farm.

"This is Dr. Buchanan." I kept it formal to remind him he interrupted me at work.

"Yes. Sorry to trouble you, doctor. Detective JR Vanderslice, CPD."

"Yeah, my wife told me to expect your call. How can I help you?"

"So, you know why I'm calling." More of a statement than a question.

"Right."

"Great. I want to arrange a meeting this week if possible."

"I'm off the next two days. The second is better. I won't be hung over from tonight." That was poor wording.

"Wednesday it is."

"Text me your arrival time. You'll find the morning flight through Atlanta on Delta is the cheapest. I'll just meet you in the Delta terminal and save you the trip into Uptown."

"That's generous of you. See you then."

I wasn't being generous. I didn't want this guy anywhere near my place. Preston Matheson fit his pecker into my soon-to-be ex-wife and himself into my robe, and other than that, I knew little of him or his whereabouts. I expected a quick meeting.

They say President Clinton was adept at compartmentalizing. Something horrendous might happen in his personal life, such as a problem with a blue dress, and he tucked it off to the side and proceeded with another thorny problem. Emergency physicians excel at this too. On most days, I can run an unsuccessful cardiac resuscitation and move on to a stubbed toe without sitting. I walked into room three.

"Moving?"

"Yes, thank you. He's back to full speed."

The mother looked less harried. I showed Brooks the candy and put my hands above my head to make a touchdown signal. He mimicked, and we clapped as if for a performing seal. I offered him and his brother, who jumped and smiled, a sucker and all was right with the world in room three.

The ultrasound techs are never happy to come in at night. Most things can wait for the next day except for twisted testicles and ovaries, ectopic pregnancies, and dead extremities.

"You nailed this one, doc," said the tech. "Barely any flow below the knee."

I started blood thinner and spoke to the sleepy vascular surgeon. Making such a diagnosis brings confidence and satisfaction. The fact that two other docs missed it was a bonus.

I went to Florence's bedside. Patty dozed in the chair, but her hand lay on top of her mother's. No pulse and no respirations. I pulled a chair next to Patty, and she stirred. "She's gone now. I'm glad that you could be with her."

"But I fell asleep."

"That's what she was waiting for."

The night proceeded uneventfully, and I found my chair at five thirty.

I walked through the Louis Armstrong Airport, mutt dog on one side and Heidi Moreau, with normal hair, on the other.

No shoes. No conversation. Just walking.
A man in a tuxedo running a floor buffer
watched us pass. A flight to Atlanta was
boarding. My wife scanned tickets.

I awakened with a start when Kathy dropped in
next to me.

"Dreaming again?"

"Yeah. That was freaky." It took a minute for the
cobwebs to clear. I coughed and rubbed my face.

"You okay?" she asked. "You are quiet tonight."

"I'm fine. Enduring the night." I had no plans to
hash over this situation my wife and her lover created.
"I hope I didn't upset you last time."

"No. I've been thinking about the dog in the road."

"That analogy should not be taken literally." I touched
her on the arm. "More about living with your decisions.
Keeping a baby is not the same as driving into a ditch."

"I got that. Your...what's the word...unsophisti-
cated story helped me to make my decision."

"Unsophisticated. Yeah, that's me. Glad I helped.
And you don't need to say one more thing." I held her
hand. "You're a beautiful and strong person."

I rested my head back, and she gripped my hand.

The charge nurse stuck her head in the door. Blank
expression. "You two are not helping to dispel the
rumors. The drunk in room six broke a finger. I ordered
the X-ray."

Terse bitch.

"I'm pregnant," Kathy blurted. "And I'm keeping it."

"So, the rumors are true." Charge stood in the doorway, one hand on a hip.

"No. Not true. I'll straighten this out right now." Kathy breezed past her.

"I'm having trouble figuring you out." Still standing in the doorway.

"My soon-to-be ex-wife says the same."

34

I AWAKENED EARLY AFTERNOON thinking of Floyd. After a smoothie made of milk and peaches, I made the quick trek to the vet office. One block toward the river, one block toward the park. Magazine Street is an eclectic collection of homes, grocery stores, restaurants, and shops. At Magazine and Delachaise, meandering branches of Live Oak trees assemble above the narrow thoroughfare, making a botanical canopy, delivering welcome cover. The smell of baked bread wafted from Mahony's as I passed. I recognized the vet receptionist and received a bright smile.

"Heidi, Floyd's dad is here."

There are worse things someone could legitimately call me, so, Floyd's dad was okay with me. In a physician's office the folksy familiarity would be off-putting. In the Uptown Vet office, it worked.

Heidi stuck her blue head out from the back. "Sam. Come back to visit your orange friend." They looked like the Denver Broncos together.

I stepped around the counter to find a pristine room

covered in bright white tile. A bank of stainless-steel cages lined the wall and a stainless exam table and sink occupied the center. An equally clean operating suite sat adjacent.

"I wish the rooms in the ER were this clean."

"Can't help you there," Heidi said. "Your boy was very dehydrated. I tanked him up and drained ten CCs of pus this morning. Looks much better now."

Floyd looked less lethargic and perked up when I scratched his fat head. An off-yellow Penrose drain protruded from the back of his neck where she shaved him. Antibiotic dripped into an IV line secured to his front leg with elastic wrap. I took his purring as a positive.

"How long do you need to keep him?"

"Let's reassess tomorrow afternoon."

"Great. I'll stop by near closing time."

"Hey," she says. "We'll be at Mahony's for dinner and drinks tonight. Join us."

"Maybe. Thanks."

———

I hoofed to the cemetery to find Ray making excellent progress. I helped when possible, but Ray and a buddy were doing most of the work. He had repaired the brick and was completing the stucco. I smiled knowing we preserved a minute piece of New Orleans heritage. In a city where sun, water, heat, humidity and wind conspired daily to decay history, every restoration had value. We talked while working, but I sensed he had more to tell me. As the job neared completion, I pushed him.

"Raymond, esta es una obra maestra. Better than I expected."

"Sí. Surprised myself."

"I'm pleased you are sticking with the meetings."

"Almost dying saved my life."

"You know, I think about why I drank. Neither of my parents were alcoholic, so I can't blame them. It was my way of pushing the emotions of everyday life off to the side, so I didn't look them in the face. I justified the drink because of a crappy day at work. That pushed me away from being engaged with my wife and my work. I missed precious time with her. I was there, but I wasn't."

Ray dropped his tools and rested next to me on a faded overturned bucket. "Funny, you say, 'Look in the face.' I drank so I didn't see his face no more."

"Whose face?"

"I killed this chico when I was twenty-five. You the only person I tell."

"You wanna talk about it?"

"I never even tell the priest, but sure, why not?" He looked at his shoes. He fingered the St. Christopher medal on his necklace, and I offered the minute. "Was walkin' one night in Gentilly. Near Elysian Fields. Guy comes out of the shadows and flash a blade. Skinny kid, maybe eighteen. Wanted my money." He brushed his hands together and then on his pants.

"I'm not much now but I was a scrapper. Didn't mess with me." He raised his fists like a boxer. "Went at him. Big scuffle. Got his knife away but he loco. Kept comin' back at me after I beat him down. I stab him right here." He pointed below his sternum. "I musta got his heart 'cuz blood…" He looked at his weathered hands and rubbed them together again. "Shit, it sprayed everywhere."

"Then what?"

"Wiped the blade and ran to a pay phone. Called the cops and disappear. Houston for a year. Knew he was dead. I just said *screw it*. It was his face. Looked so damn scared."

"He had it coming, right?"

"Sure. That don't change I wish I never did it." He tightened his fists now. "Wish I gave him the forty in my pocket. Wish I tossed the knife and beat him with my fists."

"You've been carrying that a long time."

"You ever do roofing?" Raymond said.

"No. That's tough work."

"Shit work. I worked flat roofs that year in Houston. You gotta carry buckets of hot tar. Can't let 'em hit your leg. Burn the crap out of you. It's like that."

"Sí, comprendo. Raymond, God would forgive this."

"Okay. But that don't make it no easier to forgive myself."

35

I USED THE WORD on my wife frequently. She figured out I was full of shit. Maybe. Maybe I'll be
home in time for dinner. Maybe we can attend an
event with friends. At meetings folks talk about vague
commitments they never kept. Us drunks excel at it. I
cleaned up and walked to Magazine Street.

Mahony's is a basic restaurant bar but upscale compared to the Prytania Bar. Clean lines, uncluttered,
and the combined aromas of the seafood, spices, and
fresh bread stirred my appetite. The vet tech and the
receptionist finished their drinks as I arrived, and they
departed for a party in Faubourg Marigny. Left at the
table were Heidi and a striking woman in her late thirties, pinky fingers intertwined. Deb's brunette head
reached to my shoulder when she stood to greet me.
She sported a styled neck-length bob with an asym-
metric part and wore a gray skirt, cream satin blouse,
and pearls. Deb looked like she should be partnered
with an FBI agent, not an electric blue-haired veteri-
narian. In my work, I get an inside view, sometimes

literally, at people. I learned a long time ago people are not always what they appear to be. Sometimes a positive, sometimes a negative. Deb did not fit into the lesbian caricature, nor did I fit into the mold of an alcoholic. The difference between us was she had no reason to be ashamed. Heidi introduced me as the new neighbor who lives next to Max. They live at Camp and Antonine. Nearby.

"Heidi, not that you don't look professional, but Deb, you dress like you rule the boardroom."

"I need to play the part on days I go to court. Family law."

"I see. You know, we view opposite sides of the same coin."

"How so?"

The waiter took our order. I chose a shrimp po'boy and lemonade. The ladies shared the seafood basket and a bottle of Riesling.

"I care for the drunks who fall down and cut their head. You do the divorce. I evaluate the kid with the cigarette burns on his feet. You step in for the custody fight."

"Sure. Our jobs require an intimate involvement in people's lives. Not for pussies. Right? But I do fun stuff like adoptions, so my job is not that dramatic."

"Are you seeing anyone, Sam?" Heidi said.

"Subtle, isn't she?" Deb winked.

"Yeah. No. I don't mind. Well, I met someone on a trip to Hawai'i."

I showed them a picture of her in a white bikini. I let them in on my self-improvement project.

"Oh, my. Sam, you are a stud," Heidi said. "What does she do?"

"Runs a foundation for native teens. You both will enjoy talking to her. So, tell me about Max."

"Halloween is a serious event here," Heidi said. "We do a neighborhood block party now, but, starting ten years ago, Max hosted a yearly soirée. He invited the strippers from his club and various wild people."

"We went for a few years," Deb said. "Crazy. We stopped going after we dodged getting arrested one year for public indecency."

"Heidi, were you running naked on Camp Street?" I said.

"Hardly. We kept our costumes buttoned. Most of the crowd shed theirs as the empty wine bottles accumulated. Quite a show."

Deb nodded in agreement. "So, when do we meet Kayla?"

"Yeah, I want to see if she looks that hot in person." Heidi smiled and winked.

Deb elbowed her in the ribs. "She's a flirt. That's why I love her." She placed a wet kiss on Heidi. Sam Jr., previously in hibernation, wanted in on the conversation.

"Yeah, I see that. She would say Heidi and I are both cards. And yes, you will meet her. There is more work to do on the proper human being thing, and then she will come."

"How's that going?" Heidi says.

"Well." I stopped to consider it. "I'm drinking lemonade, and I've made more genuine friends since leaving Carolina than I had accumulated there in twenty-five years."

We toasted to that.

36

I PARKED THE CIVIC in the short-term area and walked to the bright and cavernous Delta terminal. A jazz tune drifted from a piano near the growing line at the TSA checkpoint. The badge on his belt was the giveaway but this guy, Vanderslice, looked like a cop. Barber school haircut, ill-fitting suit, and unfashionable shoes made the ensemble. He looked to be fifty, lanky, with thinning gray hair. He walked with a subtle limp. I wondered if he took a bullet once. We found comfortable seats out of the flow of foot traffic and got to it.

"First, you are not under arrest. I expect you to be honest with me though. Very important if something you say doesn't fit with other accounts. Fair enough?" Southern accent, but not Carolina. Maybe Alabama.

"Preston Matheson."

"I never knew, I mean, I don't know him well." *Crap, I need to be careful with my words here.* "He's a longtime partner, so I met him at social functions many times. After I discovered the affair, I did not see him or speak to him."

"Ever threaten him?"

"I did not."

"Did he ever try to contact you?"

"Not that I am aware."

"What's the status of the relationship with your wife?"

"Pending divorce."

"Amicable?"

"She asked for it...requested it." *Damn.* "And I'm not contesting it. Fifty-fifty split. No fighting."

"Where is he now?"

"As I said. No contact. No idea."

"Did you engage the services of a private detective or anyone else to watch Mr. Matheson?"

"No."

"Do you mind if I examine your phone?"

Several scenarios clicked through my head. Simple. He's just checking to see if I'm dumb enough to call Matheson and not delete it from my call history. Complicated. They have my call history and he is checking to see if I deleted it or what my reaction to the request would be. I'm sure a lawyer would advise *no*. With nothing to hide and a strong desire to finish, I saw no harm in it. I handed him my phone. He cruised through various menus quick as a teenager and returned it. He probably figured it was the most boring call history since the smart phone invention.

"Does your wife have any reason to harm Mr. Matheson?" he said.

That came out of nowhere. Was this the reason he

came to talk? Was he looking for the pissed-off husband to tie his wife to the tracks? "First, I'm not privy to the details of their relationship. They caught me unawares as they say. And I didn't inquire about it later. Second, I can't imagine a scenario where my wife would harm someone. Telling them she was *done with them* is more her style. Like being dismissed by a royal."

"Okay." He flips to a different page in his notebook. "That covers the first one."

I shifted in my seat. "There's more?"

"Yes. Uncommon for a person to be a witness in two active murder investigations. So, I came in person."

A wave a nausea came over me. Talk about a crack-back tackle. One, isn't Matheson just missing. Two, who the hell else is dead? Three, where's the screwdriver when you need it? "Okay. Back up. Matheson is dead?" I shifted in my seat and leaned forward.

"We are unsure. High-profile case. We're going with murder until proven otherwise."

"Fine. Then who *is* dead?" My palms were moist. Worse than when I vomited on the beach. I wanted to wipe them on my pants but reconsidered.

"Lawson Jerome Gibbs, age seventeen."

I thought for a minute. It rang no bells. "Help me out here. I don't know him."

"Scooter. Caddy at your golf club."

"Oh, yeah. Great kid. What a shame. How did he die?"

"That's what I'm asking you."

In emergency medicine, the worst thing anyone can

say to you when you come in for the day is *remember that patient* you sent home last night with the...? Could be chest pain, or rash, or fever. Sometimes this was happy news. Rarely. It means you missed something. Hopefully the patient didn't die. Dread cloaked me like it fell from the ceiling, and I started to piece the memories together.

I had driven my Mercedes, for the last time, to a distant and lonely parking slot at the Columbia Hills Country Club. The late September heat rose through my loafers and a breath of steamy air floated from the tenth tee. As I walked the macadam toward the imposing white structure, no pangs of regret or waves of pleasant memories breached my mental fortress. My sole emotion was the desire to leave my life in Columbia. Feelings, otherwise, lay below a fallow field shielded from moisture and sunlight. My lack of interest in the usual emotional tilling that comes with human existence served me well over the years, or so I thought.

Wide symmetric curved steps rose to a spacious veranda covered by hunter green awnings that sported the club crest. Why two stairways remained a mystery. I always went right. I avoided an organized goodbye at work but felt obliged to attend dinner. On my way to the dining room I spied Patricia, my favorite server. For twenty years, both she and I were staples of the club. Like applesauce at family dinner. At seventy, she still didn't take crap from anyone yet managed the demands of the spoiled membership with sassy charm. She collected the club gossip, including my sad story.

"Hey, baby," I said while taking her age-spotted hand in mine. I slipped her a Franklin, and she tucked it in her pocket without a glance.

"Don't 'hey baby' me. You're leaving me to deal with your drunk friends by my lonesome." She winked.

"Well, you never needed my help before with those Neanderthals. Listen. I'm telling you this before things get out of hand and I forget." I pecked her cheek. "You'll top the short list of what I will miss. You're an important person at this place."

She set her chin, smoothed her apron over skinny legs, and looked off to the sun setting over the eighteenth green. "Nobody ever told me that before, Sam." She walked to the kitchen.

My seven golfing buddies were a half drink ahead of me and J.B. was at the punch line of a joke I told him the previous week. A shot of rye awaited me.

"And the golf pro says: Your stance is too wide." They laughed uproariously until I reached my seat. They stood and held glasses high. J.B. said, "We can find an eight handicap to replace you in a minute, but we'll never find another damn ginger mick like you. Happy hunting."

We clinked drinks and I put mine away like sweet tea. The rest of the evening evolved typically. I ordered my favorite steak, drained my whiskey and water, and another appeared. We told jokes and stories, complained about work and wives, and talked about golf. By my seventh cocktail the buzz hit hard, and the boys kept Patricia on standby for the next one.

I steadied myself leaving the Men's and met Patricia in the hall.

"Hey, Sport. You keeping the rubber on the road there?" she said.

"Yeah, well, you know how it goes."

"Somebody said, 'Always leave them wanting more,'" she said. "There's another drink waiting for you. If I were you, I'd leave it and walk out that door."

I nodded and did just that. She was right. What was the point? I would never see those guys again. As a veteran of intoxicated travels down those steps, I held the rail and paced myself. At the bottom I considered my driving ability. This was the juncture where I usually called my wife for a ride. I deemed that to be a bad idea and started to my car. Scooter, a young caddie, appeared from the shadows.

"Hey, Mr. Sam. Was lookin' for you. I was playin' catch with Joey and took one in the forehead. The guys told me to go get it checked."

"Knocked out?" I said.

"No, sir."

"Throw up?"

"No."

"Seeing straight?"

"Yes, sir."

"You'll be fine. Put ice on it."

"You're moving away, right?" he said.

"Yeah, Scooter. You're a good caddie. Stay in school. Gotta big life ahead of you. Be good now."

"You know, I like you don't call me boy. Thanks, and good luck."

Why is it we wait until goodbye to tell people we care? I drove through my pristine neighborhood. An old lady with a gold-fish bowl on the passenger seat would have passed me. I parked in front of the third garage bay and left the fob in the console. The dealership would pick it up later in the week and deposit forty thousand dollars in

my checking account. I poured pink lemonade and chugged it while I gazed past
the pool in the backyard. A sentimental
person might suspect that tears might flow
contemplating my last night in that house.
Nothing. What the hell is wrong with me?
A sliver of light escaped the master bedroom door. I turned right and collapsed on
the guest bed.

———

I turned my attention back to detective Vanderslice.
"How did he die?" I said.

"Epidural hematomato. No." He flipped through
his notes. "Hematoma." We said it together. "Went to
bed that night and never woke up."

"Son of a bitch." *In the ocean now, on my toes, feet
of bricks. Mouth just at surface pulling air against the
weight of the water.* Saliva pooled in my mouth. I
swallowed and tried to think of anything but vomiting. I spied a nearby trash can and kept that as an
option. "So, why is this a murder investigation?"

"Manslaughter. Witnesses in the dining room saw
Joey throw it, as you confirmed, and they said he and
his buddy laughed uncontrollably."

"So, teenagers laugh at that stuff. That doesn't
mean Joey tried to kill him." I recalled more as we
talked. "And your witnesses didn't see the boys come

to Scooter's aid out of view. He told me, that they told him, to get it checked."

"These witnesses did not come forward right away. One had traveled out of the country and the other was unaware that Scooter passed. Anyway, folks are all stirred up about this and they are making it a racial thing. We dug up social media stuff on Joey that is unflattering at best. Solicitor is getting ready to go to the grand jury. This will clear Mr. Watson."

I stood up and wiped my hands on my pants and paced for a minute before I sat. There was no question. Not that it mattered much since I had left the city, but my reputation would be shit. My wife would endure roguish glances and courthouse gossip with the story growing legs and a tail and by the fifth rendition, I would be a hit-and-run driver.

"Okay. I'll give a formal statement. How do we make that happen?"

"You'll need to come to Columbia and give a deposition under oath." He shifted in his chair and placed his notebook back in his jacket. "Listen, I didn't come here to jam you up. I came looking for the truth and I found it. Thanks for agreeing to give a statement."

37

I SAT IN MY car and slammed my fist on the dash. Put a big crack in it. My hand throbbed. Brain on crack. Out of control. Thoughts of the pain and misfortune I could have prevented made a re-entrant circle in my head. I needed to talk to Kayla. She would help me through this. I had put it in airplane mode for the meeting. When I turned my phone back on, three missed calls from the same number appeared. It was a local number, but I didn't recognize it.

"University Hospital Emergency."

"This is Dr. Buchanan. I received several calls from you."

"Yes, let me get Dr. Ryno."

I thought they needed information about a patient I had seen at Touro. Odd to call me on my cell for that.

"Yes, Joe Ryno here. I'm terribly sorry to bother you."

"This is Dr. Buchanan; how can I help you?"

"Oh, you're a doc. Great. We have a dead man here that we can't identify. He had your card in his pocket.

An address, a time, and some days of the week on the back side."

My problems with the prosecutor evaporated in my mind. Other possibilities ran through my mind. There was only one.

"You still with me?"

"Yes. Sorry. Describe him for me."

"Small build, barrel chest, beard, sixties, Hispanic. EMS brought him from Gentilly. Cardiac arrest from a tension pneumothorax."

Same as before. "Unilateral?"

"Yes. I saw the scar on the other side," he said.

"Right. Bilateral when I had him."

He traveled a long way from home, and I understood why. He had returned to the scene of the fight. Maybe to make his peace with it. I'd take him there if he asked, but it's something he wanted to do alone.

"Is there family?"

"Will be there in an hour with his sister."

Aside from my parents, I had lost no one else. Raymond became much more than a patient. He was my companion in sobriety and I felt responsible for him. He was a stray human that tumbled into my life. I wanted him to be safe and happy. This became part of the key to my happiness. Old Sam would never have allowed Raymond near his life or his heart and would take the news of his death like that of a washed-up movie star. I sobbed for losing my friend and for the pain and loneliness. This was a sign of success in my journey to be a better person but that made it no easier to bear. *On the beach now, hands on my knees, saliva pooling in my mouth, vulnerable.* I opened the car door and stumbled to a metal waste can two spots over. The lid clamored when it hit the ground, echoing off the concrete, and I vomited into the trash. I removed my dress shirt and then my undershirt, then wiped my face and blew my nose into my undershirt. I left it in the trash.

There was no reason to rush, but I drove like I needed to pee since Texas. There is no easy way to travel from the airport to Uptown. I took Airline Highway, with seventy-nine stoplights, to Earhart into Uptown where I found Ray's sister, Ana, at home, and explained what happened and why she needed to come with me to the hospital to identify him. She sat in her wooden rocker, a tired blanket folded over the back, and cried for a few minutes. I couldn't explain why he went to Gentilly.

"I considered Raymond a good friend. It wasn't just saving his life or working on the tomb together. We talked to each other. Not the usual man stuff. We understood each other, had a real connection. He's part of me now."

I told her it was my honor to pay for his cremation and make the funeral arrangements. She nodded and sighed. I helped her to the car.

———

A priest met us in the small room where they held Ray's body. Ryno told me they placed a chest tube, endotracheal tube, and did CPR, but a pulse never returned. He was pale and small beneath the stiff sheet. I smoothed his hair back and reassured Ana that he experienced no pain. He may have suffered but she didn't need that. The priest performed rites, and we prayed for the soul of Raymond T. Reyes. My friend. Ana and I confirmed his identity, and she signed the paperwork. The priest gave me information for a funeral home in Uptown and I gave them my credit card number by phone to cover their services. Ray did not have a family doctor. I had been writing his prescriptions, so I agreed to sign the death certificate to keep him off the coroner's table.

After the priest left, I asked Ana, "Do you want his St. Christopher medal?"

"I want you to have it." She spun the chain on his neck, released the clasp, and placed it my palm.

We hugged, and she cried again. "I'm going to miss Raymond," I said.

—

When I returned home at dinner time, I sat at the table and collected my thoughts. My need to call Kayla had intensified along with my anxiety over revealing my new problem. Even though it was a past transgression, shame and defeat sat with me at the table. I wondered when my past would stop invading my future. I touched her on my favorites list. Voicemail. I didn't leave a message.

My restlessness and anxiety made me want to escape

the house. I walked to Mahony's. I did not debate, nor did I pace the sidewalk trying to talk myself out of it. If ever I had a valid excuse to drink, today was the day. Double. I sat at the bar and told the man to line up six shot glasses and fill them with whiskey. He poured a tall glass of water as well. From my wallet I flipped two twenties onto the bar and told him to keep it. I took my time. No place to be and nothing to do was a lousy combination for an alcoholic. After the first shot, I knew I was being stupid. I continued. Four shots in, the buzz started. Faster than I expected. For the first time since I was on my knees on the beach I wanted to say *screw it*. My phone dinged. Kathy.

Wht up

                                 Ray died

Oh. So sorry. Whr r u

                                 Mahonys

Do not leave

She arrived twenty minutes later and sat next to me. I explained about Ray but not Scooter. One was enough. Possibly the story had no legs.

"Unlikely friends," Kathy said. "He was blessed to have you in his life."

"I can say the same thing about him." I nudged her forearm. "And you."

One shot remained. I clinked it to her water glass and threw it back.

"To Ray," she said. "Until you came along, I had no

close friend. I don't know what the hell's wrong with me, but I'm happy to have you. I will always love you." She turned on her bar stool toward me and touched my cheek. "And before we cry on each other's shoulders, I'm walking you home. I left my car there."

My capacity to drink alcohol had diminished and now I struggled to walk. We locked elbows, and she navigated. Small talk was unnecessary, and I was devoting too much brain power walking to divert any for conversation. After I fumbled with my keys, she unlocked the door. It was dusk and eerily quiet. The usual sounds that sifted from the neighborhood set with the sun. The scent of confederate jasmine growing on the fence hung in the air.

"Stay with me." Then I whispered, "I'll take the couch."

"I can't stay this time. Remember my ultrasound is at nine a.m. You were going to be there." She tapped on my temple.

"Right. Right. And I will be." I handed her my phone. "Set my alarm for eight fifteen, I'll meet you there."

She tucked me into bed and kissed me on the forehead. Now, who was the six-year-old?

"Tomorrow is a new day. Things won't seem so glum."

38

I AWOKE BEFORE MY alarm, mostly because of a full bladder. Other than a mouth like a Carolina dirt road in August, I survived intact. That was part of my problem. I could drink myself stupid and pay no physical consequences the next day, but for the first time I felt like a cat turd. I had betrayed my second baptism, my promise to myself, my commitment to Kayla. My choices seemed so clear that morning. I should have asked for help. What a dumbass. Had I learned nothing? Had the paddling been a waste? If Kayla had walked in the door that minute, I would not have held her gaze for two seconds. I knew I needed to tell her everything. I guzzled water at the kitchen table and considered the shit I needed to do. Call Kayla, Kathy's ultrasound, deal with Floyd, plane reservations to Columbia, go to the funeral home, talk to Wales about reworking the schedule to spend a few days in South Carolina.

The moon illuminated Hawai'i, but I called anyway. "The number you have reached has calling restrictions." What the hell. Kayla became a low-priority problem.

———

Both Kathy and I arrived early to the obstetrics unit, and I hugged her when we met. We sat in comfortable white rockers in a spacious hallway near the ultrasound waiting area. Fresh morning sun poured through the atrium windows.

"Thanks for walking me home. I'm a shit, and you are a fantastic friend. Now we've both been naked before each other, sort of."

"Right. Don't remind me. A pair we are, huh?"

"Yeah. Listen, I'm going back to Columbia for a few days. It's complicated. I need to give a deposition."

"Sure. Call me if you need a ride to the airport. Oh, I almost forgot. It was strange. I saw a lady on your sidewalk last night. In the shadows. She asked if it was your place and I said yes but you weren't well, and to stop back tomorrow."

"Name?"

"Didn't say."

"Thin, nice chest, faint accent?"

"Yeah. I couldn't place it. Irish? Oh, shit."

We said it together. *Kayla*. She had come to surprise me, which explains why she didn't answer. Now this was punishment. I can't say I didn't deserve it. Weight pressed my chest, and my shirt stuck to my back. Kathy and I may as well have had sex in the doorway. I'm sure Kayla got that impression.

"Okay. Remind me what happened at the door." I leaned forward studying my hands.

"You asked me to stay. Fairly loud voice."

I made the bird shit face. "But I didn't come on to you, right?"

"No. Perfect gentleman. You said you'd take the couch."

"Then she heard that too, right?"

"Doubt it. You sort of said it under your breath."

"I am completely screwed."

"Like I said, we are a pair."

An ultrasound tech in green scrubs, Laura, called Kathy for her test and I tagged along not caring that people figured I was the father. They didn't know me. Kathy reclined on the gurney, and Laura spread a towel over her pelvis and squirted the blue gel.

"He's not the dad. Just here for moral support," Kathy hitched her thumb at me.

I waved. "Hi. Sam Buchanan."

"Oh. Dr. Sam, I recognize your voice. We've talked at night a few times."

"Right. I'm only here to learn the gender and due date for the betting pool in the ER. I want the inside information, so to speak."

Whack. Right across the chest. "There will be no betting on my child."

"Yes, dear."

Laura worked the ultrasound probe like a teenager playing a video game. She clicked off images faster than I read them measuring the skull, the femur, and from the head to the butt. She made an average measurement of fourteen weeks. Too soon to tell the gender. Excellent heartbeat.

"Is that two I'm seeing there?" I said.

Again, with the whacking. "Remind me why I asked you to come?"

"Are you sure you two aren't married?" Laura said.

We laughed, and Laura wiped off the gel.

We parted ways, and I tried Kayla again. Same message. What the hell. I walked to the ER and found Wales in his office, a modest, windowless room, clean and uncluttered. Diplomas and certificates spotted the walls. Wales, a small stature, balding guy, with a Texas-sized heart sat in a tall leather chair that made him appear smaller.

"You work today?" I said.

"Have a seat, Sam. Yeah. It was bad. Kid fell off a scaffold at those apartments they are building off Jefferson. Broke his damn neck."

"Black kid?"

"Yeah. Family was pretty broken up about it."

My heart was in my throat. I didn't know if I could take it if it was James William. I was beginning to feel like the evil twin of King Midas. Everything I touched turned to shit.

"First name James?"

"No. Devon. You know somebody that works over there?"

"Yeah. Long story. His mom works in the cafeteria."

I gripped the handles of my chair to conceal the shaking. I was getting a feel of what parents felt like when I called them about their kid being injured. Deep breaths.

"You okay?"

"Yeah. I'm sort of responsible for James getting a job there. I'd feel like crap if he was injured."

"You know, in the short time you've been here you have more friends in this neighborhood than I do. You should run for city council."

"Ha. It hasn't been dull. I'll tell you that."

"Sam, people never leave compliments for the night shift except on you. Nurses love you. Patients enjoy how you talk with them."

It gratified me to hear it. Then I explained the problems in Columbia. He nodded and took in my sad story. He tented his fingers.

"You know, they might take action on your license over this."

My preoccupation with Raymond and Kayla put that off my radar. Shit. Wales was right. South Carolina is strict. Moral turpitude, they call it. I offered medical advice while extremely intoxicated. The state medical board frowns on this and the shit was deep.

"I'm not sure what will happen. I'll keep you posted," I said.

His picture is next to "temperate" in the dictionary. Wales tapped his pen on the blotter a few times and perused the upcoming work schedule. "Tell me if you think this is fair. I'll take you off the schedule for three weeks and cover your shifts. Let's see what happens back home. If the dust settles and there is no action on your license, then we work as usual. If things end up in the dumper, then I already did what the hospital board was going to force me to do."

I was relieved. It was only five shifts, but not having to think about getting back to work would allow me to concentrate on resolving the mess in Carolina and the bigger one on O'ahu.

———

I walked to Breaux Mart to enlist Billy's help and talk to Renée. The farther I walked, the more I realized how badly I screwed up. This wasn't a little misunderstanding. She didn't drive five minutes to find me drunk with another woman. *Oh, I'll just walk up the street, talk to her, and everything will be peachy.* She crossed a damn ocean to find me drunk with another woman who is pregnant. I wondered if I had any chance of fixing this.

Rex sliced meat for a customer as I passed the counter.

> The same feeling as when I stood in our front yard debating how to tell my father I dented his truck. It was a cool November evening, but my shirt stuck to my back. Venus low in the sky. A few dim stars. He taught me the planets and the stars standing on that spot. It wasn't the dent. It was my failure. I knew it would disappoint. I lashed my self-worth to his opinion of me.

Billy and Renée concentrated on a project in the back. I stuck my head in and rapped on the door jamb. "I'm glad you two are together because I need your help."

"What can I help you find, Sam?" Billy said. "You look like roadkill."

"Billy. That's not very polite," Renée said.

"Well, how do you think he looks?" Billy said.

"Now that she mentions it, you look tired, Sam."

"I'm okay but I need you both to sit." I gave them the five-cent tour of my screwed-up life and my new responsibilities with Floyd. Recounting my troubles ordered them in my head making the challenges less arduous. "This is going to work out, up or down, so I'm trying to prepare for the fallout."

They both slouched and looked at the floor. I'm sure they were trying to reconcile the person they knew with the one who sat before them. I did the same looking in the mirror and found no joy. In Carolina, I was a sinful person who appeared to be good. Now, I was a good person who looked bad. The latter is preferred if forced to choose.

"With your permission, Renée, I want Billy to stay at my place while I'm away and care for my orange buddy. That would lift a burden from me."

They looked at each other and Renée nodded agreement. Billy hugged me and promised Floyd would be fine. Renée joined the hug.

"We'll be here for you," Renée said. "What else do you need?"

"Well, there is good news and bad news. We

finished the tomb and it looks amazing. The brass plate is polished and back in place. Unfortunately, my friend, Ray, died yesterday."

"Oh, Lord," Renée said. "Bless his soul. I am so sorry for your loss."

"Thank you. So, he'll be cremated. I'm hoping we can put him in the caveau. No name on the plate. He'd be pleased to be in the tomb he restored."

"Oh, sure. Tell me when the service will be."

———

I carried my purchases home from Breaux Mart. Something I swore I would not do. Cat box, litter, litter bags, poop scooper, food, food bowl with the paws on the side, and toys. Billy made me buy toys. Then I walked to the vet hospital. Heidi talked to the receptionist as I tromped in.

"Hey, we missed you yesterday. Your boy is ready."

"Yeah. Sorry. Terrible day."

"If you want to commiserate, we'll be at Mahony's."

"I'll pass, thanks." The last place I needed to be was within fifty yards of alcohol.

I paid the substantial bill, pocketed my instructions, and promised to make an appointment for Floyd's man-hood excision at a future date. Domestication comes with a price. I carried his highness home pleased with his recovery. Pleasant feelings were in short supply, so I was grateful for that.

Billy, who came and went from my place like she

owned it, had moved some of her stuff over and set up Floyd for indoor living, at least for the short term. I rested him on the couch, and we petted him while he purred and flopped his tail. Billy leaned her head against my shoulder.

"Please don't leave us."

"Don't fret now. Every plan I made dissolved like salt into boiling water. So much is unknown, I'm not looking past next week. Neither should you, least not concerning me."

She put her feet up on the coffee table. "Sam, I could get used to living on my own like this."

"Yeah. Study hard, find a job, and you can do that." I poked her bony ribs. "Until then, get your damn feet off the table."

She made a pouty face then recovered. "I was thinking. When you go to Hawai'i, you should bring an assistant to shop or run errands for you."

"What an idea. That person might do my laundry, cook, attend to my social calendar, and be my chauffeur."

"Yes, sir. That's what I'm talkin' 'bout."

"Okay. I'll ask Rex if he wants to go with me."

More pouty face. "You're mean. Downright mean."

———

I thought of kayaking. I could paddle around O'ahu and still not fix anything, but I thought it would help. I tied my boots and walked. No thinking. Just walking. I took Magazine toward the city. Fourteen blocks. No shopping. Just walking. Cloud cover prevailed making the temperature favorable. I smelled rain. On my anonymous trek, cyclists weaved between parked cars and traffic, folks window shopped, and dogs walked owners of various pedigree. I turned toward the lake on Jackson, a handsome Garden District boulevard lined with live oaks. The Buckner Mansion caught my eye, and I stopped to admire the grounds and the soaring fluted columns. Thunder rumbled beyond the river, so I turned on Coliseum toward the park. I rambled past the historic homes admiring the ornate fences and cast-iron galleries common to homes of the mid to late 1800s.

As I reached Lafayette Cemetery Number 1, the densest and most punishing rain I had experienced washed the city. If I stepped out of the ocean, I would be no wetter. I remembered the morning I stood naked next to Kayla's bed trying to coax my way back in. She was right. I was thankful for her making me kayak in the rain. I knew my actions hurt her, but my determination to make it right blossomed as my boots filled with water. Like two trucks colliding in the desert at midnight, our timing sucked. Other than my lapse, I had done nothing wrong. The opposite, because I did what Kayla advised.

I zigzagged to the Buchanan tomb and stood before it, remembering my conversations with Ray. I could see him resting on the bucket baring his soul to me. Exposing his pain, the load he carried, the horrid magnet that pulled him from his wife and from God. The feel of the rough wet stucco brought me comfort and reminded me of the abiding human condition, which is not unique to Sam Buchanan. Suffering eventually touches all of us. I kneeled and prayed the peace, which eluded him through his time on earth, now shined on Raymond. No yoke of regret. I prayed for strength. When I vomited on the beach, I thought life sucked. That was nothing. Not close. That day, in flooding Lafayette Cemetery, I learned what it was to be on your knees.

39

COLUMBIA NO LONGER offered the air of home. Columbia was not home, and little connected me to the city. I lost desire to golf at the club or spend time with my so-called friends. I might have been on a business trip to Topeka. The code for the gate at the back entrance to our exclusive community still worked, and I drove the serpentine streets to my house. I parked at the curb next to the for-sale sign like a potential buyer. The contrast between this white-bread enclave and my new eclectic neighborhood hit me. I considered it before but being there again brought focus. Standing in the street, in shorts and a Hawai'ian shirt, I considered the transformation from my parochial existence. I thought I changed for the better. Time would be the arbiter of this. Rachel, my wife, stood at the front door. Her white capris pants and form-fitting V-neck sweater revealed her elegant figure. She lost weight and looked fantastic. She had a subtle aquiline nose, oval face, and long black hair. I always suspected she had American

Indian ancestry, but she never wanted to do the DNA. Her hair was in a French braid the way I like it.

"Sam? I barely recognize you without the beard."

I crossed the yard, surprised her with a hug and a peck on the cheek, and noticed her puffy, injected eyes. We sat at the kitchen table and drank tea. I couldn't count the hours I spent at that table studying, eating, playing cards, or just talking. Yet, it was not mine. My failures sat at the head of the table like a judgmental patriarch.

"What's happened? You look upset."

"This whole damn mess is my fault. I'm a fool. They found Preston in his car on a dirt road near Lake Jocassee. Shot himself in the mouth." She barely said *mouth* before breaking down.

"I'm sorry. You broke it off, but that still must sting."

"I've never felt so alone. My parents blame me for us. To the partners I'm the village prostitute."

"Listen, I'll talk to your parents. So much has evolved in my life. What was muddled before is clear now. They need to understand the guy with the beard shoulders some of the blame." I held her hand. "I forgive you. You are not alone in your transgressions and I ask your forgiveness too."

"Yes. Yes. I'm not holding any grudges here."

"Listen, when I left Columbia, much to my consternation, my shortcomings, my failures, my transgressions went along for the ride. I learned they would always be my unhappy companions until I learned to forgive myself. I found forgiving others a much easier task."

"How did you do it?"

"I had to stop drinking first. Then I exercised. Rain or shine. For weeks. The combination of exertion and solitude, plus a few friends, allowed me to cast all the crap to the tide."

"Just like that?"

My conversation with Kayla on our first kayak trip invaded my thoughts. I took Rachel's hand again in both of mine. "No. Hard work. Shoveling clay." I stared at our hands. "And I'm not done." Our eyes met. "Rachel, I know you are hurting but I also know how strong you are."

More tears and we sat quietly amongst the rubble of our relationship.

———

After I changed clothes, the original purpose of my visit, we discussed work, the sale of our homes, and the proceedings to end our marriage. Columbia holds a small community of lawyers, so she appreciated my problems with the solicitor.

"You are different, Sam, and not just the beard. Where is my husband and what did you do to him?"

"Yeah, I'll take that as a compliment."

She put her hand on my forearm. "I meant it that way."

"Except for one lapse, I'm sober. I uncluttered my life of material goods and cluttered it with a rough orange cat and genuine folks I love."

"I'm happy for you, Sam."

"I want to tell you some things."

"Sure," she said.

"I didn't go straight to New Orleans. I rented the top of the place we stayed eighteen years ago in Kailua."

"Oh. That was so beautiful."

"Long story, but I became aquatinted with this couple that lives at the shore." I had not broken a promise, but I felt like I had. I wiped my hands on my shorts and pondered the most favorable way to tell it. My plan was to say hello, pick up a suit, and be on my way. I didn't expect to stir up these feelings. "I fell in love with their neighbor. Hard. I should have kept to myself. I wasn't looking for it. Our involvement was hasty at best."

"No. Don't say that. See how you changed. Sam, you are a better person. What happens now?"

"My entire world went to shit in two days. I lost a good friend and I fear I lost her, Kayla, as well. She has the mistaken impression I am romantically involved with one of my nurses." I raised my right hand. "I am not. We are friends, but that's it."

"What are you going to do about that?"

"I am clueless where I will be in a month. I need to deal with the solicitor and then I'm going to Kailua to make things right."

40

I HEADED DOWNTOWN TO the solicitor's office at Blanding and Assembly. Joey Watson and his parents sat on the far side of the spacious, wood-paneled lobby. They stood when I entered. I shook my head and broke eye contact. They reclaimed their seats. I wondered if the solicitor placed them on purpose to see what might happen. Nobody should think I did this as a favor for the Watsons. I never met his parents, but it appeared sleep eluded them for weeks. It pleased me knowing my testimony would lift this burden and they could resume their lives.

Vanderslice greeted me and showed me to an imposing room with a stretched-out cherry table and multiple high-back leather chairs. Law books populated an entire wall and pictures of the Columbia region hung on the others. The prosecuting attorney, Horwitz, a lean man with grim features reminiscent of a mortician, followed soon after and trailing behind was the matronly stenographer.

He covered much of the same ground as Vanderslice

did in the airport, but to painstaking detail. He asked the same question multiple different ways and tried to trick me by suggesting I was answering the questions differently. It was like simultaneous root canal and colonoscopy. I kept telling myself that he was just doing his job, but this guy was a first-class dick. In high school he was probably voted most likely to be murdered. An hour later we were off the record.

"I think this matter regarding Mr. Watson is closed," Horwitz said. He picked up his notes and walked out.

He left without another word. I felt like when you put down the pen after the SAT or the MCAT. He attempted to kick me in the nuts, but I survived and was thrilled to finish. I had asked Vanderslice to give me the address of the Gibbs family. There were two more tasks to do before I left Columbia. He slid it across the table.

"What's your take on the family?" I said.

"Mom and two younger sisters at home. She's been calm through this. Let me come with you. They know me."

He told me to call him JR. I dealt with many families over the years in emotionally charged situations and people can be unpredictable. I wanted to offer my apology and condolences but not at the expense of aggravating people. Vanderslice drove, and we parked on the street in front of an apartment complex near the fair grounds. Because JR called, she was expecting us, and we found her sitting at a green metal picnic table next to a basketball court. These hoops had the nylon nets and flowers bloomed in beds along the building.

Somebody took care of this place. It was a gorgeous, partly cloudy Carolina day with a light breeze. Mrs. Gibbs, a heavyset woman, hair braided in rows, wore a flower-patterned summer dress and flip flops. JR and I sat opposite her at the table. After he introduced us, JR let me do the talking.

"Mrs. Gibbs, I want to discuss a few things if you have time."

I prepared for an emotional outburst. This might have been one pissed-off woman. I was ready to take a righteous lashing, a verbal can of whoop-ass. I can't say she appeared happy, but she seemed to be someone at peace. She shook our hands and then sat with hands folded.

"I'm glad you came to see me, Dr. Buchanan."

"Please, call me Sam. To me, your son was Scooter. Can I use that name?"

"Everybody else did, but me, so why not? His father and I spent hours and hours talking about boy names and we chose Lawson. From third grade on he was Scooter. Nothin' I could do about it."

"I am so sorry for your loss and I apologize and take full responsibility in failing Scooter when he asked for my advice. You don't need to hear my problems, but I'm troubled. A shepherd that lost a sheep."

"Thank you, Sam. I prayed on this and I don't wish you any ill will. Any of that's between God and you."

"I appreciate that. I preferred Scooter as a caddy because he tried to do more than just carry the bag. He understood the game."

She nodded and kept eye contact.

"The testimony I gave today cleared Joey Watson. I wish I had known of this sooner before it became a mess."

"I'm glad for that," she said. "I'd rather this be an accident than something a boy did on purpose."

I thought for a moment. Old Sam tugged at my sleeve, and I struggled with the words. "I was a miserable failure. Just told that to a friend. I'm working on that. I don't drink anymore. My life as it was here is a memory. But I may pay a price for my actions. Compared to what you lost, my troubles are nothing, but I may lose my medical license."

"Well, I'm not sure that helps anybody. If they ask me, I say that is not my concern. Thank you for being forthright with me. I'm gonna pray for you."

"How are you and your girls doing?"

"Kids are resilient. The girls talk about him with a smile now. I know they miss him, but their lives are moving on and they'll be just fine. They love to remember stories. We'll be at dinner and laugh about something. Then they remember when Scooter laughed so hard once a baked bean came out his nose. That's when I feel him with us."

"Lawson or Jesus?" I said.

"Oh, you gonna be okay too. You know they are both here with us."

"And how about you?"

"Day at a time, Sam. Each one a blessing."

Her picture is next to "grace" in the dictionary. This undeserved forgiveness humbled me. I needed no better role model than Scooter's mom to show me a path to redemption. While I didn't cause Scooter's death, I didn't prevent it either. These were unalterable facts. The choice before me was to drag that around for the rest of my life or cast it into the ocean and live a life pleasing to Mrs. Gibbs.

———

JR dropped me at my car, and I drove to a joint meeting with my accountant and attorney. We discussed tax issues involving the sale of property and the pending divorce. I then instructed them to work with her bank and make an anonymous deposit of $250,000 into the account of Mrs. Gibbs. We put seventy-five thousand dollars into an escrow account and I instructed the accountant to offer his services for free and use that money to cover any tax burden for the year. Finally, I instructed them to send a check for ten thousand dollars to the Leilani Foundation. If Kayla wouldn't let me pay for my treatment, the foundation would get the money.

41

I RETURNED TO MY old house, a grand low-country-style place with a deep front porch, white pillars and shutters standing watch by tall windows. I parked in the driveway this time. Rachel slept on the chaise lounge in the solarium. A novel lay open on her lap and sandals tilted on the tile below her feet. This was my favorite room. It ran the expanse of the back of the house and opened on to the yard, the rose garden, and the swimming pool. *Bearded Sam stood at the margin of the pool, hands on Rachel's knees. She had the most genuine smile on her face.* I didn't expect the memories and the tender time with Rachel. Until I held her hand and revealed my forgiveness, I did not appreciate the emotional fatigue of dragging that grudge around. I recalled my conversation with Michael on the pillbox. There is a certain freedom in having no debt. That is true, but the freedom from the animosities we hold lives in a novel dimension.

I put on my Hawai'i clothes and started my search of the kitchen. I remembered we received a sous vide appliance for Christmas one year. We never used it. I found it in the depth of the cabinet above the Sub-Zero. I pulled two frozen chicken breasts from the freezer and a stock pot from below the center island and placed them on the granite countertop. The app was easy to download on my phone. I set the device and put the breasts into a zip storage bag along with olive oil and spices while I waited for the water to warm. Cooking required eighty minutes. That gave me plenty of time to cook pasta and cut mushrooms, an onion, and peppers.

I slipped out and drove to the store for corn on the cob. In the lot of the Harris Teeter, I thought of what would have been. I know neither of us would want our earlier lives, our distant indifference. My failure to be a proper husband, friend, partner sat beside me, a mute passenger. I was a provider. Nothing more. And she didn't even need that. So, why did she hang on for twenty years? Was it social convention, habit, or hope that one day I would see her as I did that day in Kailua? See her like Charlie Scott saw his wife.

When I returned, Rachel sat at the center island drinking ice water. I dropped the ears before her.

"Shuck please."

"I'm serious now. Who are you?"

"It will be an hour until the chicken is done. Can I cut you carrots as an appetizer?"

"Sure. Usually we would be at the restaurant now and you would order steak and whiskey."

I cut veggies, and she cleaned the corn while I

recounted the events of the day. She smiled as I made an elegant display of the veggies on a tray with ranch dressing in the center bowl.

"Do you want me to nose around the solicitor's office?" she said, not using her lawyer voice. This was the voice of my fiancée.

"Leave it be. I'll take my licks as they come."

"You don't seem upset."

"Well, it helps I don't need the money. I proved to myself I can be a caring doc again. I would enjoy continuing to work but I'm looking forward. Can't change what happened."

"And you're never coming back here."

"Right. I know myself now. I'm certain."

Rachel let me prepare the entire meal save for reminding me where pots and utensils lived. We chose iced tea to drink and took our meal on the patio. She wanted to learn of people in New Orleans, so I told her about Billy.

"Everyone imagines Bourbon Street when you talk about New Orleans," she said. "You forget that it's a city with regular people."

"Regular and irregular. I meet some real characters. Hey, let's go for a walk."

"Like for exercise?"

"Sure. I walk most places I go now. I didn't own a car for a while."

We trekked a mile to the club and then started on the cart path for the golf course. As a golfer I ignored the trees, flowers, and bushes that lined the fairways.

Azaleas and dogwoods bloomed from straw beds among the towering pines. I recalled the times we could have taken this walk instead of having another cocktail and dozing in front of the TV.

"What made you and Billy so close?"

"Maybe it's because I don't have a daughter and she doesn't have a father. She helped me in the market and since then we made a tight bond."

"Did you let her in too far? I'm trying to understand your life now, not pick at you."

"No. Who else is more deserving of my attention than an orphan?"

"How will you make things right in Hawai'i?"

I told her of the fateful night of my lapse.

"I'll walk to her place and explain what happened."

"What if she doesn't believe you?"

"Then it will be a quick expedition to Hawai'i and I'll be back in the Big Easy."

"Then what?"

"I'm driving at night here."

"Meaning what?"

"I can only see as far as the headlights."

Back at home I felt mentally strong but physically tired, ready for bed. So much had been unresolved and order was finding its way back in my life. My mind settled, and I was ready to travel to O'ahu. Without discussion, I took the queen bed in the guest room. I studied the fan blades and replayed the events of the day. If I had not transformed my life before I learned of Scooter's death, my fall would have been a punch in the mouth. Satisfaction came in knowing I preemptively changed. Scooter's death didn't force me to do it. That made my transformation more genuine.

It was the middle of the night. A hand against my chest and a soft body pressed against my back. The smell of her perfume was like apple pie when you come home from college for Thanksgiving.

"Go back to sleep. I only want to hold you."

42

I CONNECTED TO ATLANTA and boarded first class for the direct flight to O'ahu. I planned to read, dream, listen to music, and avoid delivering any medical care. After declining a cocktail, I relaxed in my seat. Susan, the flight attendant, stopped in the aisle and touched my shoulder.

"Aren't you the doctor that helped the man who choked on this flight a few months ago?"

"Yes. Sam. Pleasure to be with you again. Let's see if we can make it with no drama this time."

"Sure, we can do that. What's his name?"

"Stan Hayes."

"Right. He and his wife flew a few weeks ago. Will you see them?"

"If I'm with you on my next flight, I'll tell you."

"Why do you look different?"

"I rubbed my clean-shaven cheeks."

As much as I wanted to think of Kayla, Rachel kept sneaking into my thoughts. A song in my head. Her perfume, her hand against my chest, her smile in the kitchen, our tender moments together. *I stood with Peter at Moku Nui listening to him talk about the eternal bond of marriage.* How different my life would have been had I enjoyed his clarity of vision.

No limo waited for me this time. I took an Uber to a place I rented on VRBO. A crusty old guy of German descent has a place on the beach halfway between Tree Tops and Kayla's place. A one-room efficiency apartment with a view of the pool sits at one end of his home. I met him on my last visit, and he offered to host me. I also wanted to avoid any discomfort of dealing with Jane. If Kayla was ignoring me, I would get the same treatment from the Tropical Tribe.

I arrived at dusk. Because I enjoyed the grocery delivery so much from the last visit, I called to the market and had them drop a few things. After making a snack, I traded jokes with Otto, the landlord, and put on my favorite swim suit with the fish pattern and a Guy Harvey T-shirt. During the flight I considered waiting to talk to Kayla in the morning. Emotion led the way. I wanted to redeem myself and imagined awesome make-up sex.

I walked the water's edge and let the surf run over my feet. One option was to walk the street to her front door. I thought it rather formal considering the intimacy we shared, plus that walk was longer and required shoes. It was bold to approach from the sand, but I considered it worth the risk.

> Formaldehyde. I could smell it. My first practical exam for anatomy in medical school. Thirty partially dissected cadavers lay on stainless steel tables. Professors had placed numbered pins in various body parts. Nothing was straightforward. The question was not the name of the muscle but the nerve that made it move. You had to know the first thing to answer the main question, so it was two questions in one. It wasn't the thing the closes over your airway when you swallow, the epiglottis. It was the space between the tongue and the epiglottis. Shit. I didn't know it.

Damn vallecula. Damn sweaty palms. I heard water splashing. A good sign. The breeze fluttered my shirt. The thought of her exposed in the water gave me more confidence. I stood in the shadows trying to slow my heart. Then the voices. I had almost started to speak, to ask permission to approach. I crouched and pushed foliage to the side. A casual observer might consider me a voyeur. Who could argue otherwise? I waited until they floated into view. Steven and Kayla. That snake. Rat. Weasel. I closed my eyes and waited. Slow, full-capacity breaths. My heart thumped out of my chest now. When they moved out of my view again, I made my furtive retreat to the shore.

A crescent moon, veiled partially by wispy clouds, rose in the east and I fixed on it standing at the high tide line as the vivid memory of the words Kayla and I shared rushed ashore. I stood and considered the high-altitude view of this perfectly crappy situation. I didn't assume the worst of Kayla. She thought she had firsthand evidence of my infidelity and had no reason to remain chaste. Certain I was a shit, she was done with me. Only she could explain why she cheated with a married guy and I withheld judgement. Even though she had not extended me the same courtesy, I kept an open mind.

I walked the shoreline to the public beach feeling sorry for myself. According to my logic, a one-night lapse from sobriety was a minor offense especially considering the circumstances. If life was to be just, then I viewed the cascade of events that followed as forty lashes for chewing gum. Tired and injured, I limped home and collapsed on the lumpy fold-out couch at Otto's.

43

I AWOKE BEFORE THE sun and took my orange pekoe tea by the pool, the song "Suzanne" by Leonard Cohen in my head. I feel it even though I don't completely understand it. My tea did not come all the way from China, but I imagined it did. The lyrics wandered in my head, so I found the JT version on my phone and listened with ear buds. It sheltered me from the loneliness surrounding me. A fog off the river. The rest of the *Covers* album played.

> I showed up at a house party when I was sixteen. I wore dress pants and a shirt with a collar. The other kids, older, dressed in jeans, T-shirts, and sandals, smoked pot and eyed me with disdain. I didn't belong, and I never would. I stayed a few uncomfortable minutes and drove home. My dad fixed the lawn mower in the garage, while I sat on a stool and we talked about nothing, and everything.

He helped me through a scattered night without knowing it. I'll never forget the feeling as I left that house party. That feeling of emptiness after longing for a connection and completely missing it. The smell of marijuana filled my nose.

I ate a banana and a few handfuls of granola and then hauled the kayak from the far side of the house to the beach. I needed to kayak before I talked to Kayla. Surf was low, so I entered easily and started a regular rhythm. I recalled the efficient stroke technique moving into even waters and glanced to the left not expecting to see anything of interest. The yellow kayak, black life vest, and polished stroke were unmistakable. I turned toward her and paddled faster than my usual pace. She had no reason to expect me, so she did not recognize me until twenty yards separated us. I coasted and called her name. No wave. No smile.

"Sam. You shouldn't be here. I'm not talking to you."

"Please, Kay. I can't take another breath without you knowing the truth. You owe that to me and to yourself."

"I owe you nothing and don't hold your breath."

She skimmed past me at a furious pace. I turned my boat and before I had forward momentum, she was one hundred feet away. My arms were spent from paddling to her. I paddled double my usual frequency, and she continued to gain distance, so I stopped and slowed my breathing. I thought about nothing but calming myself and returning to aerobic metabolism. Once I was no longer using my reptilian brain,

I realized I didn't need to chase. Only one way back. I kept my boat perpendicular in her expected path and gazed at the ships, oblivious to my concerns, on the horizon. I considered going back to shore, but I decided to make a stand. That's what she would do.

She approached at a modest speed. I expected her to change direction, but she kept her course. I took that as a good sign. Maybe she had reconsidered during her excursion between the Mokes. I expected her to stop paddling as she approached but she deepened her stroke. I tried to rotate parallel before the collision but only made it part way. The nose of her kayak struck mine at the level of my knees. I tried to compensate with my weight and went too far, causing me to tilt to one side and then the other before entering the bay headfirst. I swam to reach my paddle and then righted the craft. Before I sat upright again, I realized she would be in the shower by the time I reached her home. I took my time paddling back to my place.

A young Hawai'ian was surf casting near my landing spot. "Dude, that was just wrong. She didn't even turn around."

"Yeah. Take my advice. Don't piss off a woman in a kayak."

After storing the craft, I showered and put on shorts, T-shirt, and my walking sandals. I had no intention of crossing an ocean and then walking away. Good or bad, I planned to resolve our conflict that day. With no other plans for the day, I walked to the business district of Kailua and found a hair place, a storefront shop with three chairs and a 1970s theme. The walls sported album covers for the Stones, Bee Gees, Queen, Fleetwood Mac, and Chicago. I was looking shaggy and figured a fresh cut might help my chances. A cute blonde, late thirties, marathon runner body, shot me a bright smile. "Have a seat. I'll be ready for you in five. I'm Marie."

"Sam."

I sat in the other barber chair and texted Billy. All was well with her and Floyd. I agreed to fund more cat toys and a nail clipper.

"What can I do for you, Red?"

"I need a make-up-with-your-girlfriend trim. Something that shows remorse but confidence simultaneously. Can you do that?"

"Absolutely not."

"Yeah. I figured. Just a trim then."

She swung a barber's cape over my front and tightened the neck. "Women discuss their relationships all day long in this chair. Drinking, cheating, miscommunication, and not being there are the big ones."

"Okay, Alex, I'll take miscommunication for four hundred."

"Funny. You want to tell me what happened?"

I gave her the elevator ride version. "I'm at fault here but I didn't do what she thinks I did."

"Just spill it. Nothing to lose, right?" She spritzed my hair with water.

I recalled the kayak incident. "She might answer her door with a frying pan in hand."

"You know, this story sounds familiar. What's her name?"

"Kayla."

"Oh, Lord. I've heard this whole story. From the other side. My partner cuts her."

"Okay. So, I need something to disarm her, so she'll at least let me in to talk."

"She cut hair before, right?"

"Yeah. That's how she met her husband," I said.

"Right. Right. She told us the story of how they met."

Marie finished cutting and stepped to the back for a minute. She emerged with a worn cape and an old pair of scissors. "Show up with these. Very romantic."

"You sure?"

"No. You have any better ideas?"

I left with my barber supplies and newfound confidence. The convenience store up the street sold water and energy bars. I recalled Michael offering me one at the pillbox. The kid with his belongings on his back offering the multimillionaire food. I worked my way back to Kalaheo Avenue and walked the fifteen blocks to Kailuana Place. An Uber was the intelligent means of travel, but I wanted to walk even if it meant showing up sweating.

The ocean side of Kalaheo was upscale compared to the other side and the accommodations grew tonier as you approached the coast. I made a show of my barber supplies and knocked on Kayla's door. She opened it, one hand resting on her comely hip, no expression. "You don't take a hint, do you?"

"I can return every day for six months for this haircut."

She turned and left the door open.

"Let's get this over with. You don't need a haircut. And you aren't half the man Gordy was."

That was a kick in the teeth, but I stuck my chin right out for that one. We sat at the kitchen counter both facing the sink. No intertwining of any body parts. I recalled the conversations and intimate moments we shared.

"Kayla, I'm offering an unconditional apology for anything and everything I did to hurt you. But I did not commit the transgressions you think I have."

"Still listening."

"Can I confirm you were in New Orleans recently and you observed a female coworker and friend assist me into my home in a drunken state?"

"Yes. Kathy, who is pregnant with your child."

I hung my head. Her knowledge of Kathy's name suggested more observation happened than that night. I had nothing to hide. It was the lack of trust that burned like a hot poker.

"That is false. Kathy is a friend. I let her into my life along with a bunch of other people and a scruffy cat."

"Then what is your interest in attending her ultrasound?"

"Let me ask you this. If your good friend was

pregnant and alone, wouldn't you tag along for encouragement?"

"Yes, but I am a woman."

"Fair enough. Maybe I crossed a line with her. We were never intimate."

"Didn't she stay at your place?"

"She was drunk at breakfast one day and she slept at my place. I slept on the couch. I didn't want her driving."

She turned toward me with the eye your mom gives you when you are trying to explain your way out of something stupid.

"You people drink at breakfast?"

"We are day-sleepers. Breakfast is dinner."

"So, you are drinking again."

I explained the events that lead to my lapse. My friendship with Ray, the tomb, his death, my part in Scooter's death, my testimony, and the possible loss of my medical license. She listened, looking more at the stainless-steel kitchen appliances than me.

"Tremendous change has happened in a short time and that pleases me. You saw a snapshot on a terrible day. I fell, but I'm standing again. Even Rachel believes I'm a different person."

She turned her stool toward me. "Rachel." Dead face.

"My wife."

"You never called her by name. Always soon-to-be ex-wife."

"Okay. Anyway, we dined together when I was in Columbia. She says I'm not the same person."

"Did you sleep with her?" Irish accent creeped in.

Strange question coming from the person swimming naked with a married guy. Rachel, at least, is my wife. I did not enjoy the interrogation, but I stayed the course. "Are you asking if we had sex? No."

"Why are you splitting hairs?"

"She climbed into bed with me in the middle of the night. She just wanted someone to hold."

"Does she still want a divorce? Doesn't seem so."

"That did not come up in conversation."

"And you?"

Despite being caught off guard by my interactions with Rachel, my intentions remained the same. "I'm not moving back to Columbia and I want you in my life." I tired of being on the defensive and I wanted to understand the origin of our schism without being confrontational. "Can I ask what prompted you to come to New Orleans?"

"Stan said you are a con man and he had the pictures to prove it. He said only a true con man could fool him. I had to see for myself."

"Stan was spying on me." Statement not question.

She stepped around to a cabinet and removed a Manila folder. Never get on the wrong side of a billionaire. I found multiple studio quality eight-by-ten color photos of Billy hugging me, pecking me on the cheek, dancing around her car, and many shots of me with Kathy, the best being the one at my door with my hand on her boob. Also included were pictures of Heidi, Deb, and me. I'm sure his investigators learned of their sexual proclivity and I was off the hook with them.

"So, I saw for myself, turned around, and came home."

"I understand how you could arrive at a wrong conclusion when you knew only part of the story. I'm not upset about that. Just asking you to have faith in me." She fixed on the refrigerator. I didn't want to push. "Look," I said. "This has been a drink from a fire hose. I'm going to take a shower. Why don't you digest this for a while? I'm staying with Otto."

44

I TOOK AN UBER to Kalapawai and ate a light meal of smoked salmon bruschetta. I had no idea if or when Kayla would come to continue our conversation. No waiting by the mailbox or holding my breath. I wandered the shops around the restaurant knowing I needed nothing they offered. The heat of the day had passed, so I walked the uneven roads of the neighborhood back to my place. I found the homes on the town side of Kalaheo to be uninspired and the walk did little to lift my mood.

Kayla sat on the deck with Otto, a slight, balding man with large ears. I joined them at the table. He told us a racy joke and then took his leave. The light was out of her eyes and sleep debt etched her face. In a crowd, I might have missed her. I feared the conversation to come and wondered if I should have come to her front door rather than beach side. I wrestled with the hypothetical parallel universe where I was ignorant of her activities with Steven. I'm no philosopher and I don't care about the argument of whether a lonely tree makes a noise in the woods when it falls. It makes a damn noise, and it matters Kayla had an affair with a married man. I let her start, so we sat for a few minutes.

"Sam, once your heart has turned against someone, reversing that is not easy."

"I get that. After struggling with Rachel's infidelity, I forgave her. Said it to her face and felt much better afterward."

"Everything is muddled now. Everyone I trust tells me to walk away."

"I imagine Stan is the loudest voice."

"That's Stan. You're either with him or against him."

"Would you like to share anything about your life?" I said.

Kayla gazed at the ocean and crossed her arms. For me it came down to this. I could forgive it, but honesty was the prerequisite. "No."

I preferred to keep my encounter with them secret. There was nothing to be ashamed of, but I preferred she revealed their affair without forcing it. I could walk away and not say what I knew but that would be disingenuous. I was all in. "Kayla. Last night I came to talk to you. I saw you and Steven in the water. I didn't spy on you, but I can't unsee that."

"So, you're a drunk, a con man, and a peeping Tom."

"That was unplanned. You and Stan were deliberate in your surveillance of me. And I can explain my actions. Can you?"

She stood, turned her back on me, and walked to the water. "I'm done with you, Sam."

I remained sitting. Way past chasing her. *Done with you.* My wife said the same damn thing. With my wife I was ambivalent. This was a kick in the gut. If I had cheated or fallen repeatedly with my drinking, I would understand and take it as she dished it. I was the poster boy for *Life Isn't Fair.* My undeserved blessings arrived without resistance and now I had to accept this undeserved beat down. I considered what other course I could have taken. Reconciliation seemed possible if I had not raised what amounted to her cheating, not on me, but on her own morality. My accusatory tone didn't help. I could forgive her intimacy with someone else but sleeping with a married man was a character-defining transgression. I hoped she might mend this gash in the fabric of her life. Nobody else could do that for her. Disappointment hung in the air like a dog fart.

I remembered my conversations with Pastor Dan and I found comfort. The heart of my original plan, I knew to be correct, was still in place. The rest of my life continued with a job to be done. It was time to return to my new home town and get on with my reconstruction. I pulled out my phone and found Billy's number.

"Hey, Billy, I wanted to tell you I'll be back tomorrow night."

"Sam. I'm so glad you called. Bunches of stuff to tell you."

"Yeah. Me too."

"Oh. Yeah. What happened with Kayla?"

"Are you familiar with the phrase 'crashed and burned?'"

"Darn. I'm sorry. But, hey. That means you're coming back to stay, right?"

"Yes. Coming home."

I heard stomping and whooping, and she came back on.

"Ya' still with me?" I asked.

"Yes, Sam, that makes me so happy."

"Tell me how the Prince of Delachaise is doing."

"Great. Eats like a tiger. Wants me to play all the time."

"So, I was thinking. My place has three bedrooms and cats are a mystery. I need some help. What do you say about staying at my place? But you gotta clear it with Renée."

More sounds of heavy foot traffic and hollering. "Yes. Yes. I'd love that, and I'll be quiet during the day when you rest."

"Sure. We can talk later. See you soon."

45

BILLY AND I settled into a comfortable routine. I eagerly returned to work. Only Kathy and Wales noticed my absence. Patients with gastroenteritis, toothaches, heart attacks, and broken ankles asked for my help and I gave it well. I knew that the wheels turned slowly at the state medical board and a possible action still hung over me. Most days I let it be. Worry would stop it no more than autumn stops winter. Billy started summer semester at UNO and half of a steamy South Louisiana summer slipped by. Billy, Kathy, and I made dinner together at least weekly.

The tincture of time did little to help me get past my break with Kayla. Shrimp did it every time. The memory of cooking shrimp the day I told her I loved her. Cutting the vegetables. Steaming the shrimp. She put her arms around my waist, and everything was right with the world. If I cooked shrimp, peeled it, or ate it, I thought of Kayla. That same cavernous feeling of regret came to me as when I remembered Scooter. Some days I sat at the table and stared into my tea. I knew this would be trouble for me if I didn't act.

This night, Billy wanted shrimp for our dinner with Kathy. Kathy let herself in. As always. Like a bed-and-breakfast. It's true that one should never assume that a woman with a large belly is pregnant. Embarrassment will surely follow if the woman is, well, just fat. There was no mistaking that Kathy was eight months pregnant. If her size didn't give it away, her distinctive pregnancy waddle would. I greeted her at the door and relieved her of a baking pan.

"Chocolate cake," she said.

"That's my girl." I kissed her on the cheek and patted her belly.

Kathy plopped into the couch. "Billy, come quick. She's kicking."

Billy ran to her side and Kathy pointed to where she should put her hand. "This is so cool. When the baby is older, I can tell her she used to kick my hand. I'll be Aunt Billy."

Kathy pulled Billy in next to her and hugged. "I'll be her only blood relative, so she can use all the extra relatives she can get. Ha ha. I just thought of this. She'll call the doctor over here Uncle Sam."

"Oh, oh. And Sam you can grow a goatee and get one of those red, white, and blue hats. Ha," Billy said. "Uncle Saaam."

"Are you two enjoying yourselves over there?"

They looked at each other and laughed. Both Billy and Kathy needed family. So did I. Having them in my life brought joy, but I craved the intimacy that came with the relationship between a man and a woman. Not just the sex. Although that was part of it. I needed someone to hold my hand walking to a restaurant. Someone to celebrate the triumphs and commiserate in the failures of life. Someone who will share an ice cream cone, tell me to get a haircut, make dinner with me, laugh at dumb jokes, touch heads with me in a tender moment. I needed to do something to get past Kayla. A kayak was out of the question. I walked almost everywhere. That wasn't helping. A bicycle. Yes. Riding, rather than paddling, would allow me to regain the rhythm of peace I found in Hawai'i.

We enjoyed our evening and after Kathy left and Billy retired to study, Floyd and I sat on the patio and I scratched his belly. Music filtered from two houses over. The Tulane professor. English. Mozart's Jupiter symphony. The same music in my head on my last kayak trip to the Mokes. I closed my eyes, the rhythm of paddling, the water lapping, first light in my face. Peace.

"Sam, are you asleep out here?" Billy asked.

"No, just relaxing. What's up?

"I was in the kitchen and your phone buzzed. Missed call from Rachel."

"Yeah, thanks." I touched the screen and Billy retreated. "Rachel, everything okay?"

"I'm well. Listen, you'll get a letter soon from the state board. My contact there says they have a strong case against you. I'm sorry," Rachel said.

Like hearing of the death of someone with end-stage

cancer, this was not a surprise. Still it stung. Damn it stung. I was with Vanderslice again in the airport hearing it for the first time. I set Floyd on the table and paced the weathered bricks, damp phone against my face. Every negative thought, every urge to kick myself, boiled up. The idea of reliving that night in a hearing made me want to relinquish my license on the spot.

"Sam?"

"I'm here, sorry. I was foolish to hope for anything different. Could you call Stu for me tomorrow and have him get the details?"

"Sure. Sure. I'll do what I can for you on this end. You don't deserve this, Sam."

"Well, that's up for debate and there's no sense in me crying in my non-alcoholic beer now."

"Don't turn in your resignation yet. Let's see what Stu can do. So, besides this, how are you doing?"

"Not too bad. I'm sober and today was marvelous."

"Sam, I've wanted to call you for a month now. Believe it or not, the lawyer can't find the right words. I've talked myself out of calling five times."

"Rachel, I met this old guy kayaking. He said no matter what happens with a marriage you have an eternal connection to each other. Let the words go. I'm here."

"Can I come visit you? I know things didn't work out in Hawai'i and wanted to give you time. I've been feeling this way since you made me dinner when you were here."

My first reaction was to blurt out *yes*. We were

married but in practice we were not. The last time I dove into a relationship I was assaulted in a kayak. Clearly, I wasn't over Kayla if the act of peeling a shrimp raised visceral emotions. Forgiving Rachel came easily once I opened my heart. Letting her back in my life was tangible. There is a difference between saying you enjoy oranges and pulling the peel, separating it, removing those annoying strings, and tasting one. I wasn't sure I was ready to hold her hand again. I stood on the sand with Peter again, looking toward Lanikai, listening to his words and sat with Charlie, the guy who found happiness through his spouse. "Yes. Please do."

"Are you sure? You didn't answer right away."

"Did you want a knee-jerk answer, or did you want honesty?"

"Honesty it is."

"Okay. Show up when it works for you."

46

A WEEK PASSED AND no letter. It wasn't Monday, but I made red beans and rice with andouille sausage anyway. I rode my new bike out River Road to the Huey P. Long Bridge, so it was a fitting dish for the day. Billy raised a small protest, but when given the option to make her own meal, she agreed we could dispense with tradition of red beans and rice on Monday. The quality of my homemade French bread had improved to satisfy Billy's refined culinary standards, and that pleased me. After cleanup we found our usual spots in the living room. Me on the couch reading a Gabriel Allon story, Floyd stretched on my lap, and her in the chair studying for classes. I can't say I was the happiest I had ever been, but I was content and that was good enough. My riding helped already.

"Sam, I want to ask you something."

"Shoot."

"You probably saved like hundreds of people doctoring, right?"

"I never kept track, but it was more than a few."

"So, you made a mistake with the caddie. Doesn't helping all those people, plus the baby and the billionaire, sort of override that?"

I sat up and faced Billy.

"My situation is not one where God or the state medical board keeps score. Like you are winning if you stay one up. I did something a professional should never do."

"You could have just told the detective the caddie didn't ask about his head, right?"

"Right, but that would be a lie and would undermine the story told by the caddie that tossed the baseball."

"So, you risked your career to help him."

"Yes, but don't think of it as me doing him a favor. I did what a human is supposed to do. Consider how screwed up our society is and how different our country would be if people told the damn truth. A good start would be for the jokers in Washington to stop lying to us."

"How do you fix that?"

"I'm not sure you can. You'd need to raise those politicians and bureaucrats over again. All I can do is not contribute to the problem."

We heard a soft knock at the door. Most cats scatter. Floyd jumped to the top of the chair near the door to investigate.

"You gonna get that?" I said. "Your turn."

"Says who?"

"Says your friend and unofficial adopted dad and get the damn door."

I knew who was coming and wanted Billy to answer.

He had called me a few days before. Billy peaked through the window like a backward peeping Tom.

"Some guy with a backpack."

"Ya' gonna make him wait all night?"

She opened the door and stepped back with a curious countenance and half-smile. A well-toned young man with shoulder-length sandy hair entered and approached me arms open.

"Sam, great to see you. This place is awesome."

We shared a bear hug.

"Come on in, Michael. Dump your pack by the kitchen and say hi to Billy."

They shook hands and the full Billy smile appeared. She blushed, sat him at the table, and retrieved a glass of lemonade.

"You didn't tell me your daughter was here. I would have cleaned up better."

"Yeah. No. We were just discussing how to describe our connection. Billy is the second person I met in New Orleans. Like Floyd, the cat, here Billy just came with the house."

"Sam!"

"Okay. We sort of adopted each other. She tries to boss me around though."

"You make a tight team," Michael said.

"So, Michael. What are your plans? I'll be your tour guide if you want," Billy said. She refilled his glass without asking.

"Well, I want to do some fishing, but like most places I go, I work it out when I arrive."

"Billy, I never told you that Michael helped me with a plumbing job in Hawai'i. Long story but I really appreciate your help. The party was a great success."

"I appreciated the money. Easiest I ever made and the lady that paid me, wow. Worth the time just to see her."

"Who's that, Sam?" Billy said.

"Kayla. And that was not a great success."

"Sam, you didn't tell me she was that hot."

"Can we change the subject, please?"

We walked to Sucré for ice cream. I'm more of a soft-serve guy. This is upscale desert fare, but I didn't mind. I had few reasons to spend my money. Billy and I split the Richoculous, an eight-hundred-calorie chocolate-mousse-cake thing. Michael ordered the triple chocolate streusel bar. We shared a street-side table and watched Magazine Street pass. It was late July and the sweltering humidity loitered like cats at the fish store dumpster. We paid it no mind. We planned for Michael to stay in the third bedroom and to come and go as he pleased. Billy would let Michael get the lay of the land before pestering to be his tour guide. We discussed seeing a Baby Cakes baseball game. They used to be the Zephyrs. The long-term locals tell me they can't get used to the new name or the freaky mascot. Billy suggested some tours, but I could tell Michael was not the organized-tour kind of guy. We settled on inviting everyone over for a party.

—

We sent Billy off to bed since she had class the next day and I told Michael of my personal and professional disasters. Telling it was like watching a car, with a failed parking brake, roll down a hill into a lake. Once it started, little could be done, and the result was preordained.

"Did you make it back to Lanikai after the plumbing job?"

"No, she didn't want to wait."

"Crap. Now I regret pulling you away."

"Don't. If she was interested in me, she would have stayed. I had one chance to help you. We had the rest of the day if she wanted."

"You're right. Friends wait for you."

"And it worked out anyway. I walked to the public beach and hooked up with some cool people. I used part of the money I made and got a bunch of food and we cooked out."

Floyd walked around his shoulders and then flopped into Michael's lap expecting a belly rub.

"You made it around the world. Not like you walked, but it's an accomplishment."

"Making a circle was not my goal, but I have awesome stories."

"Any epiphany along the way?"

"Not like a lightbulb. I think cultures are different but what makes people friends is universal."

"Billy and I were talking about telling the truth before you arrived."

"Yeah. Fa' sure. Friends don't lie to each other, and they tell you when your fly is down."

47

THE NEXT MORNING Michael and I hiked toward the city. We walked Camp Street through Uptown, the Garden District, under the Pontchartrain Expressway, past the WWII Museum and Lafayette Square and the Central Business District, then crossed Canal Street into the French Quarter. The Vieux Carré. Camp turns into Chartres in the Quarter and we followed it to Jackson Square. At the center of the square, which graces the front of St. Louis Cathedral, sits the seventh President on his rearing horse on a massive pedestal. Andrew Jackson oversees a space the size of a city block with walkways, iron fences, cropped grass, and mature trees. The triumvirate of spires rising from the cathedral stands watch over the city that care forgot. We crossed the square and then Decatur to the steps to Artillery Park. The elevated view of the Quarter, the Mississippi, the Crescent City Connection, and the West Bank is the best spot to drink it all from the same glass. The West Bank is geographically the South Bank but since it lives on the other side of the river, it will forever be West. To make life more confusing, the bridge to the West Bank heads east. We sat on a bench and observed a freighter slip past.

"This could be Europe," Michael said.

"Yeah, after arriving I wondered if I landed in another country. Then I lived here for a spell, and I was convinced of it."

"You wanna tell me what happened on O'ahu?"

"You mean Kayla."

"Sure."

"Yeah. She said I came to her in a fever." I thought of her note stashed in my underwear drawer. "Man, it was hot. That was a spectacular three months. I might be ninety and not remember my birthday, but I'll still remember her."

I told the story of our precipitous fall and our failure to reconcile. Sometimes retelling a story makes you question your actions. This was the opposite. Though the sting lingered, I remained convinced I did the right thing. I couldn't ignore her behavior.

"What broke it?"

"We all make mistakes. I set a record on that. I wanted to forgive, as I did my wife, but she wouldn't own her failure."

"And your wife?"

"She owned it and regretted it. I love her for that, and I have no clue what will happen with her."

We descended the steps and walked to Café Du Monde where the breakfast crowd had cleared. We ordered OJ and beignets and took a diminutive circular table outside. This is a must for visitors, but I refuse to wait in line for an hour to eat breakfast. So, it was brunch. We discussed the menu for the party. Michael, unfamiliar with low-country cuisine, chose Beaufort Stew, a great meal to make for a group. Some call it Frogmore Stew. I texted that to Billy.

We skirted the square on the slate plaza, passing artists who presented their works on the iron fencing. Scruffy looking folks sat at short tables in front of their work, most of which depicted various scenes around the city. A middle-aged gal with chartreuse hair painted a caricature of a couple who appeared to be newlyweds. We roamed the next block, and turned left on Royal Street, the best street in the quarter. If your interest is bars, booze, and boobs, then Bourbon is the place to be. For me, that's not the Quarter. We browsed the Goorin Brothers hat shop, several opulent antique stores, and then stopped to listen to a five-piece jazz band on the street. High energy there. I dropped a Lincoln in the open saxophone case. We connected to St. Charles, paralleled the trolley tracks to Washington Ave. and took a left to the cemetery. I wanted to show Michael the Buchanan tomb. He admired Ray's craftsmanship as he gave it a contractor's inspection.

"We cremated Ray, and we put him below after the ceremony with a priest."

"You did a fine thing for him. What's this plaque on the side?" He crouched to read it.

This tomb restored by Raymond T. Reyes April 2019
Interred May 2019

"I didn't want to just put him below without an acknowledgement."

"I think he'd be happy with the plaque," Michael said.

We took Washington toward the river to Magazine and then stopped at Breaux Mart for supplies. No surprise to find Billy there. She sifted through fresh ears of corn to find the best specimens. Not a task to delegate.

"Where y'at, men?" Didn't look up.

"Just takin' in the day," I said. "Walking tour of the city."

"Time to get to work then. Michael, we need four pounds of redskin potatoes. Aisle seven."

We spied each other, and I put my hands out.

"Best not to argue," I whispered to him.

"Heard that. Sam, you need to see Rex. He's working on the shrimp and sausage."

We gathered everything along with shrimp boil seasoning and headed for home. Rex put it on the house, over my objection. As the three of us walked toward the back door, I recalled the first time Billy and I rolled carts to my place. A life ago.

"Who's that?" Billy said.

A slender woman, straight black hair hanging to her mid-back, braided and tied with a black bow with pink polka dots, sat at the patio table with her back to us. A roller suitcase rested beside her.

"That's Rachel. My wife."

"Did she call?"

"Last week. I'm happy she is here, and you should be as well."

"Why is she here?"

"She is here as a testament to the power of love and forgiveness. Another undeserved blessing in my life."

Rachel stood when she heard us approach, a hesitant grin. She wore the sexy black slacks she knows I like and pink blouse open to her bra line. Rachel was not a classic beauty like Kayla, but she had handsome features and understood how to accentuate them. I never lost my physical attraction to her. Introductions and hugs all around. I sent the youngsters in with the groceries, certain Billy would entertain Michael. We held a long embrace and kissed on the lips. As we sat, I spied a glass of tea on the table.

"How'd you get something to drink? Door was locked."

"Your neighbor, Max, let me use his bathroom and offered this. Very friendly."

I had misjudged Max. I didn't tell of his disrobed newspaper retrieval. Maybe later. I touched her forearm.

"I'm glad you're here. Good timing. Party tonight with friends and neighbors. We're welcoming Michael."

"I didn't mean to intrude."

"Not at all. This will be fun, and you'll get to meet my friends."

"I took a week off, so here I am. Spur of the moment. I made reservations at the Hilton Riverside."

"Spontaneity is unlike you."

"Yes. I can't say I felt comfortable making last-minute plans, but it worked out. If you can change, I can too."

I took a gulp from her glass. "I'm thrilled you are here. And you are welcome to stay with us."

"Who lives with you?"

"Well, I like to say I unofficially adopted Billy. She's in the second bedroom."

Rachel shifted in her chair and took a drink. "And what about Michael?"

"Michael is here for a short visit. Third bedroom. We connected at the pillbox in Kailua. He's a world traveler."

"How well do you know him?"

"Better than you think. We've had wide-ranging conversations."

"How many bedrooms?"

"The three."

"Maybe I should stay at the hotel."

"I want you to be comfortable, but I also want you to stay. We are still married, right?"

"Yes, Sam." She smiled and looked down.

We sat for a moment. I tugged on her pinky.

"I'm not saying this is bad," she said. "I'm not judging. You are so different now. I need to learn the words to your song."

"Then, let's do that. I'm not going anywhere."

"Love Me Like a Song" was in my head now. She knew that's one of my favorite songs and her reference to it carried meaning. A peace offering. A token. A reopening of her heart to me. I spied Max coming out his back door and walked to the fence.

"Hey, Max. We are having an impromptu gathering tonight and I want you to come."

"You sure?"

"Of course. You're my neighbor. And thanks for taking care of Rachel."

"Your wife, right?"

"Right. I'll explain later. Come at six."

Back at the table Billy and Rachel were at the deep end of the conversational pool. Billy flipped her hand at me, a la JoJo. I took the hint and went inside to start preparations. Michael and I arranged a trash can between us and shucked corn.

"That Billy is a firecracker. I never met anyone like her. And that's saying something."

"Yeah, she's full of life. She's also naïve. You traveled to Europe, Africa, and Asia." I counted on my fingers. "She's been to Texas. Do me a favor and take care with her."

"Sure. I'll be a gentleman."

"I'm not trying to get rid of you already. You can stay awhile. I'm curious about your next stop."

"Not sure. This might it. New Orleans is growing on me and I can find work in a minute."

"Super. I can always use another friend here."

The ladies came in to help with food preparations

and Rex and Renée showed up with tables and a propane outdoor cooker with an eight-gallon pot. Rex made the stew like he could do it blindfolded. Boil water with seasoning, add potatoes and cook, then slice sausage and cook, then corn and cook, and finally the shrimp. The whole process took forty-five minutes. He dumped it in a big bowl, and everybody took as much as they pleased. Wine and Abita beer flowed freely.

Heidi, Deb, Max, and Kathy rounded out the group of ten. Shorts and sandals were the uniform of the evening. I recalled the stiff cookouts at the club in Columbia compared to this group. I didn't need a drink. If I was any more relaxed, I would need a bed. I sat with Max at the far end of a table.

"You know, I could be friendlier to you. I'm sorry."

Max swigged red wine. "Everybody knows I'm an odd duck. I wait for people to come around."

"Tell me about your work."

"You might not approve of what I do."

"Try me."

"I own a gentleman's club in the Quarter."

"Those are high-end establishments, right?"

"Oh, yes. My girls and my patrons are upscale people. Come down some night. I'll give you and Rachel a backstage tour."

"I doubt Rachel would go for that."

He smiled for the first time. "Yeah. You ask a woman to come in the front door, and they say no. She'll come in the business entrance every time. She'll see more tits in the back than from the bar."

"What goes on?"

"Nothing. The girls hang out until their turn to dance. Women with regular jobs love talking to them."

"I'll ask."

"Be ready when you get home. It'll turn her on."

Billy slipped in beside me. "What are you men talking about by yourselves?"

"The stock market," I said.

Max left to fill his wine glass.

"It's settled," Billy said. "She's staying here tonight. I told her we'd make breakfast together in the morning."

"Who's bed?"

"Well, not mine. You're still married, right?"

"Oh, yeah. Right. Thanks for the heads up. Listen, I like Michael. He's a gem. Problem is, he'll be gone in a few days. I don't want you to go overboard. None of my business, really."

"Gotcha."

"Rachel is lovely. Are you getting back together?"

"Billy, you think everyone is lovely."

"You didn't answer my question."

"I would like that, but I need to hold our union like a baby bird. Don't want to hurt her again."

"I thought she's the one that hurt you."

I touched her knee. "Took me a while to get this. She made one deep cut. After I made a thousand paper cuts. I forgot this for a time, but she is the eternal love of my life. The person I promised to love, honor, cherish. I want to mend our wounds, but I must take care."

I observed the women gravitate to Rachel. Who

knows what information they extracted from her? Billy and Michael spent most of the evening in animated conversation. I think that's the only kind Billy has. I saw Kathy in serious conversation with Deb. When they broke, I stole time with Kathy, whose pregnancy could not be hidden from a blind man.

"You are avoiding me." I poked her protruding navel.

"Am not." Coy smile.

"Come on. We would have jawed about twelve things by now."

"Okay. I didn't want your wife to get the wrong idea. See how it turned out the last time with one of your women."

"Ha. My women. That's rich. Wait 'til you meet the one I keep in Arkansas."

"So, where is this headed?"

"I think this party will end near eleven or until the police arrive."

"Cute. With Rachel."

This was a conversation, so we sat.

"I miss our talks in the lounge."

"Yes, I miss our time together too. And you are avoiding my question."

"She knows that Kayla is out of the picture now and said she wanted to give me time."

"How do you measure that?"

"That is a mystery. I could hang on to my romantic fancy of Kayla's return until my teeth fall out. Or I could awaken and return to the person I have loved.

Loved more than my parents. The one I love more than myself."

"That's touching, Sam. You can be sweet when you want to. Does she want to move here?"

"Listen, you spent more time talking to her today. Yeah, and what info did you weasel out of her about me? I saw you two and I can tell when women are sharing secrets. The leaning in and the demure smiles."

"Oh, that. Never tell. Is she sleeping with you tonight?"

"I hope so. It's been a long time. So, what were you and Deb discussing?"

"I'm going lesbian and I wanted pointers."

"Ha. Let me know how that goes."

"No. Just helping me with a will. I'll have an heir to my vast fortune soon."

At eleven, Rachel said she could fight sleep no longer and headed to bed. The folks that needed to be at work the next day left soon after, leaving Kathy, Billy, Michael, and me. Billy was fading but wanted to hang with Michael. Eventually they slipped inside, and I had no interest in what happened after that.

"Tell me about your ultrasound."

"Baby looks good. Right on schedule for size. It's a girl."

"Are you happy?"

"Sure, either way."

"Money will be tight now that you have taken leave. I want to help you."

She crossed her lower leg over mine. "Thanks, but don't feel responsible for me."

"What I feel is friendship toward you. I'll give your baby an early birthday present. Any name ideas yet?"

"Lilly. She will be my little flower."

"Perfect. I'd offer you a bed, but the inn is full tonight."

"No worries. Tell me how it goes with Rachel." She gave me a tight hug, like you do when you won't see someone for a long time. "I love you, Sam."

I stripped and slipped into bed facing my back to her, the way we usually slept. She always wore pj's. She brought her hand on my chest and pulled towards me. No pj's. Her compact breasts felt warm and soft against my back. Her breathing slowed, and she drifted off. I soon joined her.

48

MY INTERNAL CLOCK rang six a.m. and faint light filtering around the blinds confirmed that. I turned toward Rachel and found her awake with a half-smile. No words. We kissed for a time and then made love with tenderness and passion long forgotten. Familiar but at the same time new, bringing a closeness that evaded us for years. We took a long shower taking turns washing each other. We had not done this in years. Shame on me. We drank tea, read the paper, and chatted about normal stuff like her work and my life in New Orleans. A door creaked. Rachel spied the edge of Billy's robe when she skulked between the two bedrooms. Not our kids. Not our business. In time we would discuss our failure, but I was content to enjoy her company.

The kids emerged by eight and tried to act naturally but tattoos on their necks would be no less obvious than their rubbing elbows and stolen smiles. Good for them. I did warn them. I hoped he had protection. I didn't want to look after another pregnant person I did not impregnate.

We enjoyed omelets with sausage, cheese, and peppers. Kids cleaned, and Rachel and I took another cup of tea on the patio. I enjoyed being outside before the heat kicked in, especially when a breeze stirred the aroma of confederate jasmine growing on the iron fence.

I sensed being inside one of those times when you look back and realize what a momentous decision you made. Where to go to college, what job to take, who to marry, what city to live in, what house to buy. If I committed to make our marriage work, I would be committing to returning to Columbia. I did not expect Rachel to leave her law practice and come to an unfamiliar city, particularly when I might not be employed. Forgiveness was not the issue. Was I ready to recommit to our marriage and could I return to Columbia and not figuratively grow a beard again?

"You're beautiful. Except a few eye lines I could be walking you down the aisle. You lost weight."

"I guess so. There're a few pieces of clothing too loose on me. I never weigh myself. You look pretty good yourself. Your belly is flat, and you've got muscles you never had."

"Kayaking. So, back to you. Are you trying to lose weight?"

"No."

"Well, I don't want to see you lose any more, okay? When did you see Christine last?"

"I love Christine but hate going to her office. Probably eighteen months ago."

"Please humor me and make an appointment."

"Okay. What should we do today?" she said.

"Let's take a tour of Uptown."

We laced walking shoes and hiked Foucher toward the trolley stop at St. Charles. We passed Touro on the opposite side I usually walked. I thought of Ray because I walked Foucher on the way home from his house or AA. We traveled through a business section of Uptown. I reassured Rachel the best views of my neighborhood lived on St. Charles.

"I haven't been hiding anything from you, but I want to tell you some things. It will help you to understand the new Sam."

"Sure."

I slipped my arm in and we locked elbows. "I saved this guy named Ray. He was a drunk like me and we made an unlikely partnership. We attended AA together, and he restored the Buchanan tomb in a local cemetery. I'll take you there. Anyway, Ray died. He and I discussed things I never thought to share with those jokers I used to call friends at home. Or with you. We shared an unconventional friendship. Let's say our positions on the social ladder spanned a few rungs. It made no matter. I still miss him and find myself thinking of something I should tell him the next time we talk."

"I'm sorry you lost your friend."

"In Hawai'i, a pastor told me I should open my heart and search for God's presence in my work. Ray was my first patient. The loss is there, but I also feel this sense of wonder for having known him. Old Sam looked past it all."

"You never wanted to share work stuff with me."

We sat on a bench next to Touro.

"Right. I thought I was shielding you from the unpleasantness. I was just shielding you from me."

She rubbed the back of my hand and leaned into me.

"Do you remember our trip to O'ahu when we first were married?" I said.

"Always. Such a wonderful trip."

"Take me on the kayak trip we made."

"Let's see. Our kayaks were bright orange. There were waves, and I was nervous about getting on mine without flipping. You held it for me. Then you flipped trying to get on yours. I tried not to laugh but couldn't stop."

"I'm better at it now." We touched heads. *Back in the truck with my dad thinking of the girl that kissed me on the cheek. Total body rush.*

"We paddled through the shallow water ahead of those islands. I've never seen that color again. Like the light came from inside the water. Those mountains against the sea and the sky. The green, the aquamarine, the blue. A few fluffy clouds. Anything was possible. We were so full of life then."

"Do you think we can recapture that?" I said.

"I'd like to try."

"Me too." I turned toward her. "I want to say this again. It's important you hear it." I turned and held her gaze. "I'm sorry for being a selfish drunk and an absent husband."

She took both my hands in hers, eyes full of tears. "And I'm sorry for cheating and for being a distant bitch."

We both laughed and held a tight hug.

"Eyes looking forward now, okay?" I said.

"Yes. Yes."

We crossed the trolley tracks on St. Charles and stood on the side headed toward the park next to a tall woman in a floral dress and with a blank face and an energetic boy in a dinosaur T-shirt. I crouched to his level.

"Are you four?" I held up four fingers. He nodded, then gave me a wide smile. "Have you ever seen a dinosaur?"

"Dinosaurs not real."

"But they used to be. Long, long time ago."

"Uh, uhhh." He shook his head, devious smile.

"Oh, sure. I wouldn't say it if it wasn't so." I retrieved my phone from my pocket and searched *T-Rex bones pictures*. "See those are real bones." He held one side of the phone and his mouth opened wide and he looked up to his mom with a beaming face. His mom mouthed *thank you* and smiled.

Electric lines ran above the tracks and live oaks reached over St. Charles. A hunter green car arrived with a round light below the tall white number 968 on the curved front. Red doors and windows provided accent. The double doors opened, and a step dropped.

I greeted the driver, used my Jazzy Pass and dropped five quarters for Rachel's fare. We sat in a weathered wooden seat, held hands, and listened to the rhythmic thumping of the motor. Like someone trapped under the train trying to get out. Tourists, students, workers, and locals entered and exited at the various stops along the way. I'm sure I did, once or twice, but I could not recall using public transportation before moving to New Orleans. I liked the trolley. When I used it, I traveled at my leisure. I suppose a commute by trolley was tiresome. I liked the people-watching best. Most people I encountered seemed happy and easy to engage in conversation. I liked to ask folks about their jobs. I could tell people coming and going from work. The trip was routine, and they paid little attention to the passing scene. I liked to ask people if they got that raise at work yet. Often, I received a roll of the eyes, a smile, and a reference to something like pigs flying. Then we talked until one of us made their stop. We passed the Columns Hotel, restaurants, apartments, mansions of varying architecture, the Academy of the Sacred Heart, Temple Sinai, Loyola, and we stopped at Tulane. The imposing white limestone building served as the face of Tulane. Rachel and I crossed St. Charles to Audubon Park.

"How are things at work?" I said.

"We seem to be past the unpleasantness associated with the affair and Preston's suicide. For a time, I considered getting out. I'm glad I stuck with it."

"Do you think *you* are past it?"

"On my way. What you said to me in Columbia helped me. I've been meditating and walking. You fill my thoughts when I walk. And my heart."

We walked a path on the outskirts of the open space. We shared it with dog walkers, bicyclists, and joggers. "You know, I'll never ask you to move here. I'll work until my commitment ends or the hospital kicks me out. Also, I want to get Kathy through her pregnancy and help her out when the baby comes. I'm more involved here than is appropriate. Just figuring out this new life as I go."

"I understand. Not jealous. So, what will you do if you lose your license?"

"Besides drive you mad?"

"Yes. That's a given."

"If this happened before I got my act together, it might have messed me up. Now, I'll be okay. I'll find something to keep me busy. I'll miss it. Can't say I won't." We crossed the park to Magazine Street. I put my hand on her shoulder. "Okay, we have a big decision to make," I said, serious face.

"Sam, I am in no rush."

"Yeah, no. I mean getting home."

"Sure." A relaxed laugh, absent from our lives for years. "What are the options?"

"Walk Magazine. Thirty blocks."

"It must be eighty degrees. Next option," she said.

"Walk back to the trolley and take it home."

"Is there a third?"

"Ah, yeah. Uber to Dat Dog and eat lunch."

"Door number three, Monty."

We sat at the bar and ordered custom dogs and sweet tea. I told the bartender "guy walks into a bar" jokes and he told me a few I did not know.

"We should take a vacation," she said. "Not just a trip to the coast. Something big. Two or three weeks."

"Now there's an idea. Where to?"

"I've always wanted to go to Australia and New Zealand," she said.

"Okay. We're going first class. Do we have any money left?"

"Yes, dear."

49

RACHEL RETURNED HOME after a week and we made loose plans for me to return to Columbia on my timetable. Michael headed east for new adventures with a nebulous promise to reconnect in the fall.

I was not obsessed with biking, contrary to Billy's assessment, but daily rides of twenty to twenty-five miles became part of my routine. My aerobic fitness was so good I felt like I could be that Army guy running on the pillbox trail in Kailua. On a Monday in late August, I biked, taking the ferry across the river, to the West Bank to a gated community in Algiers. English Turn. It sits at a bend in the river where, more than three hundred years ago, Bienville tricked the English Navy into retreat. He told one of the supreme lies of North American history. I arrived home mid-morning to find texts and missed calls from Kathy.

> SOB today. Prob jst huge baby. Going to ER
> Here doing tests
> Getting worried. Whr r u

I sprinted on my bike and left it inside the ambulance doors. Two nurses were crying by the elevator. Wales saw me from the far side of the department and came to me. He sat me on a bench outside Room 1.

"She came in short of breath. Heart rate 140s. O2 sat eighty-five. Stat echo showed right heart strain."

A pulmonary embolism until proven otherwise.

"Right after the echo her pressure dropped to eighty, and we sent her up for a C-section. That was forty-five minutes ago. I'll go with you to the OR."

We took the back steps up to pre-op. More nurses crying. Wales and I found one of the anesthesiologists. He was present for the delivery. He was unaware of my emotional attachment to Kathy and his report was dry and clinical.

"We lost mother's pulse as the OB made the cut. I did chest compressions and he got the baby out. Floppy at first but improved after five minutes. We worked on mom for thirty minutes. No response. Pronounced dead ten minutes ago."

I walked to the hallway and collapsed into a chair. Grief gripped my breath and I held my face in my hands. My body shook, the grip released, and then it echoed from the tile floor and plaster walls . . . A wail I didn't think could come out of me. Wales sat next to me and patted my back. He waited until I looked up, face mottled, eyes swollen.

"Come with me to my office. I need to tell you something."

We entered the ER to find the news had beat us.

The staff huddled to console each other. We slipped past to his office and sat in arm chairs on the same side of his desk.

"Listen. I was with her as they wheeled her to the OR. In the elevator she lifted her oxygen mask with one hand and grabbed my arm with the other. Hard, like she might fall if she let go. My God, the look of determination on her face. She could tell it was bad. She made me promise, twice, to tell you this: 'Tell Sam I love him, and I want him to adopt Lilly. Tell him to make a new life in Columbia with his wife.'"

I sat stone-faced trying to reconcile my expectations and premature conclusions with the events of that dismal day. "Thank you for being with her. I'm glad I wasn't working but I wish I would have been there for her."

"We both look chance square in the eye every day we work," Wales said.

"Yeah, I'm getting better about not second-guessing myself."

"I'm sorry for your loss. Stay here as long as you want."

"Thanks. I need to go check on my new daughter."

"Is she your biological child? People will ask, and I want to set them straight."

"No. But I will treat her that way."

———

I rode the elevator to the OB floor. I remembered our conversation sitting in the hall waiting for Kathy's first ultrasound. And I thought that was a crappy day. I lost count of the families I sat with to deliver *the* news. A girl struck by a car, a father who choked on taffy, a man shot in the head in his office. The question was always why. Why him? Why now? As Pastor Dan said to me, these are questions for the ages. Just as before, I had no answer. I left the elevator and stood near the rockers in the hallway. I could see Kathy with her hands across her belly, crooked smile. Tears filled my eyes again. She was a blessing in my life from the day she stood in the doorway, dirty scrubs, a knee bent, one white clog resting on the toe, asking me to come save a man's life. I would remember her that way. She was the person who always swerved to miss the dog in the road.

Laura, the ultrasound tech, came up beside me and locked her arm with mine. "Gossip is you are adopting this baby."

"Word travels fast."

"Yes. Come with me. I want to introduce you to your daughter. This is a sad and difficult day, but we can rejoice in this new life."

I donned a gown, washed hands, and entered the nursery, a serene place with pastel paint populated by dozing babies in clear bassinets. The sun illuminated a rocker in the corner and a nurse directed me to sit. A nurse, Sarah, placed Lilly in the crook of my arm and she wriggled and sighed. Peace. I realized that instead of relaxing in the doctor's lounge I should have been coming to the nursery. I rested my head back and rocked with my foot. Nothing else in the universe mattered at that moment. We belonged to each other. Thirty minutes passed in a breath and I awakened to her cry.

"I realize this has been a day, but you two are a postcard for happiness." Sarah handed me a bottle of formula and Lilly took hold. "Before discharge, we'll need a name. No rush."

"I'm not sure how this works with an adoption. I need to talk to a lawyer. Lilly Katherine Buchanan."

After the feeding, I placed Lilly in her bassinet. I needed to talk to Rachel. The rockers in the wide hallway sat empty, so I took one and called. Her secretary answered and put me through to her office.

"Hi you. How is your day going?"

"Are you alone?"

"No. Working with Ben on a case. What's wrong?" She asked him for a minute alone. "I'm scared now. What happened?"

"Kathy died in childbirth."

"Oh, Sam. I am so sorry. And the baby?"

"Doing well. Lilly Katherine is seven pounds and has a healthy appetite. Just fed her in the nursery."

"Thank God for that. How are you?"

"I need you now more than ever."

"Of course. I'm on the next plane."

"One more thing."

"Okay."

"Kathy's last words were that she wanted us to adopt Lilly. I want to come home now, but we come as a pair."

"On my way."

I rocked, amnestic to time, knowing I would not need

to look back to fathom the events of the day. Thoughts of Lilly filled my mind. Not the pedestrian chores of raising a child but the high-altitude view of our lives. I saw her singing, laughing, making friends, going to school, learning to ride a bike, learning to win and to lose. This collision of hope and despair drained my energy. If I sat much longer, I might fall asleep again.

When I walked through the ER, the day charge approached.

"Were you aware Kathy had no living family?"

"Yes."

"She listed you and a Deb Tarka as her emergency contacts. Can I give you this?"

She handed me her purse. I told her the name of the funeral home and gave her my number. The funeral home was in my favorites list. What the hell.

50

WHEN I ARRIVED home my neighbor, Deb, was getting out of her car. The family lawyer. She hugged me, and we walked to the house.

"Sam, I am so sorry. Kathy said you were the best person she ever knew."

Billy stood in the doorway to the patio and read our faces. "Sam, what's happening?"

We went inside, and I sat next to her on the couch. She was crying but didn't understand why yet. I explained and held her. My Billy, lost in the grief over her friend, the woman she let into her heart, the one that gave her a measure of having something of a mother again. Watching her suffer was almost as painful as losing Kathy. She calmed enough to sit back on the couch, and I poured lemonade for us.

"Billy, this is a terrible thing, but I want you to take a few breaths now. On the worst day of my life, I am filled with joy. Lilly Katherine was born today, and she will be my daughter." Saying those words made me consider the momentous changes ahead of me.

One year before, my attention to my own life proved to be inadequate at best. The changes I made were a piss in the ocean compared to our adventures to come with Lilly.

More tears and nodding of her head. We moved to the kitchen table.

"At the party, Kathy made a time to meet with me at my office," Deb said. She pulled a file from her briefcase and placed it before me. "She harbored a fear that, if she died, Lilly would be alone in the world. Kathy wants Lilly raised by a good person. I don't think she expected to die so soon but her foresight was prescient." She spread four documents across the distressed wooden table. "This first document grants you power of attorney for healthcare for both her and Lilly. The next, power of attorney for financial matters." She lifted a single page and held it between two fingers. "This is an affidavit from the biological father renouncing any claim for custody. Very important. Finally, you, through the adoption, are the beneficiary in her will, and you are granted custody of Lilly in the event of Kathy's death."

"Well, this confirms in writing her last words in the ER."

"Normally this is a lengthy and difficult process. What she set in motion a few weeks ago will make this a breeze. I'll submit the paperwork tomorrow if you choose to proceed."

"Yes. The only question will be if it is only me or

my wife and me making the adoption. Rachel arrives tonight, and we'll discuss it."

"Sure. And this." She handed me a sealed envelope with my name lettered in Kathy's hand. "This is to be opened in the event of her death. Also, she wants to be cremated and have her ashes spread in the Mississippi." Deb left, and I promised to call the next day.

I left the papers on the table. I stood behind Billy and put my hands on her shoulders. "Billy. I know this is hard. We are both going to miss her. We will mourn her and then we will carry on."

"Sam, this hurts so much. Same as when I lost my mom." Floyd jumped on the table and she pulled him close.

"I know, baby. All we can do is cherish our time with her and care for Lilly. Come on. I want you to meet her."

I put Kathy's keys in my pocket and we walked to Touro fingers mingled, my mind racing with thoughts of preparations for Lilly. Renée never had kids, so she was no help. I called my landlord.

"Maria, Sam here. Hey, do you have kids?"

"Three of them. I'll loan you one."

"Thanks, no. Too much to explain now, but I'm wondering if you stored baby furniture."

"We got the whole ensemble. Rob can deliver it tomorrow. He's been after me to get rid of it."

"Super. Ask him to text me. Thanks."

Billy and I took the front entrance to get to the nursery. I couldn't endure any more encounters in the

ER that day. Lilly slept as we viewed her through the glass. Perfect round head with wispy red hair. Nurses waved us in so Billy could inspect close-up. She touched the back of a finger to Lilly's cheek like she might break her with too much pressure. I wondered if she ever held a baby. We stayed a short time and then found the rockers in the hallway.

Billy stared at the atrium windows and wept. The rails spoke a soft rhythm and she gripped my hand. Tight. "I'm missing Kathy so bad, but I can't stop thinking about my mom too. One is bad enough. Now it seems like my mom has been gone just a week."

I couldn't help but feel anything but inadequate. An emotional midget awakening from alcoholic stupor barely able to say *there, there* without stuttering. "If it's any consolation, I'm as lost as you. I may look okay on the outside but I'm not." I turned in my seat to make eye contact. "Listen, when you walk with someone in a damp, murky tunnel, you hold hands. I'll hold yours and you hold mine."

"Okay," she said. "Please don't let go."

"Promise. We'll find the light." We touched heads unleashing emotion, tumbling shelves in my head. I thought of my time on the beach with Kayla, limping out of my addiction. Touching heads, giving in, knowing that alone I was lost.

We dried our eyes on our sleeves and rocked in unison. I felt Kathy's presence. His too. That feeling of love, forgiveness, and acceptance. *I held my breath.*

Underwater at the Mokes. The motion of the water.
Pastor Dan at my side.

"It's a slim slice," I said.

"What."

"Our time here. Our time together."

"New Orleans?"

"Earth."

She nodded. "Sure."

———

We found Kathy's car in the ER patient lot. She was scared if she parked there. We stood facing each other, the heat of the day radiating from the steel and the pavement.

"Listen, we can sit around, or we can take our mind off it and get something done. We'll have a baby at home soon and there's lots to do." I looked up at the hospital. "Lilly has no thoughts about this. The events of the day have not altered her primal needs and desires."

She nodded, and I tossed her the keys. Billy drove to St. Charles, and we crossed the tracks and turned left. Toward the park.

"I like driving an SUV," she said.

I flipped through the glove box and found the title and registration. She owned it outright.

"Lilly's now. You have your own car." I nudged her shoulder. "I'll need it to cart Lilly over creation and back."

We pulled to the curb in front of Kathy's place. She owned a two-bedroom shotgun out past the park in Carrollton on Short Street, which meant that Lilly and I owned it now. The name of the street is apt because it runs a block and a half long from the far end of St. Charles to the river. A modest front yard full of blooming annuals spread before a porch with a traditional two-seat swing hung from the ceiling. The paint was yellow with powder-blue shutters.

"Let's walk before we go in."

We strolled to the end of the street, stood shoulders touching, and looked across the tracks to the Mississippi. Two freighters rested on the opposite side of the river. A tug churned its way west. I thought of Kathy wanting her ashes spread in the swift current. The temperature was cooler by the river and pleasant breeze came off the water.

"Rachel comes tonight and will stay with us until the adoption is underway and then we go to Columbia."

"Okay. I'm scared, though."

"I promised not to let go. I won't. Rachel and I still need to mend, and Lilly just tossed a big wrench in the works."

"Strong baby."

"You said it, darling. I want you with us if you want that too. Just give me some time with Rachel. I'm sure her head is about to explode. She does very little without a plan. And this is…"

"Definitely unplanned."

We walked back, and I fumbled with keys at the

weathered blue door. It opened into a cozy parlor, ahead of two bedrooms along a slender hallway that opened to a kitchen and dining area in the rear. A home destined to be full of life, now silent. On a distressed pie crust table in the parlor sat an array of pictures. One with people I assumed to be her parents, several of her first child, and one Heidi took of us at the cookout. I touched the edge of the frame. "Picture in a Frame" in my head now. *I love you, baby, and always will.* That harmony kills me.

I put my arm around her shoulder. "In a situation like this people often say everything happens for a reason. That's crap. Sometimes events get past us. Disrupt our lives. No grand plan. It just happens and you take it in. You deal with it. Best you can. You know this because you lived it once. Right?"

"Right."

"You are Billy strong and we'll get through this together. I love you."

"You too, Sam."

We entered the kitchen and a calico cat jumped from the refrigerator, scaring the crap out of Billy. I forgot about the cat. She rolled at our feet and we scratched her head. Billy found a cat carrier, and we corralled Tuesday, the cat.

"Another orphan," Billy said.

"I guess I have two cats now."

"What's Rachel going to say?"

"Well, I've learned that cats are independent creatures who don't make plans."

"Say no more," Billy said.

We dumped milk in the sink, tossed perishables, emptied the cat box, and took out the trash. Like fixers for the mob. Mr. Winston Wolfe. In the second bedroom we found a bassinet and a boat load of baby supplies. *That's my girl, organized.* Three trips to fill the back of the SUV. I returned to use the bathroom. A midnight blue terry-cloth robe hung from the door. I held it to my face and breathed the hint of her perfume. *How I loved her.* I grabbed the picture of us on the way out.

"Now we are off to the vet."

"For what?"

"Spay. This is a female."

"How can you tell? You didn't even look."

"I couldn't tell even if I did. All calico cats are female."

"Really."

"Really. And you understand what happens when males and females live in the same house."

"Sam." She whacked me across the chest with the back of her hand, blushing. *What is it with women whacking me in the chest?*

"A baby is trouble enough. I don't need kittens. You want kittens?"

"No."

We stopped at our place and picked up protesting Floyd to drop them both at the vet for fixing. We ran to Domilise's for food, near Tchoupitoulas, by the river. If it were a bed, it would look like two German

Shepherds had been playing on it. The front door is cut into the corner of the building and a hand-painted wooden sign hangs next to it. You don't find it by accident. Inside is no more inviting, but they make the best po'boys in Uptown, maybe the city. Three shrimps, and we were out the door. I figured Rachel would be hungry when she arrived. We unloaded the SUV and ate our sandwiches at the kitchen table.

"Sam, do you believe there is a heaven?"

"Sure. And you?"

"I do, but I can't tell you why."

"If it helps, I can't either."

Billy picked at her sandwich and studied her plate.

"What do you think it's like?" she said.

"Let me ask you this. When you fell for Michael, did you have an unusual feeling?"

She looked at me and smiled. "Oh, Lord. Have you had it too?"

"Yes. With Kayla and recently with Rachel."

"I can't describe it. Warm and peaceful. I felt so happy."

"Right. I think that's what heaven is like. Unconditional love," I said.

"Is Kathy with my mom?"

I held her hand and smiled. "No question. And they are smiling."

I took Kathy's letter to my bedroom. I made the bed since Rachel was coming and reclined with my head on a folded pillow. I found a single folded sheet.

The paper they use for wedding invitations. She wrote it in elegant cursive.

> Dear Sam,
>
> I planned to revise this letter after Lilly arrived, so if you are reading this I'm gone, and she and I never met. I pray she is alive with you. My wish is for you, and Rachel hopefully, to raise Lilly as your own. You are the best person I know and I'm certain she will enjoy a wonderful life with you. I love you, Sam. My heart was always yours. You became a part of me. The best you can say about someone. When Lilly is playing, and she looks over her shoulder at you with a crooked grin, I hope you'll think of me.
>
> Eternal Love,
> Kathy

I sat on the edge of the bed and put my face in my hands. There was no place to put this pain. In time, I would make room for it. In my narrow moment, I'll never understand it. Did the events and decisions that led to our friendship carry me to Lilly? Stan, Kayla, Michael, Steven, Dan, Billy, and Kathy. Was there a complex celestial plan? I don't believe so. Our lives are not a pre-planned chess game with a certain destiny. We find ourselves in circumstances throughout our lives that require us either to choose to engage or step away. To open our eyes and our hearts or to walk past and miss both the triumphs and the tragedies of life. I chose to open my heart at every turn since I left Carolina, and Lilly was no different.

A quiet knock at the door. I opened it and we embraced. Rachel held me tight. "You are all I need right now," I said.

We sat on the bed and she put her arm around my shoulder.

"I love you. I'm sorry I've complicated our lives with this," I said.

"And I love you. Don't be sorry. Together. Together we can do this."

"We have so much to talk about." I handed Rachel the letter and she read it.

"Yes," Rachel said.

"What?"

"I'll adopt Lilly with you and we have plenty of time to talk."

"You sure?"

"I should ask you the same. This won't be easy. We'll be in our sixties when she's in high school."

"I'm sure."

We walked to Touro, so Rachel could meet her daughter.

51

THE NEW DAY brought the excitement of bringing Lilly home and a tropical storm that jogged course overnight. Hurricane season had been busy, and the storm trackers were already up to the Js. Jay was headed toward the Mississippi coast but lurched west toward the city that rests below sea level.

Maria's husband, Rob, delivered the baby furniture and helped us clean and assemble. Billy and Rachel unpacked and washed the baby stuff Kathy purchased. By eleven a.m. we were ready for Lilly. We expected rain by two. I sent Billy out for batteries, candles, extra food, water, diapers, and baby formula.

Under threatening skies, Rachel and I drove through random gusts, to Deb's office in the Garden District. We parked at the curb in front of an orderly white shotgun on Toledano Street near St. Joseph Cemetery. Originally it was a wide duplex later converted into the current office. We sat on a couch in the parlor holding hands.

"Nervous?" I said.

"I never shared this with you." She turned toward me and pulled her leg onto the couch. "We both said we didn't want kids from the start."

"Right."

"When I turned thirty-nine, I wondered if it was too late." She coughed into a tissue and tossed it in the trash.

"Why didn't you say something?"

"I planned a special meal at home one Saturday. You called me from the club because you drank too much to drive. That was it. We ordered Chinese."

She put her index finger on my lips.

"I didn't tell you this to rub your nose in it. I want a child. I want Lilly."

Once again, I was humbled before God asking why this undeserved bounty filled up my life. I understood the grace offered to me and the people in my life come with the certainty that pain and loss cannot be cheated. As planets move, tides lift ships, and one season yields to the next, those we love can leave with no more warning than a summer rain shower. I found comfort in this inescapable reality that has ruled every generation. No blessing comes divorced from this.

Deb called us to her office, and we signed the paperwork and she provided the forms needed to take Lilly home.

———

Hospitals are the most inefficient institutions outside

the federal government. They were not ready to release Lilly and a hospital attorney needed to approve the forms we submitted. We sat in the wide hallway with the green wooden rockers and viewed murky clouds swirl above the atrium. Rachel and I were veterans of sundry hurricanes and tropical storms. Ten inches of rain caused us little concern.

"I'm planning on being the house husband."

"Really." She turned and smiled.

"You say that like you don't believe me."

"Well, I know you changed but let's just say I'll believe it when I see it."

"Hey, I can cook now, and I'll figure out this baby stuff as quick as I can strip the clothes off your lithe body."

"And you'll still have energy to skinny dip with me after we put Lilly to bed?"

"Energy to do more than that."

"Again, I'll be a believer when we are naked."

Before I could utter a snappy retort, Sarah from the nursery appeared with Lilly swaddled in a purple, green, and gold blanket. Mardi Gras colors. An orderly stood behind a wheelchair.

"Who wants to ride?" Sarah said.

Rachel put her hands out to her side. "You're the house husband."

I sat in the chair and cradled my daughter. Rachel took a thick stack of papers and a bag of starter baby supplies. I directed the orderly to take us through the ER. Nobody paid attention at first until Wales directed the nurses our way. They needed to see that part of their sister nurse lived on. After sufficient oooing and ahhing we left to beat the rain. The night crew would meet her another time.

At Camp and Delachaise, wind whipped horizontal rain and lightning cracked like it struck next door. We scooted inside to find Renée and Billy stocking cupboards. I rested on the couch while the ladies settled Lilly in her new bedroom. Plenty of time for me to be alone with her.

Despite the tropical weather, the mail arrived. I heard the distinct rumble of the truck. Instead of the usual sound of the box, a knock. "Sign please." Registered letter. South Carolina Medical Board. Not a greeting card. *Dear Dr. Buchanan.* They scheduled a hearing in one month to determine if they should revoke my license. Even though I expected it, that pang of regret settled in my gut. Just when I tucked away Scooter's death, something like this letter knocked it off the shelf. I wondered if my license was worth the fight. Wales had taken me off the schedule at Touro. No going back. Given my recent promotion to house husband, I weighed my responsibilities with Lilly versus my remaining professional desires. Like comparing a four-course meal at Drago's to rice cakes. I came to New Orleans to change my life and prove my worth not in the number of dollars I could produce but the number of patients who want me to be their doctor again, the number of patients who healed emotionally as well as physically. And that is the answer to whether anyone would miss me. I believed so and the feeling was mutual. I walked to the bedroom and opened the sock drawer. I lifted socks and found Kayla's letter. I slipped the new letter in and tossed hers in the trash.

52

I LAY IN BED at five a.m., Rachel's back pressed against me. With a child in the house, I experienced everything new again. The Christmas decorations, the fresh tree, the smell of cookies baking, the lights glimmering on the bannister. Each day the time between my awakening and Lilly's brought peace. I stopped looking back at my failures. They took my medical license without a fight and a sense of freedom lived in me. I remembered Kayla without regret. I saw Kathy's eyes each morning when I fed Lilly her bottle, and instead of grief, I felt joy. Christmas was a week away, and I anticipated it more than a seven-year-old.

To my surprise, Billy decided to stay in New Orleans and continue her studies at UNO. She and the cats were finishing my lease at Camp and Delachaise.

Through the baby monitor I could hear Lilly stir, so, I flipped the switch and slipped out of bed. I pulled the comforter over Rachel's shoulders and padded to Lilly land. On her back in her crib, she fixed on the mobile of amphibious animals above her. When I came into view, she smiled and kicked her legs.

"Are you ready for a big day, Miss. Lilly?"

More kicking. She took her bottle and I my tea in the rocker by the tree in our vaulted living room. We agreed not to go crazy with presents for a sixteen-week-old, so three presents for Lilly and a gift each between Rachel and I tilted beneath the tree under silver and gold wrapping paper. I played a Willie Nelson Christmas CD. Lilly liked country music already.

"I didn't hear you two get up," Rachel said. She tied her robe, descending the broad steps.

"I fear you are underestimating the sneakiness."

"Don't make me guess which goofy movie."

"Do you want a hint?"

"No." Not only did Rachel not share my love of country music, she did not enjoy my stupid comedies. I still loved her. After making coffee she curled her legs on the couch. "You two are the picture of happiness."

I thought about what Sarah said the first time I held Lilly in the hospital. "Are you awake yet?"

"Sure."

"Did you lose more weight?"

"Maybe. Do I appear thin to you?"

I put Lilly over my shoulder and patted her back. "Your breasts feel smaller."

She flashed me. "You like them this size, huh?"

"It's twue, it's twue."

"Okay, even I know that scene from *Blazing Saddles*."

"Very good. But any more weight loss has me

concerned you could have high thyroid or something like that. Plus, you've been coughing at night. You should make that appointment with Christine."

"My last appointment she ordered a hundred tests, and all were normal. That colonoscopy prep nearly killed me. I told her it was just a hemorrhoid."

"She should examine you and do blood work."

"You examine me thoroughly two or three times a week."

"Nice try. Not the same. Humor me."

"After the new year."

I was hiding something from Rachel and today was the day to spring it on her. Lilly and I waved as she left for work. First came the usual baby stuff of bath and dressing. We played in her room and then nap time. I called the caterer and the balloon guy to coordinate an eleven-thirty delivery. We arrived at her lawyerly looking downtown office at Bull and Lady Streets, with the cherry paneling and weighty furniture, early for our surprise visit. We circled to the back hallway, and I presented Lilly to the associates and paralegals. Ben, one of her partners, called her into the conference room, where a buffet awaited consumption, and she found the entire firm there to congratulate her.

"What is this? My birthday is in March."

I handed her a sealed envelope from the court in New Orleans. She opened it, scanned the legalese, dropped it on the table, and walked into my arms. Rachel seldom cried or displayed emotion. From the time she asked for a divorce, I had seen her cry one time. Her eyes filled; a few tears traversed her high cheeks, then dropped to her silk blouse. Someone unfamiliar with Rachel would call it a muted response. Some women can cry watching a soap commercial. For Rachel, this was a big deal.

After a festive lunch, Lilly and I drove to the airport to retrieve the second surprise of the day. I paid for Billy to fly from New Orleans to spend her holiday break with us. We put her bags in the guest room, which overlooked the pool and the back yard.

"Sam, I love this house. Your neighborhood is so...what's the word?"

"Sterile?"

"No. Clean and tidy."

"You're not in Uptown any more. The culture here is what I call *buttoned up* compared to NOLA."

"Well, buttoned up is not so bad."

"Tell me about school."

"I enjoy my classes and the professors. Difficult to make friends when you don't live on campus."

"Sure, it's a different experience when you work and go to school. Not going to be a party for you."

"I get lonely at night. I miss you."

We surveyed the yard, and I put my arm around her shoulder. "Listen, you were kicked around some. And you know how to do something few of your contemporaries can do."

"Pull myself up out of the mud." As if reciting in school.

"Right. I'll put that person on my team every time."

She squeezed tight. "I love you, Sam."

"And I you."

"Hey, is that thing heated?"

"It is. Find your suit."

I put the baby down for a nap and found Billy floating on her back, spitting fountains of water in the air. Entering the pool with trunks on seemed odd.

"This is like a bathtub," she said.

"Yeah, it's great when the weather is chilly."

"So, how are you doing?" she said.

"We have a comfortable routine. Things are great."

"Okay. But I want to know about you."

She was growing wise. "Sure." I thought for a moment. "I was naked in the water with Kayla…"

"Sam." She splashed me in the face.

"Stick with me here. I told her I had never been so happy in my life. That was true then. Now, when I sit at the table with Lilly on my lap, talking to Rachel, that happiness is magnified tenfold."

I left the front door unlocked knowing he was coming that afternoon. He rode Amtrak from the sunshine state to Florence and walked from there, refusing a ride from me. For the guy who walked the Appalachian Trail alone, this was a day trip. An eighty-mile, three-day walk in practice.

"Hey. Some guy is coming in your front door."

"Sandy hair and a backpack?"

"Oh, my Lord. Sam, you are the best."

"Hey, this was his idea."

Billy exploded from the water like it was electrified,

tore through the sliding doors and tackled Michael in the foyer. Once she finished smothering him, they ran to the pool. Cannonballs.

"Tell us of your adventures," I said.

"While not as much fun as New Orleans, I had a blast rambling along the gulf coast. I walked Alligator Alley to Miami, spent time there and then tagged along on a fishing boat to Key West."

"Oh, oh I want to go to Key West," Billy said. "They say it's a lot like New Orleans."

"Yeah. I met some characters there. Nobody like you. You're a genuine original."

Billy blushed and gave him a smooch on his scruffy cheek. Lilly squawked on the monitor and I left the two genuine originals to reacquaint.

53

CHRISTMAS EVE BROUGHT a bliss and optimism unimagined months earlier. The firm took the day as a holiday, so Rachel and I prepared the meal while Billy and Michael streamed movies and doted on Lilly. We made twice-baked potatoes. After seasoning I handed a spoon to Rachel for tasting. The spoon hit the floor.

"I'm sorry. I thought you had it."

"Yeah. So did I. Clumsy lately."

"What do you mean clumsy?"

"I dropped a thick file yesterday. I just need a few days off."

She sat in a chair and I performed a neurological exam in the kitchen. There was nothing of concern. "Any other symptoms?"

"Now that you mention it, I've been a little dull at work. A little forgetful, not as sharp as usual. I think I'm just tired."

I sent her to the living room to rest and enjoy the kids. I planned to enjoy the holiday and sort it out later.

"Sam!"

Emotional and boisterous were the default setting for Billy, so I strolled to the living room unconcerned. I found Rachel on the couch in a generalized seizure. She stiffened and shook rhythmically, bloody saliva and grunting sounds flowing from her mouth. I turned her on one side and kept her from flopping on the floor. I saw hundreds of patients seize and found it easy to watch with clinical detachment. Shit. Tough to do with your family. I called 911 and then called to notify the community front gate and waited.

"Sam, I'm scared. What's happening?"

"She's having a seizure. Should stop soon on its own."

"Why is this happening?"

"We'll know more after tests. I need you guys to stay here with Lilly. Okay?"

"Sure. Anything."

The seizure stopped followed by rapid and deep breathing. Sweat soaked her hair, and she was gray. Now her brain needed to recover from the electrical shitstorm of the seizure. Some people awaken quickly and reorient, others take their time or become combative when they awaken. Paramedics, familiar by name, arrived, placed an IV, and transported her to the hospital. I followed in my car.

My mind raced and I struggled to make sense of why she had a seizure. If I didn't know Rachel, and I listened to the story, it would probably all come together. This is why doctors should not take care of family. My emotions jumbled my brain and I felt stupid. And scared.

I observed while the ER team, well known to me, did their job. Not that I could help anyone. The MD after my name was just for show. Nurses placed pads on the side rails of the cart to prevent injury should she seize again. Her monitor showed a fast pulse with elevated blood pressure. I expected that. She was slow to awaken, which was not a bad thing if you are getting an IV, blood draws, and a Foley catheter. They worked efficiently, and she spent only ten minutes in CT. She awakened a few time zones away. Phelps, my closest colleague when I worked there, pulled me from the room. He had the look on his face. The look when you tell a family member something horrible. Something you can't fix. We sat in chairs outside the room. He spoke as if in church. "I'm sorry buddy. Mets in her head. Three of them."

Metastatic cancer. Son of a bitch.

"She's going back for another head with contrast plus chest, abdomen, and pelvis and we'll figure out what's primary."

I sat there with a Parkinsonian countenance, immobile with fear of the unknown and fear of what was likely. He didn't ask if I had questions. I knew the answers. This was cancer of lung, breast, uterus, or ovaries. I was on my knees again. Phelps left me, and the tears came. This was it. The beginning of the end. We were screwed. There was no fixing this. I wanted to scream but there was no need to make a scene, so I sat alone and sobbed, not asking why but praying she wouldn't suffer. I wondered if God figured me to be particularly dense and needed one more whack on the head just to be sure he had my attention. Ray, Kayla, Kathy, and now my wife. Each one more devastating.

Rachel awakened enough to ask questions and I reentered the room. She appeared less gray and the nurses cleaned her face and neck. Medication to prevent another seizure dripped into her IV. "Sam. What happened?"

"A seizure."

The elevator was not going to the top. She stared at me with a vacuous expression. "Sam. Why am I here?"

"It's okay. I'm here with you. Can you close your eyes for a while?"

She drifted off and they rolled her back to radiology. One of my favorite nurses, Kelly, the one who never gets flustered, the one who wouldn't say *shit* if she stepped in it, sat next to me and held my hand. "I know this is too much at once. Don't think too far ahead."

We sat there as we had for years at lunchtime. Sometimes listening to the radio, sometimes talking about her kids, sometimes enjoying silence together. She understood me better than anyone at the hospital. Didn't need to say a word.

"Being on the other side of this business sucks," I said.

"What are ya gonna do." Statement not question. We said that to each other many times before. It brought me comfort. She patted my hand.

Rachel slept while we waited for CAT scan results. I fixed her blanket, smoothed her hair, drank water, used the bathroom, flipped through a magazine. Anything to move the clock. Phelps again with the face. We walked to radiology to talk with the guy I'd consulted hundreds of times for abnormal CAT scans.

"I'm sorry, Sam. None of this is good."

He scrolled through images and stopped at the pertinent findings. First the lungs.

"Here in the right upper lobe. This is primary. Large lymph nodes in the chest. Down to the liver now. More mets there. Both adrenal glands too. This lumbar vertebra may be involved as well."

Back in the room Rachel was more herself. She was sitting up, Kelly by her side. "Sam. What the hell. Kelly says it was a seizure."

"Right. Seizures are under control now. How do you feel?"

"My tongue hurts."

"Yeah, you bit it."

"Where's Lilly?"

I realized that I needed to text something to Billy. "With the kids."

"Sam, I don't have seizures. What caused this?"

I pulled a chair to the bedside and held her hand. "There is lung cancer and it spread to your liver, your adrenals, your bones, and your brain." Better to say it, not dance around it or use euphemisms. If somebody died, they didn't pass or slip away. They were dead. If it was cancer, I said it. It's not a spot on an X-ray. "I'm so sorry, Rachel."

"Oh, crap. How can this be lung cancer? I never smoked."

"Fifteen percent."

"Damn. This can't be good if it spread."

"You're right. Let's hear what the oncologist has to say tomorrow."

"No sir. Dammit. I'm not spending my last Christmas here. Give me the meds so I don't seize and get me home. We can see them next week."

54

CHRISTMAS WAS ROUGH, but Rachel was right. Better to be home. The following week we visited the oncologist who, when pressed by Rachel, admitted the prognosis was dismal. She refused chemotherapy but agreed to palliative radiation to the tumors in her head and back. Michael needed to attend to things in Ohio and left after the New Year.

Billy, like a squatter, refused to go back to school. "Sam. School will be there forever. When else can I help you?"

"Fine. You must promise me you will start back in the summer."

"Promise." She held up her right hand. She told me later her fingers were crossed behind her back.

"This will not be pretty or easy."

"Easier if we do it together," she said.

So, Billy and I watched Lilly grow and Rachel recede. The first two months brought us time to talk, and to love Lilly, and to laugh, but time for rational conversation grew short, and on a mild March morning we reclined in the shade by the pool, her cachectic frame covered with a blanket.

"Rachel, soon the tumors in your head and the ammonia in your blood will make thinking difficult."

"Yeah. I can feel it already."

"I regret many things in my life. Wish I had been a better person."

She lifted her hand to my mouth, and I held it.

"I'm not looking back any more. That said, loving you and Lilly is the best thing I've done. If I had never saved a life or relieved someone from misery, I would be no less fulfilled than right now. I'll be eighty-five, driving Lilly crazy, and you'll still be with me."

"I'll be waiting for you. No rush."

"Sure. For you it will be time enough for a deep breath."

We held hands, and both drifted off. When I awakened, she sat on the lounge facing me with her hand on my heart.

"What happens if I stop the steroids and the seizure med?"

"In a day or so you'll seize, and it may not stop. Are you ready to die?"

She nodded, her face steeled. I sat up and held her.

"You tell me when."

"I haven't taken my meds today."

We involved home hospice early on, but Rachel did not want to go to inpatient hospice. She wanted to skip the last step entirely. I understood her desire to avoid the final stages of cancer. The confusion, the restlessness, the pain. I would choose the same. The seizures allowed her a way out without actively ending her life. There was risk in having repeated intermittent seizures that didn't kill her, only cause misery. We both desired a quick exit, so she stopped her meds.

We enjoyed three days of lounging around the pool. Rachel monitored as Billy and I played with the baby in the shallow end. We listened to Mozart and Jackson Browne and ate ice cream. I savored the time but found the abrupt loss of Kathy easier. That Band-Aid ripped off in an instant. Like someone sneaked up behind you. Watching Rachel skeletonize and drift into a cognitive wasteland tugged and stung more each day. One of those square Band-Aids stuck to your chest pulled off three hairs at a time.

I carried her to bed, like lifting a kid, and surrounded her with a fortress of pillows. I slipped in beside, rested my hand on her belly, and we drifted off.

> I returned to the gate, the lanky grass, the blooming trees, the gardenias, the warm feet. Rachel, on the far side of the gate, facing away from me, peered over her shoulder. She appeared more radiant than the day we married. Her bright eyes conveyed a sense of hope and peace. I felt a fluttering at my hand, pleasant at first, then forceful and urgent. Then my body shivered, and I saw her face.

The violent seizure seemed as if it might break her fragile bones. Blood and saliva dribbled from her mouth accompanied by beastly grunting and rhythmic rattling of the bed frame. I flipped the light. Ashen skin was hot and wet. Up on my knees, I wiped her face with a pillowcase and smoothed her hair back.

"Sam, what's happening?"

"Come in, Billy. Come sit with us."

Billy climbed into bed on her knees opposite me. "Is this the one?"

"Yes. She'll be gone soon. This is her brain running out the tank. Are you okay watching?"

She nodded. No tears.

We held her hands for another twenty minutes. It passed like an hour. Her lips blued and sweat pooled in her navel.

"She's not aware now."

"You're sure?"

"Certain. Be happy for her now. She didn't want the slow death."

Just twitches now. I had been mourning her for weeks. I viewed a painless death as an uncommon blessing. My sadness for the loss was eclipsed by the knowledge she escaped her disease to walk through Elysian Fields.

Random, shallow, agonal breaths. I thought of Lilly. She won't remember her two mothers. And I won't remember Rachel as a cancer patient. I'll remember her face as she opened the envelope that said Lilly was our daughter.

Her faint pulse drifted to asystole. Peace.

55

CHILDREN DIVERT YOUR attention from your grief. Babies and semi-adopted twenty-year-olds. At ten months, Lilly cruised furniture, loved the water, and was not shy about making her demands known. For someone who lost two mothers in her first year of life, she thrived. Each month, I recognized more of Kathy in her face. The hazel eyes. The cockeyed grin. Her head filled with auburn curly locks and time for a haircut approached.

Billy expressed demands of her own. Cats coming to live with us. Not going back to NOLA. Waiting to start school until the fall. She transferred her credits to USC and they accepted her for the fall semester. Marketing. Watch out, Corporate America.

I used the sous vide to cook chicken and then seared it on the grill. Billy cut up the meat, onions, peppers, and mushrooms and we mixed it with pasta and white wine sauce. I drank my tea at the table contemplating my next bike ride. Billy entertained her sister, as we now referred to her, in her high chair.

"Sam. We should take a vacation before I start school this August."

She had a point. I welcomed the idea of a few days away. "Where to?"

"Hawai'i." That confident smile.

"I was thinking Hilton Head."

"Oh, come on. You and Michael told me all those stories. I want to see it for myself."

"There is a rule for traveling with little kids."

"What?"

"The smaller you are, the more stuff you require."

"Sam, you are a multi-millionaire. Order online for delivery there and you can donate it later."

"You can be pushy."

"Assertive."

"Fine. You win." Psychotic hip-hop dance. "And I'll do one better. Rex and Renée can come too. My treat."

"Oh, Lilly, this will be so much fun."

"Eyes here, please." She turned but couldn't suppress the grin. "Don't for one minute think anything will happen between Kayla and me. That train left the station on a one-way track."

Nodding. Smiling.

———

Rex had never taken over three days of vacation since opening the store. After much convincing and cajoling from Renée, Billy, and me, he agreed to come for a week. The rest of us stayed two weeks in the Tree

Tops house. Rex and Renée planned to stay upstairs. Jane no longer owned the property, and I wondered what happened to her. All connected in Houston and we traveled first class, Lilly in her own seat.

Billy leaned over Lilly's seat and whispered. "Are you going to talk to Kayla?"

"I should tell the flight attendant you are bothering me, and she will move you to coach."

"Won't you try?"

I was gaining immunity to her pouty face.

"If I see her, I'll be cordial. I'm not seeking her out. Remember her last words to me."

"Fine. Did you hear from Michael?" she said.

"Last was Philippines."

"He's not returning my texts."

———

O'ahu, Hawai'i

Aside from takeoff and landing, Lilly was a perfect first-class passenger, and she monopolized the flight attendant's attention. We rode in a custom van to Kailua and everyone unpacked. We walked to the beach to enjoy the late afternoon. The shadow of the mountains encroached, so we sat near water's edge, and I put Lilly on a blanket.

"Oh, Sam, this is such a treat. I could study those mountains all day," Renée said.

I elbowed her to point out the trim, sandy-haired dude with the backpack walking from the public beach. He touched his index to his lips, stole to the shade, dropped his pack beneath a tree, and stripped to his hiking shorts while Billy flapped her gums about visiting the pineapple plantation. He probably played safety in high school, the way he lifted her. He sprinted to Billy's blind side and plucked her from the sand like a stalk of corn. Billy shrieked as if she was being carjacked. They crashed through the surf then came to the surface in a full embrace.

———

The next day I let Michael choose the hike. Maunawili Falls. We took a cab to the trail head. This is a long, flat hike on uneven and muddy terrain through rain forest. Every step was an invitation to an ankle sprain or a precipitous journey to the mud, plus a minor risk of infection with leptospirosis. None of us fell going in but our boots filled with mud. More aggravating than difficult. The prize came at the end. From a rocky outcropping, water cascaded into a refreshing lagoon surrounded by rocks and vegetation. A dinosaur might have emerged from the forest to take a drink and a snack. We swam around the waterfall and rinsed off the mud and sweat.

"Michael," I said. "Since you traveled around the world, I'm interested where you would live if you could go anywhere."

"Well, I *can* go anywhere, so the question is more than hypothetical." We swam from the waterfall to escape the noise. "There's too many to mention. I'd be happy lots of places. It comes down to who you want to be with, not where you want to be."

"Billy, you came to Columbia to be with Lilly and me, right?

"No, it wasn't humid enough in New Orleans."

I splashed her in the face and tried to dunk her, but she was too quick.

"Yes, Sam. You two are where I want to be."

We air dried and then slogged back to the trail head. Each of us fell once, so we were the mud people. The Uber guy appraised us warily. I gave him an extra Jackson for his trouble.

56

RENÉE, BILLY, THE prized child, and I awakened early because of the time change. We carried coffee, tea, and formula to a blanket on the sand and viewed the sunrise. At first the edges of high clouds ignited, then as the margin of the sun broke the water's edge, the clouds colored with reds, oranges, and purples. And the memories flooded back like a spring tide in a hurricane. Moments in her pool, at the shore, laughing at dinner. I had tucked them away neatly only to scatter like toys on a toddler's bedroom floor.

Billy wanted to walk the beach, so we walked. Billy chose to go left. It was chance because she didn't know Kayla's place. We took turns carrying the baby as the girls marveled at the land and seascape and Lilly clapped at the rolling surf. When we reached the end of the sand at Stan's place, we turned and walked toward the sun. I thought of my intimate connection to Stan and JoJo. The guy whose lungs I filled with my breath. They probably wouldn't return a wave of hello. I felt it deep in my gut. Losing their friendship and their faith in me. I wondered if they had similar regrets.

Low clouds burned off leaving the fireball to blind us. I saw backlit figures walking toward us. One walked with a familiar gate. They appeared to be holding hands, but I was not sure. When we reached Kayla's place the figures cut toward the house.

"Sam Buchanan."

I turned and shielded my eyes. Fifteen feet away. Kayla stood with a buff guy who appeared to be forty. He wore slacks and a dress shirt. Overdressed for the beach, but possibly just watching the sunrise before work. She wore a white sun shirt and white shorts, attractive as ever.

"Kayla. Hi. I hope you are well."

She didn't move any closer.

"Yes. Thanks. How long are you with us?" She cocked her head the way she does.

"Two-week family vacation. This is Renée, Billy, and Miss Lilly."

"Hi. What a picture you are. And this is Ric." She pointed to the guy.

We were going to step into the deep end and learn what was happening in our lives or the conversation needed to end.

"Yes. Hi. Well, we don't want to keep you from your day. Great to see you."

"And you. Enjoy." It seemed she might say something else because she hesitated, but then turned away.

The girls walked a few steps beyond of me. Heads

tilting to each other, whispering, sun peeking through between them. Lilly, over Billy's shoulder, eyed me with a grin.

Billy turned back, a hand on one hip. "For someone you once swam naked with, you weren't very engaging."

"Billy, you're being a bit forward, now," Renée said. "She's graceful, Sam."

"Graceful? That's like saying the Grand Canyon is a minor crack in the ground. She's movie star gorgeous."

"Billy, who do you think that guy was with her?" I said.

"Friend?"

"Do friends, who don't spend the night, show up to watch the sunrise?"

"I guess not." Billy handed me Lilly, and I perched her on my elbow.

"Billy, we've shared our secrets and our hearts. If she had any desire to rekindle our relationship, she would hug me and put a wet kiss right here." I pointed to my lips. Kayla crossing the deck naked flashed in my head.

"Why not stay and talk a while? Ask about her life."

"And what's the point? Damn it. This is not a casual relationship with an old classmate. The switch is on or off with her."

"Sorry. I didn't mean to upset you."

I brought Billy close, and she rested her head on my shoulder.

"You two are my life now. I love you both. Losing

Kayla left a mark and I'm not picking at it. Big day today. Let's go enjoy it."

We found Michael and Rex standing at the blanket drinking coffee from tall mugs. The girls took Lilly in for a diaper change. I couldn't make out the words but Renée was using her mom voice.

"I'm glad you two are together," Michael said.

Rex raised an eyebrow, and I reciprocated. "Tell me how you knew your wife was the one." I raised my chin at Rex.

"Good question. When I was young, we raised hell. Drank, hunted, fished, raced our cars. When I stopped wantin' to do the stupid stuff to spend time with Renée, I knew."

"How did you know she wanted to be with you?"

"She hung around for two years, whilst I did stupid shit, waiting for me to get my act together."

"So, what's the common denominator?" I said.

"English, please," Michael said.

"What was similar between them?"

"Right. Right. Ah, they both gave up something."

"There you go," I said. "I'm not sure early days, but I can tell you what happened last year. You know Rachel and I went through a rough patch."

"Sure."

"She asked for a divorce and then changed her mind. She recognized that I transformed my life. We were both willing to forgive each other's transgressions. We loved each other despite our failures and shortcomings."

"Thanks. That helps," Michael said. "I'm not going

to do something crazy and propose, but I want to settle in Columbia and see how things go. When I travel now, I miss her bad."

"All right, dude. You can stay at my place one week and then settle in to your own place. Deal?"

"Deal."

Columbia, South Carolina

57

W

E ENJOYED HAWAI'I but getting back home into our Lilly routine brought stability and contentment back to our lives. Billy cared for her sister while I showered after a bike ride. Laundry had not been a high priority, so I was down to my last pair of underwear. Beneath that pair was a card embossed with a pineapple. The card I tossed in the trash the day Kathy died. The card Kayla gave me the day Stan and JoJo renewed their vows. Billy.

I dressed and stepped into the kitchen where she was teaching Lilly to catch Cheerios in her mouth. I held the card between two fingers.

"Do you recognize this?"

"No. Sam, watch this." She tossed one, and it hit Lilly in the forehead. They both laughed. Lilly giggled that full throttle, no cares, laugh that only little kids do. "Darn. We did it a minute ago."

"Billy. Are you sure you didn't put this card in my underwear drawer? I'm not mad. I just want to know."

"Let's see." She read it twice and handed it back.

"Wow. This is amazing. Sam. I had no idea. I thought you guys had a fling. Would you have married her?"

"It seemed like it. This is why you take time to truly know someone before you devote your heart."

"Do you mean Michael and me?"

Lilly banged on her high chair and Billy absently tossed more cereal on the tray.

"I'm making a general point. You two seem to screw your heads on straight. Am I right?"

"Yeah. He's sort of a wild horse now."

"Excellent insight. If you are patient, things will work out," I said.

"So, back to this card. If you tossed it in New Orleans, and I didn't bring it here, who did?" She lifted Lilly from her chair and held her.

"This is not something Michael would do," I said. "There's only one other person at both places. Lilly."

"Funny. That is so sweet. Rachel was telling you to fall in love again."

"Yeah. You're right. Before our troubles, this is not something Rachel would do. She changed more than I imagined."

I pulled open the trash cabinet door.

"Oh, no, no, no. You can't throw it out now. The card is not from Kayla anymore. It's from Rachel." She made her twirly finger. "Back in the drawer."

"Fine. Listen now. This is not an invitation for you to fix me up with your professors, women you meet at the grocery, the cute chick that reads the electric meter. Got it?"

She handed Lilly to me. "Fine. But what if Lilly and I go to the park and meet this buxom brunette, angelic face, bubbly personality?" She did a pirouette like a drunken ballerina.

"Text me a photo of her and pigs flying, then we'll talk."

—

I called to be sure she was home. She bought a small place out near the Army base. I pulled to the curb and found her on her front porch swing. A young dogwood and a bed of black-eyed Susan, Xenia, and rosebushes accented the yard in front of the red Cape Cod. She hugged me, and we shared the swing.

"Your yard is beautiful, Mrs. Gibbs."

"Thank you, Sam. You know, not long after you and I talked the first time, the bank called me."

"Is that so?"

"Yes, indeed. They wanted to talk about the money in my account."

"That sounds like a blessing."

"Oh, yes. That ring any bells with you?"

I turned toward her. "Well. I am experienced with blessings, and I learned to not question them but to receive God's grace with humility."

"Sam, I'm surprised to hear you say you are blessed. I read in the paper that your wife passed. I prayed for you and I hope you are doing well."

"When I was drinking, I would have told everyone

I'm cursed. I lost three people important in my life in a short time." I swallowed and took a deep breath. "My wife and I reconciled, and we adopted the child of my friend who died in childbirth. These blessings, unasked, undeserved, filled me when I could only anticipate the next tragedy in my life. They seem to come just past the difficult turns."

"My son was there to greet your wife in heaven. I believe he told her he loves you. No grudges or looking back in heaven."

We held hands and rocked.

58

I AWAKENED BEFORE THE sun and rode my bike across Broad River and back. While riding, my grief rested by the pool. One day I hoped to find it dead on the bottom like an elderly cachectic aquarium fish. The rhythm, the breeze, and the burn in my thighs showed the way until then.

After my shower I found a scribbled note askew on the kitchen table.

Off for a stroll w Lilly
XOXO

I poured tea and sat on the front porch in a wooden rocker absorbing the October sunrise. The sun cleared the roofline across the street, and I dropped my sunglasses to my nose as a red Mustang convertible approached without commitment. People familiar with the neighborhood cruise by without a glance. I watched the silhouette of the driver peer from side to side. Once stopped, the figure emerged and looked across the rag top. I felt a catch in my chest, and I walked to the shade of the live oak.

"Hi. Can I help you?" I asked.

"Thanks, no. I'm sorry to disturb you. I was just admiring your house."

She walked to me and I extended my hand. "I'm Sam."

"Vicky. My pleasure. The realtor said to drive around the neighborhood before meeting her at the club."

"Sure. Welcome. You'll find some others with similar architecture."

"Well, it's a stunning home."

"What brings you to hot Columbia?"

"I'll be working as an anesthesiologist at the hospital. I've come to start my life over."

"Now that's something. Best of luck."

"Thanks. Nice to meet you, Sam. Maybe I'll see you around."

Billy and Lilly returned from their walk as the house hunter walked to her car. We settled into rockers and Lilly ran around the yard.

"Who was that?"

"House hunter."

"She's attractive. Did you get her number?"

"I hadn't noticed, and no, I did not get a number."

She punched me in the shoulder. "Get out of here. She was cute and you know it."

"If you say so." I winked at her.

"Sam, it's hard to believe what's happened since you first left here."

"True. I try not to think of that man."

"You talk like *that man* is someone else."

"He is and I'm glad you never met him."

She rested her hand on my arm. "Well, I'm glad I know you now."

"I think of the people who have come and gone from my life," I said. "Can't pretend to understand it. I do understand this. I didn't know how to love someone until I went to Hawai'i and surrendered. I let go of my self-centeredness, my unwillingness to forgive, my short-sightedness. I accepted God's underserved grace and learned to appreciate my blessings."

"You and Lilly are blessings in my life, Sam. I can't imagine where I would be without you. After all that's happened it's hard to think where we'll be a year from now."

"Indeed. So, we love each other in this slim moment since our path is a grand mystery."

Author's Note

THE PEOPLE AND events in this story materialized as a hybrid using my thirty years of experience in emergency medicine caring for nearly one hundred thousand patients. None of the patient scenarios were embellished. Some of my patient encounters have been so unique or sad that I told a milder version to protect the identity of the patient or family member.

This story is not autobiographical. I have cared for thousands of alcoholic patients and have known a few but am not an alcoholic. Over the years I have flirted with burnout but never made a commitment to it. Burnout, depression, and addiction, however, are significant problems in the medical community. The suicide rate among physicians is 1.41 times higher for men and 2.27 times higher for women. I knew two doctors who took their own life. The corporatization of medicine, high workload, loss of meaning in work, the threat of litigation, the electronic medical record, and insurance companies place a great strain on doctors. This hinders the delivery of sound and compassionate care. These problems affect everyone either directly or indirectly. At your next visit to your doctor, tell her you understand how difficult practice is today and thank her for being there for you.

Rachel was diagnosed with late-stage lung cancer. This was not dramatized. I have made the diagnosis of advanced cancer in patients many times. These folks usually had symptoms, but none were specific enough to seek medical care right away. Rachel chose palliative care. That is a decision that should be made carefully in consultation with oncologists and palliative care specialists. Cancer care is changing rapidly, and we are on the cusp of momentous change in the field of oncology. And the future looks bright.

Thank you for reading. I hope you enjoyed the book. Connect with me on Facebook @dbaehren or visit me at www.davebaehren.com

Be Happy,
Dave

Acknowledgements

THANKS, AND LOVE, to my wife Sonja for her patience and support. Writing while working full time was challenging. Her devotion to me helped to make my work enjoyable.

I received an excellent education at Ottawa Hills High School in Ottawa Hills, Ohio. Alice Lora, Barbara Wagner, Patricia Smythe, and Vance McCarter taught me English. All, I am certain, are surprised to learn that I wrote a novel, and possibly surprised that I read novels.

Thanks to Paul Huffman, my now deceased junior high math teacher, for the joke about pi. Thanks to Frank Oelerich for the shoe scuffing and to Dan Hanson for the lesson in statistics.

Thanks to Linda Dolan of Write to Sell Your Book for her expert and compassionate editing and to Sonja Baehren, Kym Lemieux, Lori Dixon, Lydia Schafer, Laura Burzynski, Heidi Glosser, Jill Hayes Deckebach, and Michael Deckebach for their help with the early manuscript.

Also, thanks to Diane O'Connell and her team at Station Square Media, including Cristina Schreil, for her expert copyediting; Steve Plummer for the beautiful cover design; and Janet Spencer King for her deft shepherding through the publication process.

Finally, thanks and best wishes to all the doctors, nurses, clerks, techs, and EMTs I have worked with over the years. Some of your names made it to this story. Y'all will be with me always.

Made in the USA
Monee, IL
13 July 2020